THIS IS
HOW IT
STARTS

Grant Ginder

Simon & Schuster Paperbacks
New York   London   Toronto   Sydney

Simon & Schuster Paperbacks
A Division of Simon & Schuster, Inc.
1230 Avenue of the Americas
New York, NY 10020

First Simon & Schuster trade paperback edition June 2009

SIMON & SCHUSTER PAPERBACKS and colophon are registered trademarks of Simon & Schuster, Inc.

For information about special discounts for bulk purchases, please contact Simon & Schuster Special Sales at 1-866-506-1949 or business@simonandschuster.com.

The Simon & Schuster Speakers Bureau can bring authors to your live event. For more information or to book an event, contact the Simon & Schuster Speakers Bureau at 1-866-248-3049 or visit our website at www.simonspeakers.com.

Designed by Davina Mock-Maniscalco

Manufactured in the United States of America

1   3   5   7   9   10   8   6   4   2

Library of Congress Cataloging-in-Publication Data

Ginder, Grant.
This is how it starts / Grant Ginder.
p. cm.
1. College graduates—Fiction. 2. Interns (Legislation)—Fiction. 3. Self-actualization (Psychology)—Fiction. 4. Washington (D.C.)—Social life and customs—Fiction.
I. Title.
PS3607.I4567T47 2009
813'.6—dc22   2008031312

ISBN: 978-1-4165-9559-5

For my family

I

So this is how it starts:

I'm watching Chase Latham lift up the edge of my cousin's skirt beyond what can be considered polite or appropriate, and I'm just starting to regret introducing them to each other two years ago at that bar in Philadelphia when I see the horse stumble, before buckling at the knees and then collapsing—dead—in an equine pile of hoofs and hair and teeth. Unfortunately for the horse, at that particular moment every man in the Latham, Scripps, Howard, LLP tent is quietly wishing he was one of Chase Latham's sly, tan fingers, and every woman is fantasizing about being a patched square on Annalee's madras skirt, so time ticks by for a languid three minutes before anyone notices that the unlucky beast has died.

A man's voice crackles and breaks over a loudspeaker and when the feedback finally clears he announces that a horse named Prep School has won, Sophie's Choice has placed, Enola Gay Ol' Time has shown, and Light of Our Lives—who was trailing in seventh place—has failed to finish due to sudden death. A wave of low murmurs passes throughout the tent and its exterior and

when—thirty seconds later—it's quieted, it's been publicly decided that Light of Our Lives was blessed with a fine life and has
died honorably: for God, for country, for Gold Cup. I sip my gin
and tonic and watch, half curious, half drunk, as a small cluster of
girls in pretty flower dresses and boys in navy blue blazers with
shiny buttons starts gathering at the rail closest to the horse's lifeless body. After a few minutes, the congregation of eight-year-olds
grows and multiplies to about thirteen mourners who vigorously debate the cause of the horse's debilitated state ("sleeping,"
"tired," "horsey heaven" seem to be receiving the most votes). It's
a funeral service of sorts, I suppose. It's something. Poking sticks
and giggles aside, these are undoubtedly the best-dressed second
graders in northern Virginia: brass buttons just polished and bows
freshly tied. They're not grieving, that's true, but I'm sure that if
they knew any better, they would be, and besides, the Gold Cup
is this lavish affair, a celebration of sorts, and if there's a way to go,
this is probably it, among the hats and the cigars and the pearls.

But then a fly lands on Light of Our Lives' black marble eye
and the first of the eight-year-olds lets out a long, bellowing wail,
which causes a mother to stop whispering about Annalee's lifted
skirt long enough to intervene and disband the flock ("sleeping,"
it's decided, is the most probable cause). And I shake my head and
I look at a single melting cube of ice in my empty cup as, around
me, the world continues apace with some universal metronome
whose beat, at least today, I've been unable to match.

The crowd's doing the waltz, see, and I'm tripping through a
tango.

Maybe it's the bow tie, I think. After all, I've never worn one
before and this one (pink seersucker) isn't even mine, it's Chase's,
and the lesson he gave me in tying it was hurried and unsatisfac-
tory, at best. I could loosen it, maybe, give my neck a bit of slack,
some breathing room. But on second thought I'm not sure how
these things work and a little slack could cause the whole thing to

unravel and fall apart all together. And I'd ask Chase for his advice, but his hands are otherwise occupied.

Or maybe it's the empty cup. Yes. That's it. That's what it is; it's this sudden lack of gin, which I've always thought vaguely tastes of pinecones but for some reason seems to be more distinguished, *classier,* than vodka. No matter it's likely that intoxication has played accomplice to this sense of *mal dans ma peau* in the first place. At least if I'm blitzed I've got something else on which I can place blame for my disheveled hair and ill-fitting khakis—something other than myself.

Latham, Scripps, Howard, LLP's tent is situated inconspicuously along an endless row of white cabanas that are hard to distinguish from one another, if distinguishable at all. In the Tanqueray + sun haze, I wander back into the tent's populated interior ("LSH Welcomes You to Gold Cup: Eat. Drink. Race!"), which, if a person didn't know any better, he could easily mistake for a modern re-creation of Versailles, circa 1665. I stumble through the throngs of plunging necklines and correctly constructed bow ties and make my way to the bar that, surprisingly, is empty, which I take as a sign of providence so I order another gin and tonic. As the bartender lets the Bombay waterfall into a clear plastic cup (one finger, two fingers, three fingers . . .) I brush my blond mop, which has become matted with humidity and sweat, away from my forehead and lean against the bar's high, wood countertop. The bartender—a young man about my age wearing a white dinner jacket—hands me my drink and gives me a nod.

"So, where's your money for the next race?" I say as he rearranges a series of bottles. We could be friends, this man and I—buddies. Both intruders in this club of modern nobility.

"There's no formal betting at Gold Cup, sir," he says with a sneer. "Enjoy your fifth gin and tonic." Then again, maybe not.

I finish the drink in a single prolonged chug and order another before leaving the bar. *Sixth gin and tonic, thank you very much.*

Comparisons to Versailles may be unfair—*exaggerated*, I think, as I make my way through the crowded space. After all, there are no kings here, no divine monarchs or bejeweled thrones. There are votes and elections and a healthy and sedated middle class.

"And so I said, Madam Pelosi, my apologies, but my cuff links are being polished, so you'll have to settle for a shirt without French cuffs. But it's flattering that my reputation precedes me." Chase's father—tall, impeccably dressed, Kip Latham's voice cuts above the din of the crowd. I spot him in the tent's opposite corner, surrounded by a sea of fans who erupt with laughter after each of his sentences. Kip thanks them by flashing a smile that's been crafted by an intimidating team of orthodontists and dentists from only the best practices along the eastern seaboard. For the past two and a half decades, Latham's been crafting his reputation as the District's most prominent Republican lobbyist. And from the looks of it, his blueprints have proven to be one of the more booming examples of social construction. The man's a caricature of success. His hair, flecked with streaks of silver that reflect the sun's glare like some precious metal, hasn't changed tones in twelve years. He has a collection of loafers that has received pictorial treatments in *Washington Life, Capitol File,* and *Esquire.* To date, he's the only man I'm aware of who possesses a preternatural knack for bullshitting that's actually feared, if not actively avoided, on both coasts and in portions of the Midwest. A lunch, a night at the theater, a Nationals game, eighteen holes; they all meant the same thing to a Republican congressman: he was about to be Kipped. He was about to be had, about to be convinced, beguiled, *manipulated*—even if not for a single second he believed any of the words swimming gracefully from the man's mouth and into the open air. If Mr. Latham had been operating when Jesus was preaching his monotheistic madness, there would have been no cross or martyrdom or moving rocks. There would have been a misunderstanding; something that could be smoothed over with a little bread and a little wine and maybe (if the mood called for it) some dancing. No one would've had to share a cup.

And so maybe Versailles wasn't far off, after all.

Standing next to Kip like two silent Mazarins are the Pauls—Scripps and Howard, respectively. If Latham hosts the palace feasts, these are the men who kill the boars and stuff the pheasants. They're stoic, I think, as I watch them maintain tight lips and stern faces through Kip's raucous (and likely inappropriate) jokes. Specimens, really; some kind of nod back to an old guard that I thought, at least before today, was a dying breed. They wear their graying hair—which isn't nearly as brilliant or as coiffed or as godlike as Kip's—in the same plantation-inspired southern "swoosh." Word is they both came from the Hill, where, a decade ago, they worked as chiefs of staff for two senators who had rhyming names. Kip managed to get ahold of them in a skybox at a Knicks game, which was provided courtesy of another top lobbyist, and since then both Pauls have narrowly escaped indictment on four separate occasions (one of which involved the death of a puppy). To soften their image as political assassins, both have had their wives (Bunny and Kitty) featured three times (holding puppies) in *Southern Living*. While Chase's father has spent the past fifteen years sculpting the face of an empire, these two men have been building the gears and pulling the strings and flipping the switches that make shit work. It's impressive, if not menacing and intimidating and—according to Chase—likely illegal.

And so I move, careful not to attract the Pauls' laser gazes, toward the mahogany table set at the center of the tent and start to forage as politely and inconspicuously as my current state of intoxication will allow. For the most part, the spread's what you'd expect at an event like this: expensive cheeses, fresh fruits, scallops wrapped in bacon that are kept warm on an elaborate chafing set fueled by tiny devices whose source of power and heat I can't quite comprehend. At the center of the table are two large

pewter platters featuring mountains of dark caviar. I stare at the
tiny eggs. Thousands and thousands and thousands of them. Murder, I think, before piling a large mound onto a tasteless cracker
(spilling at least half down the front of my white oxford) and directing it into my mouth. Absolute murder. At least an entire generation of sturgeon has been wiped out. If only the little bastards
could know how delicious they are. The Pauls start looking at me.

"Don't let the feds get ahold of that shirt, champ." I stop picking the tiny beads off my shirt and look up to see Chase (sans Annalee, hands respectfully in pockets). His lips start curling at the
corners to form that Cheshire-cat smile. "Evidence of that caviar
could get you five to ten." I stop chewing and consider spitting
the roe out while trying to mentally calculate how many tiny un-
developed creatures are already swimming in my digestive tract.
"I don't know how those sons of bitches do it," Chase continues,
"but they do. Dad says something like 'wouldn't it be great if we
could get our hands on something none of the other tents will
have, something a little edgy.' And fucking voilà! The next day the
Pauls show up with *ten goddamned pounds* of illegal fish eggs from
Iran—this shit the UN's actually *banned*. Can you believe that?
Fucking illegal caviar. From *Iran*. Iran! Ten fucking pounds of it.
Awesome." Chase pauses for a moment to reflect on the power
and the beauty and the contraband, and then starts noticing how
much of those ten pounds are staining my shirt and how my eye-
lids have started dropping a little more than they should in the
early afternoon and adds, "Well, it looks like someone's been having a good time."

A man in all white carrying a tray of champagne flutes walks
by and Chase grabs two of the glasses and shoves one of them
into my chest. "Tough gig, huh?" he says, motioning toward the
field. A pickup truck has pulled close to the track and Light of
Our Lives' dead body lies in its bed, covered by a green tarp. "I bet
Vance Alexander fifty bucks that fucker would win, and then he

has to up and die on me. Goddamned *horse*." The truck rumbles, then jolts, and then drives slowly through a crowd of spectators who nod to the deceased beast in deference. *He gave it his best shot.*

Even though the champagne's become lukewarm, I finish the glass in two swallows before asking him where Annalee has gone. (I half expect him to tell me that she's waiting for him—madras skirt off; a crumpled ball of orange and red—in an empty bus on the outskirts of the field.)

He laughs. "She's fine. She's with her friends. Look." He points to another corner of the tent, where Annalee and two other girls who look just a little too much like her are talking in a circle that's as tight as their large hats will allow them to form. Big hats. Everywhere. We wave and she waves back. "Man, I thought Californians were supposed to be laid back! Maybe you should be the one we're worried about, huh?" He gives me a playful punch on the shoulder that, in my opinion, is a little too hard, a little too brash, coming from someone who's fucking my cousin. But he's mostly right, I think. He's mostly right because I'm the one who just moved here (forty-eight hours ago) and I'm the one who took a year off and went back to California after Chase and I graduated from Penn and I'm the one who's in a new place, new city, new job. I'm the one who's becoming increasingly aware of my own displacement. Annalee's been living comfortably and happily in Washington since she graduated Duke in '03, making her two years older than Chase and me. She's a pretty girl, I think, as I watch her awkwardly adjust the floral arrangement that's been strapped precariously to the top of her blond head. Stunning, almost. Though, really, she's never known it.

The flawless product of a mother whose obsessions include *Vogue* and cayenne pepper–based diets and a father who'd wished for an Aston Martin—*not* a daughter—Annalee spent most of her childhood staring into a mirror scrutinizing whatever inadequacy had been pointed out to her that day. (Too thin, too fat, too many freckles, not enough freckles, too *much* Gwyneth, not *enough* Gwyneth, etc., etc., etc.) It wasn't a particularly uplifting activity, though it was one at which she certainly excelled. While many young girls spend their days committing Hannah Montana songs to memory, Annalee could—without stuttering—give you a rundown of the stats surrounding her blemishes: this mole's grown 0.18 inch in diameter since last summer. Seven hair ends have split since breakfast yesterday. When we were younger, I'd found it impressive, if not entirely disconcerting.

As kids in Southern California, we'd always gotten along well, Annalee and I. Our parents—namely, my father and his brother—lived close enough to each other to allow for at least one play-date each week. We'd spend these mornings and afternoons and nights on the beaches of Orange County, dodging not only the Pacific's crashing waves but also her mother's attempts to convert us to whichever fad diet she'd read about that week. (During one such excursion, I'd returned home and had announced to my own mother that I had pledged my digestive tract to veganism. She responded to my proclamation by cooking veal for dinner and telling me that if I wanted tofu, I was more than welcome to eat it with the rest of my burlap-sack-clad friends, but that while I was living under *her* roof, I'd best check my dietary restrictions at the door.)

When she turned eleven, Annalee's family moved to Chicago. My uncle, who had slid comfortably into personal wealth after inventing an obscure (yet highly expensive) bike lock used by nearly every East European cycling team, cited business needs and promptly plucked his wife and daughter from their comfortable California lifestyle and set them down in the wild, wild Midwest. He bought a sprawling mansion in Lake Forest—a decision that at once pleased his wife (thanks to the house's sheer size) and horrified her (thanks to the house's location in a region of the country known for its meat-and-potatoes approach to dieting).

"Business needs," as it turned out, though, translated roughly to "abandonment." After the move, Annalee's father was all but present, opting to spend time with his family solely on long weekends and national holidays and the occasional birthday celebration—visits during which he'd forgotten his daughter's name after four fingers of scotch and two illegal cigars that he'd obtained during his latest international jaunt. It was hard, she'd tell me in her monthly letters and during our weekly phone calls, but she had faith it'd get better. Although he'd never said it, although he'd never *expressed* it, she was certain that she was still his princess, still his little girl. Because, really, that's all she'd ever wanted. She was right, I'd tell her, even though it hurt my stomach to do so. He was just a busy man. Always traveling. Always working. What with the bike locks and all.

Despite the infrequent visits from her father and the constant harassments of her mother—despite all that—Annalee turned out all right. She passed through adolescence with unprecedented grace and crystal-clear skin, luck that my aunt would attribute to specific portions of kale she ate during her third trimester of pregnancy. Upon graduating somewhere in the top quarter of her high school class (she wasn't the brightest in our family—though she certainly wasn't the dumbest), she attended Duke University, where, despite meager protests made on my part, she traded her judgmental mother in for sixty judgmental sorority sisters.

She took the hazing in stride, though, and laughed when the older sisters wrote "FAT" across her visible ribs with a red marker during pledging. ("They obviously haven't met my mother," she said during one of our weekly phone calls—a tradition we maintained through her time in Durham.) Four years later, she graduated, sandwiched somewhere in that same top quarter of her class, except this time she was armed with a Bachelor of Arts in cultural anthropology—a weapon, my brother claimed, that would be less useful than the paper on which it was printed.

And it was. Or it wasn't, depending on how you look at it, I suppose. Using an article she had written on the cultural signifi- cance of colored loincloths among tribes in Papua New Guinea, Annalee managed to land a job as a "fashion assistant" at a Wash- ington lifestyle magazine whose name I can never remember, and whose circulation can't be more than three digits. Together we laughed at the prospect—at this *job*—and she told me that it'd just be a stepping-stone until she found something she deemed more worthy.

But this was when we were still talking weekly, before Chase had met her and had called her princess for the first time, before Belize.

I catch her eye again, and this time we share a smile and she rolls her eyes at me as she points to the bouquet strapped to her head.

Chase finishes his champagne and tosses the empty flute to the ground and as he calls me "champ" it dawns on me that I can't remember the last time he called me by my real name. "Let me explain Gold Cup to you. First, you've got the south gate." He points to the left. "It's for folks coming from towns like Lynchburg and God-knows-where-else. Towns where people wear, like, J. Crew and American Eagle, and *Abercrombie.* I'm not talking about, say, Great Falls, Virginia. Or McLean. I'm talking about *Virginia* Virginia. You got me?" I don't have him but I nod. "Good. Then, you've got the north gate." He points to the right. "That's where the D.C. folks generally come in. But—and my bet is you'll learn this sooner rather than later—not all D.C. folks are created equal." He laughs at his own joke. "For instance, you've got the kids who split the cost of a party bus to get them out there, throw on their only pair of Nantucket reds, pack a picnic, and call it a good time." He pauses. "It's cute. It's nice. And there's always some hot ass over there. State school girls. But it's not us, champ. It's Gold Cup purgatory. You've managed to escape *hell* with the Virginia trash, but you're still sitting on some shit blanket eating Doritos and drinking brut. You follow?" This time he doesn't wait for my response. "Then, you've got *us*." Chase makes a wide, sweeping gesture with his arm as if he's some feudal aristocrat showing some guest his plots of land. And I'll admit, amid the madras and the seersucker and the tans, the plots are impressive. "Every year, Dad manages to throw together the best private tent at Gold Cup. Check out the *Cap File* this month, I'll bet you a night of drinks that there's a write-up on it, sans mention of the Iranian delight, if you know what I mean, compadre."

"What about the actual races?" I ask.

"The what?"

"The horse races."

He throws his head back and howls. "You kidding me, champ? No one watches the races. *No one.* Think about the Derby. You think Jessica Simpson goes down to Kentucky to see some god-damned horse run around a track? No. She goes to wear some hat that cost her a grand and throw back a few mint juleps. I swear," he says, shaking his head, "sometimes you kill me. Absolutely *kill* me." And then: "C'mon. Let's introduce you to the masses."

If I wasn't exaggerating, and if the Latham, Scripps, Howard tent is, in fact, a castle and Kip is its reigning king, Chase its dauphin, and the masses their loyal subjects, then I am the distant relative who's a product of inbreeding gone very, very awry. By any legal standard I'm drunk. My shirt's covered in illegal caviar. I forget the name of every Susan, Bryce, Hunter, Valerie, etc., whom Chase introduces to me almost before I shake their outstretched hands. And then I step on a six-year-old. I manage to spill the remainder of my gin and tonic down the front of an LSH associate's wife's Lily Pulitzer dress. I stare for a *little* too long when the cocktail forms a sticky river of booze and lime and carbonation that runs through the bronze canyon created by her mostly inorganic breasts.

I'm embarrassed. For her. For me. And in a moment of self-awareness, I worry that this situation, that this scenario and I may not be the best fit.

But Latham Jr. doesn't flinch; he doesn't blink. He's confident and cool and smooth. Standing at a perfectly proportionate six two, Chase Latham looks like he's carved from marble and walks like he skates on air. He keeps that Cheshire-cat smile and continues introducing me to a sea of pastels and Polos that seems to worship him only slightly less than his father. Each introduction is prefaced with a series of disclaimers: This man—a prominent right-wing pundit—is rumored to have made a habit of receiving oral sex in the men's sauna at the Sports Club L.A. That woman—who used to be a Democratic strategist but has since jumped ship—leaked the Kerry/Botox rumor back in '04, which landed her a six-figure job at LSH. These three girls all slept with the same White House press secretary ("twenty years older than they are, a Dem, and not the least bit attractive").

It's impressive, I tell Chase, how much he knows about these people and their skeletons.

"Currency," he says, grinning. "Secrets are currency." He points a tan finger into my chest. "The sooner you learn that, the better." And I'm reminded of my first semester at Penn, and the seven terms thereafter, when Chase taught me the difference between Andover and Exeter, loafers and lace-ups, pink vs. salmon, etc., etc., etc. ("These things are important, champ, and you're not going to learn them in a classroom, I can guarantee you that.")

We continue to bob and weave and cheek-kiss and high-five our way through the crowd. But such are the politics of a friendship with Chase Latham, I think, as I watch him shake hands with a twentysomething in green pants with tiny blue whales embroidered on them. He could be publicly disrobing your cousin, who passes for a female Forrest Gump on her smartest days, and you could be on the verge of throwing him under the hooves of a stampeding horse, but then he slips his arm around your shoulder and he gives you the patented smile and he convinces you that his world, which is really a mirage that you've been on the verge of touching for six years, spins entirely around *you*. And then suddenly you forget about your cousin's lifted skirt, and that overpowering urge you have to protect her by telling her how many times Chase had gonorrhea sophomore year (four). You forget about the time you invited Dianne DeWitt to your senior spring formal—after that whole Caroline mess—only to find her, an hour after the event had ended, snorting cocaine out of the creases in Chase's abdominals in a booth at that club in Old City. And even though you and he are both about 93 percent heterosexual, you suddenly become a little jealous of your cousin and how she's blessed enough to be intimate with Chase on a daily basis.

So he's a drug, really. Grade A, uncut, pure, top of the line. Served up by only the slickest dealers in high-class clubs. Sure, he's a little dangerous. And yeah, there's a hangover—mornings and days and nights wondering why and telling yourself it's not going to happen again. But rehab's a joke. It only works for something like 12 percent of addicts, anyway, and you're certain beyond any kind of doubt that you fall safely in that other 88 percent.

I wander around, high and happy in Chase's orbit, until I'm standing with him before his father and I become sincerely concerned that a Latham overdose may be in my cards.

"Taylor!" Kip slaps me on the back. "So glad you got in town in time for our little tradition." The Pauls, who have since collected their wives, aren't smiling. They're staring at the brown specks on my white oxford.

"He'd originally planned to move two weeks from now, but I convinced him otherwise," Chase says.

"Well, we couldn't be happier." Kip turns to his associates. "Mr. Mark was a classmate of Chase's at Penn. Inseparable from day one. In fact, they lived together all four years, two of which were spent in the Phi Delt house, my old stomping ground." He smiles, but more for himself than in honor of our shared past, and the Pauls nod knowingly, as if they've heard this story countless times before. "In any event, Mr. Mark just spent a year in Southern California, which"—the smile—like father like son, "certainly explains his tan."

"Welcome to the District," Paul Scripps (or is it Howard? And moreover, does it matter?) says coolly, keeping his eyes on my shirt. "Paul Howard." *Damn.* "And this is my wife, Bunny." He puts his hand on the back of the woman standing next to him, who, for lack of a better adjective, is blond—just very, very blond.

"I just *love* Californ-i-a," Bunny sings in some southern accent that I can't quite place but that most likely falls somewhere between Columbia and Charleston. "Is that where you're from, Taylor?"

"I am. From Laguna Beach."

"*Oh* . . . how *exotic.*"

"Not particularly."

"Taylor spent the past year at home taking care of his mother," Kip chimes in, the bass line in Bunny's song. "This young man's got *character.*"

"Well, now. Is everything all right?" Bunny puts her hand to her chest.

"It's getting there." I sigh. "She wasn't doing well for a while." The Paul, who has become bored with the conversation, whispers something to the Other Paul.

"Oh, *dear,* I'm sorry to hear that. May I ask what's wrong? Is she ill?"

"I suppose you could say that."

"Is it . . . cancer?"

"Divorce."

Bunny and Kip nod, as if to say *sometimes that can be even harder.*

"You know, a girlfriend of mine in Nashville got divorced two years ago," Bunny says, as if the crumbling of marriages was a rare thing, as if more than half of American matrimonies don't end in legal fees, therapists, and seeing-the-kids-every-other-weekend, as if it was, in fact, cancer. "And I don't know how your mother's coping, and I don't mean to impose, but Candace, my girlfriend, she really turned to Jesus." She smiles. Out of the corner of my eye I see Chase swallow his laughter and mouth "more champagne" to one of the servers.

"Yes, ma'am. Religion's really helped Mom, as well." I decide against telling Bunny Howard that, for Katie Mark, my mother, the word God is spelled P-R-O-Z-A-C and that His Holy Son, contrary to popular belief, is named Glenfiddich. A matter of semantics, I figure.

The introduction reaches that awkward point where neither of us has anything more to say about divorce or cancer or religion, so I'm relieved when Paul Scripps leans in and tells Bunny that the next race is about to start, and that her favorite horse, a mare named Pretty in Pink, is running. She squeals and claps, and she mentions something about Molly Ringwald changing her life back in '86 before she begins making her way toward the rail.

"So, Taylor, when do you start your new job with Congressman Grayson?" Kip asks, after Bunny and a Paul move closer to the course. Chase answers for me.

"Tuesday," he says, handing me a champagne flute. "Champ becomes a Hill rat on Tuesday."

"Well, that'll be great. Just great. John"—Kip catches himself—"sorry, Congressman Grayson, is such a close friend of mine. I'm so *happy* that it all worked out." He grins and allows me to recognize that I'm indebted to him for my current state of employment. Which, indeed, I am. Three months ago, between driving my mother to therapist appointments, to the pharmacy, and to Neiman Marcus, I slowly—and then instantly—lost grip on my own sanity. And then, finally, after ten months, there was that night with the pot and the broken wrist and Jack White and I finally broke down and explained to my mother that I'd be leaving California; that I was too young, that it was too early for me to be playing nurse in a convalescent home for one. Against her best wishes, she understood, she *had* to, so we made an arrangement with my aunt and I began for the first time since graduation, looking forward. At Penn, I had majored in political science and French literature, and while the latter captured a greater portion of my interests, in-depth knowledge of Camus—while impressive at Ivy League reunions and UN receptions (neither of which I've attended)—is not exactly a marketable trait on the job market. So I brushed off this unopened copy of the *Federalist Papers* that had been assigned reading in at least six classes and set my sights on Washington. It'd be good, I thought, *rewarding*; an exercise in service and duty. I called Chase the next day, asked if his father had any connections (a pointless query, but a formality nonetheless), and precisely thirty minutes later I had a job with Congressman John Grayson, of California's Forty-first Congressional District. They say that good timing is everything, and indeed it is, because an assistant legislative aide was going to be attending law school in the fall, and had decided to spend the remainder of her free life teaching art to disabled children in Ecuador. I told Chase I didn't care about the details, as he excitedly relayed the news to me over the phone on a warm February morning. I would no longer be "Driving Ms. Mark."

"And what a coincidence that Congressman Grayson represents your district back in California, eh?" I nod and say yes, yes, it's wonderful—*really* wonderful, but silently I'm thinking how, truthfully, it's not such a mind-blowing convergence of events; that, really, Kip is close friends with the entire Republican caucus.

"Yes, sir," I say and take a sip of the champagne. "I'm very excited for the opportunity."

"Enough with the 'sir' nonsense." The king pats me on the back again. "You're like a second son to me. Like a second son."

Two hours later and my blood alcohol content levels have elevated from officially wasted to lethally toxic and I'm sitting, Indian-style, on the grass outside the LSH tent, and the sun's beating down relentlessly on the back of my neck, causing the alcohol to boil and simmer and thin in my veins. I pick methodically at the green blades, which is truly the only action that seems to suppress the mixture of champagne and gin and bile that's mixing in the back of my throat.

"And Moscow was absolutely *gorgeous,* which I didn't really expect from a country that used to be *Communist.*" I have no idea where this girl has come from, nor an inclination why she thinks I'm in any mental state to hear about whatever time she's spent in the former Soviet Union. "It's just a fantastic opportunity— doing advance for the vice president." If I could just get my hands on some water, I think, that'd help. And where has Chase gone? "What people don't realize about Cheney is that he's really like a big teddy bear. *A great big teddy bear.* He loves to give hugs. He's just a kind, kind man." *Paternal* is the word she keeps using.

"Yeah. I really get that vibe." And Annalee? Where's Annalee?

"He didn't *mean* to shoot that friend of his. Mr. Whittington just got in the *way* of Dick's gun. I mean, *Christ*"—she lights a cigarette—"it was an honest mistake, really."

"So," I say, tired of hearing about the vice president's honest mistakes with guns and lawyers, "how do you know Chase?"

"Chazy? God, I've known him *forever*," and I'm suddenly sorry I've asked. "Kip and Daddy both worked for ExxonMobil, in government relations, at the same time. Then Kip left to start LSH and Daddy stayed on board with Exxon. Chase went to St. Alban's and I went to the National Cathedral School. You've heard of NCS, right? I was two years above him. He dated my closest—well, three—of my closest friends when we were in high school, and then of course he went to Penn"—she gives me a nod—"and I went to Princeton but we just stayed the absolute *best* of friends." She stops abruptly. "I'm surprised he never mentioned me to you."

But I'm not in the mood to hurt any feelings so I assure her that it's likely he did and that I'd just forgotten. *So many names,* you know.

"Oh, I know exactly what you mean. Just the other day I was at this happy hour at Daily Grill that was arranged by Princeton's D.C. alumni association, and I was utterly *appalled* at how many names I'd forgotten in a span of three years. I mean, D.C. *is* small and all, but you really don't run into as many people as you think you would. I suppose it's a matter of—" I cut her off and ask her if she knew my older brother, Nathaniel, who had graduated from Princeton the year before her.

"Nathaniel—what's your last name? Mark? Nathaniel Mark . . . hmm. Was he in an eating club?" She stops and feigns embarrassment. "*Ugh.* I absolutely *despise* asking that about people. 'Was he in an eating club?' It's just so *juvenile* and faux *pretentious.*" The girl's penchant for speaking in italics, combined with the thought of my family, begin to mix disagreeably with the Veuve/gin/bile cocktail, so I tell her that I'm not sure if Nathaniel belonged to a club or not—which is a lie—and I excuse myself from the conversation.

Standing, though, doesn't prove to be as easy as I had expected, and I sway and teeter before the gin takes over and I crash in slow motion to the ground. I apologize to the girl, who is now staring at me in italics, and I hoist myself up and brush off my khakis (now stained with green patches) before giving a weak, defeated smile and staggering off. My father always used to tell me that a man didn't get a second chance to make a first impression, which I always chalked up to him taking fortune cookie advice a bit too far. "They're like business cards for twenty-year-olds," he told me over steaks at a small restaurant in Laguna Beach the night before I left for Penn. "Your generation doesn't understand that. They think that being on *The Real World* is somehow going to impress people." He poured himself another glass of pinot noir. "Well, it's not, Taylor. It's just *not*. I don't care what coast you're on, or who you're dealing with; nothing impresses someone more than looking him in the eye and giving him a firm handshake. Ask Nathaniel. He'll tell you the same thing." He hesitated, and then poured me a glass as well. "Don't tell your mother."

I run over the conversation again and again and again in my head but nowhere in it can I uncover the part where my father explained the importance of caviar or grass stains or nine gin and tonics. These are the obstacles, though, that parents don't disclose when they give their lectures on What Makes the World Go Round. Dad never mentioned the Pauls or Kip or St. Alban's School for Boys. There was a handshake, and a bit of eye contact, and a world of eternal respect.

But then again, look how he turned out.

I make my way back to the tent and take post against one of the steel beams that's propping up the taut white canvas. There's a possibility that the beam won't bear my weight, I suppose; there's some likelihood that, thanks to me, all this will come crashing down on the hats and the glass flutes and whatever's left of the felonious hors d'oeuvres. But thanks to my grand jeté in front of Ms. Princeton a few moments ago, it'd appear that my feet are skipping out on their anatomically devised job of supporting the gin and me, of *keeping us up,* so I roll these dice and take my chances. Water. That's what I'm searching for: water; something to detox my thoughts and provide some clarity. Or some trace of Chase and Annalee, whom I haven't seen since the third race (the sixth and final steeplechase is about to start) and who seem to have been consumed and digested by the mob around me.

"Excuse me, young man," a lithe finger taps my shoulder, "you wouldn't happen to have a light, would you?" I turn around and am greeted by one of the more spectacular pair of breasts I've encountered in my twenty-three years of breast-scoping. They're large, but not unnaturally monstrous. Real, that's for certain. Not a trace of silicon or salt water or whatever it is doctors are pumping into mammary glands these days. What's attached to the heaving mounds is no less impressive: five feet, eight inches of feminine sexuality. She's older than I—in her thirties, maybe. Dark hair falling down past her shoulders in rolling waves. I reach into my pocket for my Bic lighter—a cheap orange number whose flame doesn't seem to be glamorous enough for this woman's cigarette. She takes a drag and exhales a steady stream of smoke.

"Thanks."

"Taylor. Taylor Mark."

She smiles. "It's a pleasure." She extends a hand and I can't decide if I should shake it or kiss it, so I do neither. "God, don't you just hate these things?" She looks out over the crowd.

"Absolutely. They're the worst." She could have told me the world was as flat as a pancake and I would have agreed with her. With this woman, no questions asked. She lets out another stream of smoke, as if to tell anyone who will listen that the PSAs are all wrong, that smoking is, in fact, sexy. Especially when being done by a woman like her. "Can I get you a drink?" She laughs and her breasts heave up above her dress's plunging neckline.

"That's nice of you to ask, but I think I'd better sit this next round out. Lord knows what I'd say to these women if I got any more vodka in me." She motions over to Bunny and Kitty, who have started taking notice of our conversation, and have, in turn, started spinning a conversation of their own. "I forgot to wear a hat today, and apparently these women consider that a capital offense." It's true: she is the only woman under the tent's canopy lacking some oversize headpiece. All things told, her attire is, at first glance, rather understated: a simple and unassuming white linen dress. But then, after watching her for a moment more, after watching the hair and the figure and the way the streams of smoke seem to finish the ends of her sentences, it's safe to say she chose the gown without those two particular adjectives in mind. "It's not that I mind, per se." She drags in on the cigarette. "I mean, Jesus, can you imagine carrying on a conversation with one of these women for longer than two minutes? You'd start sounding like some goddamned Jane Austen character." Another plume of smoke escapes her lips.

"Oh, I don't know," I say, shoving my fists into my pockets. "They don't seem all that bad. I met Mrs. Howard. She seemed nice."

She throws her head back and laughs. "So tell me, Taylor, is this your first time at the Gold Cup?"

"Yes. Yes, it is."

She taps the ash off the end of her cigarette and nods slowly and smiles.

"And are you enjoying it so far?" She eyes my shirt. "It looks as though you are."

"I am enjoying it. Hard not to. I'm afraid I may have drunk too much gin, though, to be honest with you."

She laughs again and tosses her hair to one side. "You're fine, I'm sure." She nods to Kitty, who is attempting some sort of hand-stand in what can only be a two-thousand-dollar dress. "You could be in worse shape." She drops the Dunhill to the floor and crushes it beneath a high, thin-strapped sandal. "But you're obviously not from around here." She looks me up and down. "Your bow tie needs a bit of work."

"It's my first time wearing one," I say, fingering the edge of the seersucker cloth. "It's falling apart."

She grins. "Let me help you." She leans her body against mine and wraps her two tanned arms around my shoulders. As her fingers work to untangle the tie, her lips graze my neck and her breathing—warm and controlled—against my cheek sends my groin into electric frenzies. After a few moments that seem to linger dangerously long, she backs away from my sweat-drenched body, holding the bow tie.

"I never liked these things, anyway," she says, folding the tie into a small square and placing it into a small gold clutch she's holding. "Well," she says with a grin, knowing exactly what she's done and exactly what will not be happening. "I suppose it's time for that drink. It was a pleasure, Taylor. A real pleasure." I watch her walk out of the tent and down a patch of grass, her hips swaying with the attitude of a woman who knows that (a) she doesn't belong at an event like this in the first place and (b) that if it weren't for the way white linen hugged the figures of women like her, moments like this, moments where young men were reduced to pubescent catastrophes, would cease to exist.

"That's Juliana. She's beautiful, isn't she?" I turn to see Bunny Howard, who has suddenly materialized as some pink and green and bedazzled juggernaut spilling champagne and eyeing the crotch of my khakis, which now features a small bulge that my fists (which are still in my pockets) are trying to conceal.

"Yes, Mrs. Howard. She's very attractive."

Bunny nods. "It's nice to see that you're getting along with all of Congressman Grayson's family. I'm sure that'll be helpful in the office."

"Is that his daughter?"

"No," Bunny says, giving me a flute of champagne that's been topped off to the brim. "That's his wife."

The races end and I still haven't found any water. I'm standing with Chase, who has missed a smudge of lipstick on the left side of his mouth and whose shirt is unbuttoned to a point that lies somewhere between "casual" and "tacky"—a very un-Latham move. With one hand, he holds up Annalee, who is giggling and drunk and basically just this messy rag doll, and with the other hand he starts directing the guests back toward the LSH fleet of chauffeured Lincoln Navigators that are parked at the edge of the grounds. Thanks to alcohol and noise and general confusion, it's slow going. When we finally make it back to the cars, Chase, Annalee, Ms. Princeton, another guy I haven't met, and I climb into one.

"Taylor," Chase says once he's slammed the door shut, "this is John Alexander Buchanan. Call him Jack. We went to St. Alban's together." Jack shakes my hand with little interest and forgoes any attempt at learning my name. "He writes that gossip column for *Politik,* so watch where you're dropping your pants, if you know what I mean." Chase laughs and edges me in my rib, which causes my stomach to stir and jolt. Jack, bored, takes a BlackBerry out of his back pocket and starts typing.

"What are we doing tonight?" he says once he's sent his message.

"We could do something different. Like the Black Cat or *something.*" Princeton (whose name I still don't know) manages to force at least one italic word into the sentence.

"Too many fags and hipsters," Chase says. Annalee giggles. Jack rolls his eyes.

"Yeah, you're right. All ugly people in *black.*"

"Let's just hit up SP. You know that's where everyone's going anyway." Ms. Princeton nods her consent. "Hand me that bottle of Veuve."

"Chazy, you can't be *serious*."

"C'mon, Caitlin, we got to pregame. We'll be the only sober ones at Smith Point." *Caitlin*. I make a mental note of it.

"We've been pregaming since ten this morning, Chase." She looks unsure.

"Pregame, postgame. Whatever. We've got to game," he responds.

"And seriously, I hardly think any of us are sober." We all eye Annalee, whose head is drooped at an awkward angle and who may or may not be drooling.

"Speak for yourself, babe. I could drive a school bus of Down syndrome kids with one eye closed." Annalee lifts her head and points to her empty glass. "See? We're fine. We're all fine." Caitlin sighs. Chase wins. She reaches into a cooler branded with LSH's logo and produces a sweating bottle of France's finest. The driver keys up the ignition and Chase fumbles with the wiring choking the Veuve before he finally removes it and pops the cork. Bubbles shoot up like geysers.

Annalee gasps and champagne drips like amber tears from the ceiling. As Chase fills each glass I can't help but think of how the sound of the cork exploding from the bottle's neck sounds like some sort of starting gun, and how the low growl of the Navigator's engine rapidly accelerating sounds eerily like the grunts of strain and adrenaline at the beginning of a horse race. And I think back to Juliana's lips brushing against my cheek, and then back to Light of Our Lives and his black marble eyes, and I start wondering if he had it right all along.

May 22, 2007;
8:30 A.M.

So here's what I know about John Grayson: he's a tall man with chiseled features and congressional hair; which is to say that it's not bold enough to be presidential, nor distinguished enough to be senatorial, and so: congressional.

In the same way that some celebrities end up in prison, whereas others get their own reality shows on MTV, Grayson landed in the U.S. House of Representatives through no fault or accomplishment of his own, but rather through a series of unforeseen circumstances, accidental accolades, and healthy roots and no split ends. The younger son of a wealthy, second-generation land developer (practically a Vanderbilt by Orange County's nouveau-riche standards) in Newport Beach, California, Grayson had gone to the University of Southern California on a football scholarship. Unfortunately, halfway through the first season, a drunken incident involving a rusty keg led to an infected ingrown fingernail. What started as a pesky inconvenience led to gangrene, which led to surgery, which led to the amputation of the little finger on his right hand, which—to the distress of his mother, a Trojan through and through—resulted in the downfall of his PAC-10 fame spiral, and then—finally—the subsequent death of his scholarship. The money wasn't the problem, but the diminishing glory was, and Grayson spent the next three years drinking and screwing and mourning the loss of that damn little finger, all the while planning on simply taking over his father's firm, pending graduation. He'd get a secretary to do the typing.

What Grayson hadn't considered in his grand plan was that his older brother, who, while not as follically blessed, was certainly the more business savvy of the two. Rupert Jr. (you win some, you lose some) graduated two years ahead of John and made use of that 730-day head start at Grayson and Co. by leading the development of two new shopping centers and an upscale housing complex—which, in the Rupert Sr. Dictionary (second edition), translated roughly into "hugs," "kisses," and "favoritism." By the time John left USC's gated brick campus things were not looking good on his road map to wealth and comfort and pretty young secretaries transcribing his memos.

So he chalked it up as a loss, as just some other signifier of his less than perfect role in this world. He settled in as second in command with a noncorner office and an elderly secretary named Florence who, while she was not the nubile, youthful thing John had imagined, was competent enough to be ignored until she was needed. He toiled away for nine years, his time consumed with strip malls and low-rent condos and cheap hotels while his brother managed much of Newport's booming residential scene. Eventually he bought a house in Corona del Mar (on one of the flower streets on the beach side of Pacific Coast Highway), where he and the rest of his friends who had managed to escape marriage would drink and occasionally get high and try to recollect the details of their nocturnal college conquests. Things were fine, comfortable. They weren't great or spectacular or really how he'd imagined, but they were *fine*, and when things are *fine*, John knew, they really shouldn't be trifled with because—while there's a slim chance they can get better—probability and general experience showed that they are more likely to get worse.

Then, on the eve of his thirty-second birthday, John Grayson saved a life, and fine and comfortable went to shit.

It started out per usual: the birthday, John's, in Grayson tradition, was an opulent affair on Rupert Sr.'s yacht, which patrolled the Newport harbor like some glittering sentinel powered by so many tiny lights. Rupert Sr. was a stern man with broad shoulders and a tight mouth that rarely showed teeth, who had garnered most of his friends and acquaintances through monetary threats and favors, both of which had heavy price tags attached. That said, on that fateful night the yacht (an eighty-five-footer with a spa and a helipad) played host to more of the father's friends than the son's. So John ran a hand through his near-perfect auburn hair and opened a beer for one of his two college buddies in attendance and watched from a distance as Rupert Sr. cut the cake and handed the first piece to his eldest son, the one who handled mansions instead of movie theaters, the one whose birthday wasn't being celebrated. And maybe it was this distance from the center of things, or maybe it was destiny that caused the younger Grayson to hear a faint scream, followed by a splash, and then a woman from the crowded deck shriek "my baby!" He turned in time to see the red head of a young girl bob up and down like an apple in the boat's wake. Women gasped. Men took longer than normal to take off their Rolexes and empty their pockets of keys and wallets and money clips. John dove in the cold Pacific brine and, in four wet minutes, became a local hero.

The girl, incidentally, was Erin O'Brien, the ninth of ten children fathered by Hannity O'Brien, a successful lawyer who had escaped his Roman Catholic roots by being born again, and who was an influential member of the Republican Party of Orange County. Even more incidentally, the following year was an election year, and the Orange County GOP was looking for a likable, photogenic candidate to challenge one of its district's few incumbent Democrats—who, in the years directly following a scandal involving a president, an intern, and a little blue dress stained with DNA—seemed to be a healthy target for guilt by association. Background checks into the first three prospectives had turned up some less than desirable information (pedophilia accusations, pestering cocaine addictions, and money laundering, to be exact), and so Hannity and the rest of the committee were still searching desperately for a winnable name to get on the ballot before the primaries, which were but months away. In John Grayson they found what they were looking for: good pedigree, a stint in heroism meaningful to constituents, and—above all—prodigious hair. Two months later he was on the ballot, and fourteen months later, in a beauteous example of American democracy, John Grayson and his nine fingers were headed to Washington. For two glorious weeks Grayson—the young, fresh face from Orange County— was showered with the species of attention that had been reserved for Rupert Jr. for the past decade. Pundits lauded his frankness; fashion magazines lauded his widow's peak.

Washington, though, is quick to forget a new kid, and after he was sworn in at the beginning of January, Grayson found himself barely treading water, fighting for seats on committees that he knew nothing about but that held the key to his future success as a legislator. It was a tough gig, and Grayson didn't have a playbook, so privately he found himself wishing—over glasses of scotch at a one-bedroom apartment on Capitol Hill—that he had let that little girl dip up and down one more time, that he had let someone else be the hero, that he had cited his own inebriation or his own past indiscretions as handicaps for saving drowning children.

But we can spend hours and days and years wishing away our brief flirtations with greatness and the unexpected and unwelcome places they've taken us, yet in the end our races have been run and our winnings have become embedded in our blood, eclipsing our secret desires for defeat along the way. So John Grayson stayed put—the victim of his own heroism—as he won elections every two years, as he became another permanent feature in that great white building on the hill. After four cycles and eight Novembers, his presence became as expected and as uneventful as those oak benches that arc across the floor of the House of Representatives.

He managed minor accomplishments along the way. After two terms, Grayson—under the guidance of his chief of staff—secured a position on the House Armed Services Committee. It wasn't Appropriations—or Ways and Means, for that matter—but given the clusterfuck in Iraq, it did carry what appeared to be an increasing amount of prestige. Over the years, he received invitations to speak at local universities—an honor he particularly enjoyed. His staff would write the speeches and walk him through the harder-to-grasp legislation, while his own hair and charisma would (for the most part) hide his rather impressive lack of knowledge.

One thing he did find: now at home, when he spoke, people listened. Undeserving or not, the title "Congressman" gave him some credibility, some *oomph,* at family gatherings where—at least for the past two decades—he had been but a fly on the wall. His father and his brother and his mother would nod intently as he waxed poetic on what needed to be done to correct the deteriorating conditions in Baghdad. They had faith in his beliefs on health care and education, and believed the facts that he presented—often wrong—on how global warming was a sham.

Or at least he thought they did. At least he was *pretty* sure they did.

<hr />

And I'm sitting under the Great Seal of California in 1224 Longworth, the cubby that serves as John Grayson's office in the long, dense neoclassical maze of structures that's inhabited by the 435 members of the House of Representatives. The space itself is small and cluttered and dusty and looks nothing like what I expected after idealizing my political debut à la *West Wing* marathons. My desk sits in the front of the office, which also serves as a miniature lobby/meeting space for guests, constituents, and other visitors. There's a bluish-green cloth couch, which can comfortably sit two and a half people and is just short enough to make napping on its faded fabric impossible (something that I discovered when the office was empty on Friday afternoon of last week). Above the couch hang these tacky pictures taken from California's Forty-first Congressional District: here's downtown Laguna Beach on a perfect summer day; here are waves crashing over the Newport jetty; here are surfers staring vacantly off into the Pacific. Regardless of their kitsch, they're a nice touch, these pictures, I think as I search for any news clips of Grayson on the websites of the *Orange County Register* and the *Los Angeles Times* and a myriad of other papers, both local and national. (There are no clips. There haven't been any since last Thursday, my fourteenth day of work, and the day before I attempted my intraoffice nap.) As the lowest-ranking member of Grayson's staff, rummaging for clips each morning is part of my job. On my first day of work, I'd suggested to a more senior staff member that the clips—these news nuggets—could be easily collected using one of the many wonders of technology. *"Google!"* I'd said. *"Or Lexis!"* My problem-solving enthusiasm was greeted with glares and scorn and a largely undeserved speech about how everyone—*everyone*—has to search for clips when he first starts out, and no technological advancement was going to change that. And so, the clips. I'm also required to answer the phone; open the mail (twice a day); sort the mail; file letters from angry constituents; occasionally (and if I'm lucky) respond to said letters with form statements in which I fill in a series of blanks ("Dear Mr. [x], thank you for your letter regarding [y]. I've taken your letter into careful consideration, and am taking every possible action on [z]."); organize the newspapers, fetch coffee and chili fries for Peter Branson, the thirty-six-year-old bald chief of staff who sits directly behind me; and, when there are no interns present (there rarely are), I give tours of the U.S. Capitol to groups of Grayson's visitors. I'm the office manager, the workhorse, the prole, the bitch. In a move of good faith, Peter knighted me unceremoniously as an assistant legislative correspondent, though I have no issues I cover or legislation on which I correspond.

I tackled my first two weeks in the office with a severity and an earnestness that's normally reserved for new enlistees in the Marines or Olympic athletes, because the future of American democracy depended on the morning clips. Late-night study sessions were employed to read and to learn and to commit to memory little-known facts about the Capitol's dome that I then imparted upon those fortunate enough to embark on one of my tours. Each time the phone rang, the world stopped. I was fighting for the freedom and the liberty and the voices of the upper-middle-class constituents in California's Forty-first. And although that enthusiasm's started to fade, my quixotic intentions remain. Last week, after my failed attempt at an intraoffice nap, I sat up partially guilty but really more amazed by the fact that Washington was still standing despite my thirty minutes' worth of restless and uncomfortable shifting. Government proceeded at its glacial pace.

So I read the local session of the *Register,* half looking for news about Grayson, half wondering how reading *Les Misérables* (twice) in French, coupled with $160,000 in tuition fees, prepared me for this task. There's a heat wave in Southern California. Temperatures are spiking well past what can reasonably be expected for mid-to-early May, which has firefighters concerned that the dry season will be longer and brush fires will be more prevalent, etc., etc. There was a gang skirmish in Laguna Niguel, which has prompted a local woman to fear that southern Orange County may start looking like Garden Grove or—worse—Los Angeles. A high school student in Aliso Viejo has written a book that documents the horrors of being young and blond and wealthy and anorexic. The Angels' starting lineup is expected to be stronger than last year's.

The door to the office swings open and knocks back against the adjacent wall and shifts the placement of one of the pictures. Peter stands in the frame, coffee already in hand, saddled down with files and reports and a leather shoulder bag that's seen better days.

"Morning, Taylor," he grumbles. He's a nice man, Peter. I like him, and I get the sincere feeling that he likes me, too. "Any clips?" I shake my head: no, no, there aren't—not today. "Goddamn it. City Council members in Newport get more press than we do." Peter lumbers through the front room and sets the stack of file folders on his desk and half of them tumble to the floor. He's sweating a little too profusely for eight thirty in the morning. "How was your night." It's more of a statement than a question; a kind of acknowledgment that we're the only two in the office and I'm still the new guy and that these awkward questions are always better than those awkward silences. I tell him that it was okay, that I did some laundry and watched a rerun of a reality show on TV—something about a plastic surgeon in Beverly Hills. Peter grumbles and effectively stops listening when I say "rhinoplasty." His computer boots up and I ask him how his night was. He sighs and shakes his head and taps his desk as he waits for his antiquated PC to come alive.

"Fine. It was fine. Grayson's plane to Orange County was delayed, which of course he didn't care about, but of course I did because he had that damned panel at UCI on preserving the Back Bay, and you know how he doesn't sleep on planes." As it turns out, I didn't know that. But I don't blame him. They're impossible to sleep on without some kind of chemical assistance, so cramped and such. Then again, I'm sure he flies first class. I used to fly first class. Before the Belize thing. "We don't get these opportunities too often, Taylor. So we've got to strike 'em while they're hot." Peter takes off his glasses and rubs his temples and (I imagine) thinks back to a time when all this was so much more exciting; when he was on the campaign trail in '96 or when he was press secretary for someone much more important, someone in the leadership. "Anyway. I had to cancel dinner with my wife, which is strike two for this month. He got there in the end though, so . . . you know, crisis avoided, I guess."

Shrugging, I give my best "wives just never understand" look to let Peter know that he and I are pals, see, in that great, old Fraternity of Men, even though I'm relatively certain that marriage does something to one's membership status that I've yet to grasp. In anticipation of Grayson's panel appearance, I'd printed out an *Orange County Register* feature from two months ago about a ragtag group of preservationists and their battle to preserve Newport's Back Bay—a muddy swath of land that's coveted by environmentalists and developers, though for largely different reasons. When Peter seems settled I hand it over to him and he says he read it when it was published, but then thanks me for my initiative.

"It's just so goddamned problematic," he says as he hands the article back to me. "Those bored housewives in Newport think there's some *grand gesture* in protecting the Back Bay. Only problem is their real estate–developing husbands are the ones who want to kick out the herons and build more houses and condos. Got to make everyone happy, Taylor. Or, at least make one person happy while figuring out how to get the other ones to believe that they're happy."

I'm impressed with how succinctly he's managed to express

something I've been suspecting for the past few weeks and I watch him for a bit longer as he gets lost in his e-mail in-box before I turn back to a story about a young girl with leukemia in Corona del Mar.

The next time the door swings open, I'm not nearly as happy. Kelly Hawthorn—Grayson's press secretary—and Janice Wagner—his scheduler—strut into the front office with the kind of authority that's reminiscent of runway shows, though neither of them could be any traditional kind of model. Kelly's young and thin, which, while those are two desirable qualities in a city known as "Hollywood for ugly people," do not exactly land her in the "attractive" category. She attended UC Berkeley, where she was the star of the debate society, and, I suspect, never got laid. At twenty-seven, she's a political wunderkind of sorts. Peter found her a little under year ago doing local politics in northern California, where she managed to turn a small-town mayor's sex scandal into a reelection campaign. She's cold; the girl who, in high school, never managed to infiltrate the ranks of the charismatic and popular, and who thus uses her newly acquired authority to remind you how unimportant you really are. And I suspect that regardless of my education and earnestness, she is less than confident of my intellectual abilities—a belief that Janice Wagner shares.

If—in Chase terms—Kelly borders on "bone-able" in the right light and with the correct amount of makeup, Janice eludes the label entirely. She hasn't seen the inside of a gym or even a pair of running shoes in years. She insists that she eats healthily and wisely and "only for energy"—a proclamation that's severely compromised by her habit of getting nachos with extra cheese daily at 4:00 P.M. According to D.C. lore, things had been going well for Janice, who started out as an office assistant before she graduated to a congressional campaign. She was married by age twenty-five, and was headed toward occupational success and pearls and a nice town house in DuPont Circle. But indiscretion be damned, her husband fell in love with a *Post* reporter (from the Style section, no less) and by age twenty-seven, Janice was back to a studio apartment in a less-than-desirable part of town, where she dealt with depression and loneliness and loss by eating too much ice cream and wearing too much makeup. And when the clouds finally cleared, she was seventy-five pounds heavier and her career hadn't just fallen off the track, but jumped it entirely. Now, having endured thirty-five years, Janice handles the congressman's schedule—which, while normally a prominent and fast-paced job in a political office, is rendered rather slow by Grayson's status. Which is all fine by Janice. More time for the cafeteria, I suppose.

At first I felt sorry for these women, both in their own masochistic ways fighting for lost time that'd been poisoned by uncontrolled velocity and the cruelty of others. And so truth be told, I'd probably still feel sorry for them if they hadn't made a routine of referring to me as "you" and demanding that I refill their staplers. But one's got to pay one's dues, I'm told. Then they brush by my desk without the faintest trace of hello: those fucking bitches.

The Sisters Grimm settle into their desks, which are behind me and next to Peter's, and I settle back into childhood cancer. Lori, the Corona del Mar girl, was diagnosed a year ago, at age six. Since then, she and her parents have taken the battle against pediatric illnesses to the streets, where Lori has befriended underprivileged children diagnosed with diseases similar to her own. Through funding provided by her parents, Lori hosts picnics and playdates in the family's beachfront manse, where clowns and magicians and musical guests entertain the children once a month. "We don't have to wear our wigs here," one of the party's attendees is quoted as saying. There's a picture of him—a young Hispanic boy proudly sporting a bald head that's been robbed of its hair by chemotherapy. "And I like that because my wig is really itchy. I have to wear it at school, otherwise people get scared. But I don't have to wear it here because no one's scared and everyone's nice. Even the clowns."

Lori and her clash with pediatric carcinogens have gotten me a little teared up, a little sad, and I write this off as a lack of caffeine, so I ask Peter if it's all right if I take five minutes to grab some coffee from downstairs. He tells me it's fine just so long as I grab him another iced-no-water-Americano and one of those "goddamned scone things that my wife is always telling me not to eat." I smile and tell him sure, that it's no problem, that it's my treat, and head out the door before Kelly and Janice direct me to buy anything else.

As the morning drags on, the marble halls of Longworth have become increasingly crowded with frantic young staffers determined to convince anyone and everyone that they belong there, that they've been there all along. Politics aside, it's an impressive structure, I think: a perfect example of neoclassical revival; a nod back to the folks in Athens who did it first—and maybe a little better. Five porticoes flanked with looming Ionic columns that support a grand entablature that cuts across the building's exterior like some stone razor. Two stories in some places, four in others—an architectural phenomenon that's got a sloping foundation to thank. I can't help but think of Grayson each time I climb the stairs that lead to the building's main entrance. Staring up at the pediment, it's difficult not to feel emasculated. It's difficult not to recognize, to pay deference, to the fact that two kinds of people have filed through these columns: those who have made a stamp on history, and those who haven't. And that first group's got a steep entrance fee that—chances are—you're not willing to pay. I imagine Grayson had some conflicting emotions the first time he stepped into these hallowed halls; at once exhilarated by the prospect of self-worth, of *importance,* while quietly wondering if neoclassical revival was really his style; or if maybe he was better suited for the glass and steel and silicone that formed the buildings and the characters who tower above the Pacific.

But back to the building: like everything else in Washington, what's most impressive about Longworth isn't what you can see. It isn't the columns or the pediments or the limestone worn thin by decades-long stampedes of loafers and heels. Rather, it's the secrets that teem below the structure's diagonal foundations. Longworth's basement isn't a basement; it's a fully functioning, self-sustaining community. Aside from the standard cafeteria and Starbucks, the basement (it just feels so wrong to call it that) boasts:

- a post office,
- an office supply store,
- a bank,
- a dry cleaners,
- a gift shop,
- a photo-developing store,
- a gym.

So if God forbid the terrorists did get their vengeful hands on a nuke and if it did explode in America's District of Columbia, Congress could continue as normal, fueled by cheap turkey sand-wiches and skim lattes and freshly pressed trousers, all thanks to this community within a community. The complex is connected to the other House buildings and the Senate buildings and the Capitol through a series of tunnels that enable pale congressmen and their overworked staffers to conduct business without ever having to be troubled with the light of day.

Grayson prefers to walk outside.

And so I walk down three flights of stairs into the under-ground city and filter through the hordes of legislative aides and interns in cheap, boxy suits until, ten yards away from Starbucks, I'm accosted—*tackled,* really—by Anna, one of Grayson's legislative aides who is searching for her caffeine fix before heading up to the office.

"*Taylor,*" she says and she grabs my arm. Her nails dig into it. "Thank *God* I saw you before I got to the office." Anna, with her frazzled brown hair and horn-rimmed glasses and never-ending supply of black knee-length skirts, is more of an exaggeration of a person than a person herself. "Did you hear what happened at Tapatinis last night?"

"No . . ." I answer with hesitation. As the newest member of the congressman's team I have not only been assigned the role of de facto outsider, but also the role of de facto Deep Throat—a holder of secrets. It's a position that I've come to learn is bestowed upon those of us who have yet to learn the names or the faces or the places in this town and thus couldn't spread poisonous facts even if we tried. I walk with her to Starbucks, her nails still ripping away at my flesh, and I order my coffee and Peter's no-water-venti-ameri-whatever as Anna rattles off her latest discovery.

"*Well.* You know John, who works in Miller's office?" I tell her that no, no, I don't. "Whatever, it doesn't matter. Anyway, we all thought that John was sleeping with this girl Rebecca who is an aide on the Ag committee because we'd seen them out together a few times at—God, where was it they liked to go—that's right, Fin MacCools. Anyway, turns out that *last* night, he was at Tapatinis with *Julie* from *Hershorn's* office."

"And?"

Anna stops and rips off her glasses and her mouth goes agape. "*And it's so obvious they slept together!*" she yells. I tell her to quiet down and then she says "Oh, God" because she thinks that John is behind her or something, but I assure her that no, no, he's not, it's just that she's speaking rather loudly. See, for as hard as these Hill staffers work, their libidos work harder. And because they never leave this mound of democracy, the only sources of hormonal relief they have are one another, which I'm quite certain will result in some sort of Tudoresque genetic disaster in the years to come.

"Shit," I say as we're walking back up the stairs to the office.

"What? It's John again, isn't it. He heard me. You were lying before." I shake my head in irritation.

"No, no, he didn't hear you. I forgot to get Peter's scone. He asked me to buy him one. Fuck."

"I hear they're going to get a divorce."

"Who?"

"Peter and his wife. That's what people are saying at least."

"Anna . . ." She holds up both hands.

"You didn't hear it from me."

"Stop."

When I get back to the office, the remanding members of Grayson's staff—the rest of his team of BlackBerry-armed legislative aides and correspondents—have arrived and are umbilically attached to their computers in a room that's adjoined to the front office by a hallway littered with copy machines, printers, and a door leading to the congressman's personal office. I give Peter his coffee and feign realization that I've forgotten to get his scone. I apologize and he tells me not to worry about it, and assures me his wife will thank me later. Kelly and Janice shoot me daggers for not asking them if they wanted anything.

When I settle back into my desk, the clock reads nine-fifteen. Seven hours and forty-five minutes to fill with mail and local news. The phone's still silent. I log into my personal e-mail and see that I've received 147 pieces of spam. And then, among the offers for naturally enhanced penises, mail-order brides, and Cartier (Super cheap! Super real!) watches, there's one personal message, from my brother, Nathaniel.

I open the e-mail, which—per his signature style—is composed entirely in abbreviations and incomplete sentences as if to remind me that his correspondence is something he'd elect to do on his own, if he only had the time; that, really, when it comes down to it, he's too busy to be dealing with this shit ("not shit in the derogatory sense, but, Jesus, Taylor, you know what I mean"), but I'm his little brother and after all the crises and catastrophes of the past two years, he's obligated to fill the role of patriarch that our father so recklessly abandoned.

To: Taylor.Mark@gmail.com
From: Nathaniel.Mark@gs.com
Subject: chking in

taylor,
hope all's well w third (?) wk of work, in dc, etc etc etc. have been looking but havent found anything re: grayson in news. Impressive still you're working on hill. Am v proud. NYC becoming hot and filled w more tourists every day. Work's work, still making rich richer. Gotta love banking. Would love to see you in nyc some time this summer let me know weekends you're free and will work something out.
re mom: pls call her. Know you're busy w new job etc etc etc but you know I cant take her calls at office. Know its difficult right now and that youve done enough already but pls do me this favor. Spoke to dad two days ago. He says he misses you would like to hear from you too——but know that's between you two so will do best not to get involved. he's leaving for anther trip sat and doesn't know when he'll have phone access again. Keep in mind. Be in touch.

Love you
N

I shut the window and go back to Lori and her cells and her wigs and her clowns.

By lunchtime I've sorted one load of mail and the phone has rung a total of seven times. Twice, the calls came from the party whip's office, which means they were transferred immediately to Peter. Twice more they came from lobbyists who did not have the direct number of the legislative aides they were trying to reach. And three times they came from constituents, which meant the callers were either (a) members of America's aging demographic that has little more to do with their time than become politically active and shop on QVC, or (b) bloggers.

At one thirty, I'm reading lewd e-mails on my fraternity's listserv ("Kristen Harper's banged four bros so far—one more and she gets a set of steak knives." And "N E one know when Lorena Palmer stopped waxing?") when the phone rings once again. I let it continue for two more chimes as I reach the end of the e-mail (Lorena Palmer, as it turns out, stopped waxing after she got back from spending a semester in Senegal, much to the disappointment of Penn's Greek community), but then Kelly calls out and reminds me that phones don't answer themselves, and I roll my eyes and reach for the handset.

"Congressman John Grayson's office," I say and I hear Kelly sigh on the other side of the office.

"Hello, yes, can you transfer me to Peter, please?" The man's voice is hurried and flustered. Older than I, but younger than my father. "I can never remember his direct dial." I turn around and look at Peter, who's engrossed in an e-mail and is shaking his head.

"He's on another call," I say. "Would you like his voice mail?" This, I've been taught, is how you deal with callers such as this man. Democracy, see, doesn't have time for all Americans—just the ones Peter wants to talk to.

"He is? I suppose I could leave him a voice mail. How about Janice? Is Janice there?"

"Sir"—I do not have time for this American—"is there something I can help you with?"

"Maybe. I'm supposed to meet a man for breakfast. Someone from Deidrich and Howe. And I can't remember for the life of me where I'm supposed to meet him. Somewhere in Newport, but I'll be damned if I can remember where."

"Sir?"

He starts again and then laughs self-consciously. "I'm sorry, I should have introduced myself at the beginning of the conversation. You must be one of our new interns. This is Congressman Grayson."

My heart sinks and I begin wondering if making an ass of oneself is a genetic trait; if *Belize* has something to do with it. "I'm sorry, Congressman, I'm relatively new, and we've only been introduced once before, and I couldn't rec—"

"Taylor!" Grayson's voice rises and his laughing grows in sincerity. "I was wondering if that was you. How are things going so far? You'll get used to the humidity. It might take a few months, but you'll get used to it."

"Okay."

"I was telling Peter the other day how happy I was to have a fellow Californian in the office. I tell you, the weather out here is *gorgeous*. Why'd we ever leave?"

"I'm . . . I'm not sure, sir."

He laughs again. "That's what I always say. We must be crazy, right?" I tell him that yes! Yes, we must be! And we laugh briefly until silence takes over and he says, "I suppose I should find out where I'm supposed to meet this guy. Is Janice still busy?" I tell him no, she's not, and that she really never was, and he laughs and congratulates me on perpetuating the myth of productivity that's come to define D.C. "Always tell them you're busy," he tells me. Noted, I say, duly noted, before I transfer him to the larger of the Sisters Grimm. I hear her squeal and giggle—two techniques that I imagine were entirely more effective when she was seventy-five pounds lighter. She tells him where to meet the man, and I go back to Lorena Palmer and her newfound au naturel take on hygiene, until I hear Janice bellow out a disgruntled "YOU!" from behind the partition that breaks the front room into three distinct sections.

"Nachos," she says, when I ask her if she's called my name.

"Pardon?"

"Speak English? I said nachos."

I stutter. "Well, to be honest, Janice, 'nachos' isn't really an English word."

"Save it, Cervantes. Get me some nachos." She starts slathering on lipstick and looking into a mirror that's set on the edge of her cluttered desk. "And make sure there's extra cheese. It's been a rough day, what with the congressman calling so early and all."

Back downstairs, back in Longworth's basement, the cafeteria's lunch crowd has largely cleared out. I order Janet's nachos and cover them with four large scoopfuls of creamy Velveeta cheese. Fun fact: Velveeta is actually still considered pasteurized cheese by the FDA, believe it or not. Actually, to be technical, it's "pasteurized process cheese food," which means it's only got to contain 51 percent of cheese ingredient, by weight. I Googled it last week, the first time I was commanded to retrieve snacks for the fatter of the Sisters Grimm.

It's amazing what you can get away with around here.

I get a turkey sandwich for myself and take my tray over to one of the open registers to pay. In the line ahead of me, a girl close to my age reads the Style section of the *Post* as the cashier asks for her money. After waiting for a moment, and after seeing that the staffer has no intention of paying anytime soon, I clear my throat, which, I'll admit, is an obnoxiously passive form of protest. But so is holding up a queue of busy people in the name of reading an 850-word story about Anna Nicole's children.

"What?" she says, without looking up. "Worried that your nachos might get cold or something?"

"No. It's just that there's a line. And you're holding it up."

She looks up. "Is there?" Behind us, a lone aide pounds relentlessly on his BlackBerry, unaware of the confrontation unfolding in front of him.

"Yeah, there is. Me. Now, can you please pay so I can get back to work?"

She smiles. "Oh, yeah? And whose office are you running?"

I think back to my fraternity's listserv. Lorena Palmer's waxing habits don't exactly constitute running an office—or a reason to be offended, at that. I break down and I hang my head and I laugh. "Grayson, from California. You're keeping me from sorting his mail, you know."

"Ah, yes, the Republican." She finally reaches into her purse. "Great hair."

"What about you?"

"Reyes. New York."

"Right, the Democrat."

"The one and only."

"She get a lot of mail?"

The girl laughs and brushes back a dark strand of hair off her olive face. "Tons. Those women from Spanish Harlem can get pretty feisty."

The cashier gives her a handful of change.

I grin. "Right, I bet. Well . . . good luck with that."

"Nice pants," she says, glancing downward before walking off.

A puddle of yellow (pasteurized) goo has dribbled onto the folds of khaki covering my zipper.

Janice asks what took me so long but then she cuts me some slack after taking notice of the inconspicuous stain. I apologize for the delay, and I tell her that there was a long line in the cafeteria. "Tourists, you know." She rolls her eyes as she shovels the first chip into her gaping mouth.

"The afternoon mail got here while you were gone. It needs to be sorted."

"Where is it?"

"Taylor," she says with a sigh, letting out noxious fumes, "it's by the mailboxes. Where it *always* is."

I nod and tell her of course, and then I say sorry for interrupting her lunch before I head over to the mailboxes, which are really nothing more than a series of cubbies on a wall in the adjoining room.

When I walk into the room the legislative aides briefly look up from their computers and give me nods. Anna keeps her head down but says, "So you guys hear about John from Miller's office last night at Tapatinis?"

"Yeah," another one answers, and Anna gives me a look that says, "See, idiot, I told you." "I always thought that chick he brought home was a lesbian, though."

"She *is*?" This is Anna, who is already frantically typing an e-mail, and I roll my eyes and get back to the mail. The twice-daily mail deliveries are not necessarily good news for them, the aides. Generally, the bundles of envelopes and packages mean nothing more than an increased workload: angry constituents who need prompt responses, passport requests from housewives with poor vacation planning skills, reports that need to be read from the ever-growing army of foundations and think tanks that've formed around town.

"Don't worry, guys," I say as I cut the plastic band holding the bundle together, "there's not too much this afternoon. Just about four thousand letters from bottled blondes fighting for the Back Bay."

They give me quiet chuckles and thumbs-up.

"What happened to your pants?" one of them asks after I've sorted about twenty-five letters.

"Cheese accident."

"Fuckin' Janice," he mumbles. "One of these days that bitch is going to turn into a nacho." The aide sitting next to him laughs and gives him a high five and I imagine Janice, a giant, cheese-covered chip (I don't think she'd be pasteurized), BlackBerry in hand, and the seven-year-old in me grins along with them until my phone starts vibrating in my pocket. Startled, I grab it through the cotton. "You sure it was the nachos?" he says, raising an eyebrow and getting back to his work.

I roll my eyes before stepping out into Longworth's hall and flipping open the mobile. "Hello?"

"Sir, this is the FBI, and we've obtained evidence that a Congressman John Grayson has been harboring douche bags in his office."

"Nice, Chase. Funny. Hilarious, in fact. What do you need? I'm at work." He starts laughing.

"Jesus, look who's suddenly important. Got some votes to cast, champ?" He's right. The only thing I've got to do, now that the second load of mail is sorted, is sit and wait for the phone to ring. And maybe, if I'm lucky, refill Janice's stapler.

"I just want to make a good impression, that's all." This is something Chase won't understand. He's working for his father at Latham, Scripps, Howard, where, as I understand it, his days are comprised entirely of expensive three-martini lunches with clients and the occasional golf trip.

"Right, right. Anyway. We're going to Café Milano for dinner tonight. And by 'dinner' I mean 'drinks.' Reservation's at seven thirty. Early, I know. But it's a school night." I sigh. So far I've made a determined effort to avoid interactions with Chase during the workweek. While the outings are no doubt fun, they're hard on my productivity and even harder on my liver. Our apartments—mine in Woodley Park, his in Georgetown—are far enough apart that they've made the goal seem reasonable—obtainable, even. But Chase has caught on, and has been pushing back hard.

"I don't know, man. Grayson's back in the office tomorrow afternoon and things are going to really start picking up."

"C'mon. Caitlin, Annalee, and Jack are going. We'll get a bottle of wine, tops. You'll be in bed by ten thirty."

"Chase, it's *Tuesday*." There's a silence on the other line, and then for this moment I'm relieved because I've won, I think. I've changed the course. But then:

"You're right. Reservations were probably a bit much."

May 22, 2007;
7:45 P.M.

By the time I get to Café Milano I'm fifteen minutes late but the first to arrive.

Not that it matters, but I suppose I could have been on time had I not decided to walk from the Metro. Had I not suspected the group's general tardiness, I would have taken a cab from the station to the restaurant in an attempt to bypass the crowds that gather in swarms outside the cookie-cutter bars and bistros and pubs along M Street. But I've known Chase for five years, and the past two weeks have been enough to gain a basic understanding of his friends' modus operandi. So I watch as four empty taxis pass me heading south—just in this uniform line—down Pennsylvania Avenue, and I know perfectly well that my appearance will be at once fashionably late and casually early, depending on one's perspective.

Regarding weather: the beginning of May is one of the few pleasant times of year in Washington. Never too long and always too short, it's sandwiched tightly between a winter that seems to outstay its welcome, and a summer that arrives inappropriately early. The days are warm, but haven't yet been saddled down with the kind of oppressive humidity that makes you curse your forefathers for founding a nation's capital on a swamp; the nights are cool but not biting.

I cross the bridge over Rock Creek and Potomac Parkway, and Pennsylvania Avenue ends, and I pass by the Four Seasons, outside of which a long line of black Lincoln town cars with diplomat license plates has started to twist and snake. Each vehicle pulls out of the hotel's driveway carrying one or a few of the world's more powerful people and so I straighten my tie, which has become slack during the day, and walk with a more pronounced gait. Behind me, Pennsylvania Avenue's a straight shot to the White House. And it's hard not to become wrapped up in it all—or, maybe, what's more: to not *want* to be wrapped up in it all, I suppose, but then my phone vibrates in my pocket and my shoulders slump as I read the mobile's screen, which screams KATIE in capital letters.

"Hi, Mom," I say into the phone as one of the town cars rolls in front of me, almost over my toes, and honks.

"Hi, Taylor, it's Mom." I think I hear the rattling of ice against a glass and I look both ways before crossing the hotel's driveway.

"I know; that's why I said 'Hi, Mom.'" I rub my free hand over my face, over the sweat that's gathering over my eyebrows. And I tell myself not to get frustrated because, really, I don't know how sane I would be if I were sitting alone in that sprawling Spanish-style villa with Pacific views and countless balconies that's starting to crumble at its foundations.

"Of course, right, I'm being silly." She pauses and this time I hear, without mistake, the clang of ice in tumblers. "Anyway, I'm sitting out on the veranda with Suzanne and I wanted to call to see how your day has been." In the background, I hear Suzanne instructing my mother to tell me hello. "Suzanne says hello."

"My day has been fine," I say. "Busy. Tell Suzanne hello for me, too."

"Anyway," she says, her voice becoming—and this is not a word I'd use comfortably with Katie Mark on any frequent basis—*giddy*. "You won't believe what Suzanne and I did today."

"What?"

"We went shopping at the *swap meet*."

"That's fantastic." *Have I passed Prospect Street?*

"*The swap meet*, Taylor," her voice gets louder. "Aren't you proud?"

"Yes. Very." I rub my face again. "Did you find anything?"

"Well, no." And then: "Actually, that's not entirely true. Suzanne found a chew toy for Princess Grace." Princess Grace is Suzanne's Pomeranian, a nasty little creature that my mother has always said would make a better appetizer than a pet. Katie whispers into the receiver, "I hope the little bitch chokes on it, frankly."

"Mom, look, this is all great. And I'm proud you're cutting costs, but I'm about to walk into dinner, so I've got to—"

"I didn't say I hope she chokes on it, Suzanne," I hear Katie say as she falsely defends her statement. "I said I hope she—" and I hang up the receiver.

I make my way up M Street and then bank right on Wisconsin, headed up to Prospect. Outside of Third Edition, a small band of men who could be fraternity officers, or could be thirty-five-year-olds still dressed as fraternity officers, are smoking in a tight huddle.

"Cavanaugh said he's going to Daily Grill. He says there's some happy hour or something for skinterns tonight." Skinterns. Clever.

"Cavanaugh's a fag. No one goes to Daily Grill anymore."

"Dude, I'm just telling you what he told me."

"Well, what he *told* you was fucking wrong. Last time I was at the Grill some bitch mistook my boat shoes for loafers. I told her to go back to Adams Morgan." They all laugh and they punch their fists together and they revel in the sartorial mistakes of the socioeconomic less fortunate before calling someone else a fucking whore, which changes the conversation completely.

So, like I said, no one's at Café Milano when I walk in. The hostess tells me that I'm the first of the party to arrive, and she suggests I get a drink at the bar as I wait, and so I tell her that I like the way she thinks. She giggles and flips her hair before busying herself again with seating arrangements. At the bar, I take an open seat and I order a Bombay and tonic. Ten minutes later, one drink's turned to two, and I'm starting to think I've mistaken the time of Chase's reservation when Caitlin, cell phone attached to her right ear, breezes through the double glass doors and past the hostess station. She spots me at the bar, smiles, and makes her way over to me. "Hi," she mouths, kissing me on the cheek. She continues her conversation, which is in a different language—Arabic, I think. It's an almost uncomfortable dichotomy: pretty young woman, Polo dress, Stuart Weitzmans, David Yurman, perfectly symmetrical freckles arranged along sun-tanned cheeks; the language of Muhammad and Mecca and Bin Laden. I suppose I just hadn't expected this from her at Gold Cup.

She continues her conversation in a flourish of hand gestures and nods as I order her a glass of rosé (it really is the new pinot noir, she told me a week ago, the pink's back, but only the most sophisticated winos know it. Seriously, she read about it in *Gourmet* as she was planning a dinner party in April. Give it a year. I allow her, then, to convince me, and I decide not to say that Nathaniel had told me about the unfortunate rosé epidemic that held Manhattan in its grip a few years back, and that it was only a matter of time before the culturally less astute made the discovery on their own). Finally, she sighs and hangs up the receiver.

"Sorry about that," she says, tucking the phone away in a giant Fendi spy bag. "*Really* I am. Future employers." After doing advance work for Dick Cheney, Caitlin attended Georgetown's School of Foreign Service. She is finishing the two-year program this month, but until now I hadn't heard anything of her future plans.

"Congratulations," I say, clinking my glass to hers. "I didn't know you'd landed a job."

"I was debating among a few of them," she says, bringing the glass to her lips. "Good wine. Anyway, I was debating. I had some offers with a few banks. Some consulting firms. I don't know, everything just seemed so *typical*. And then this offer came along and, frankly, it was just too exciting to pass up. I'll be moving in August."

"New York?"

"Baghdad." I spit out my gin and tonic, but she doesn't correct herself. Instead, she pulls a compact out of her purse and checks her hair and her makeup and just sort of purses her lips. How does one answer such a statement? I rack my brain for appropriate responses: Cheap real estate? Booming nightlife? Both seem insensitive at best, downright wrong at worst.

"Well"—I'm trying my best—"that should be . . . fun."

She snaps the compact shut and returns it to the depths of her bag. "It'll be fascinating. Absolutely *fascinating*. I'll be acting as deputy attaché to the Treasury Department. Would you like to try this rosé?"

"Sure." I sip the wine and try to imagine this girl cradling an M-16 in one hand and a cosmopolitan in the other and, I'm realizing slowly, it's becoming unnervingly easy.

"It's not quite as light as, say, a sauvignon blanc. But it's nowhere near as heavy or acidic as a red. It's a shame that rosés are associated with Franzia, because they really are delicious wines." She turns in her seat and surveys the restaurant. "God, just *look* at this place. It's always such a scene. I think *Esquire* or *Vanity Fair* or some other magazine once drew up a seating chart that detailed where all the big lobbyists and politicians sit when they come here. Daddy said it was mostly fabricated. I don't even think the food's all that *good*. Last time I was here I ordered the gnocchi bulgari, which was *so* overcooked I could barely eat it. I could have sworn the chef left it boiling for at *least* an hour. But Chazy loves this place. He always has. Kip's good friends with Franco Nuschese, the owner. Chase had his sixteenth birthday here. *God* knows why. He sees all these people every week *anyway*."

"Do you think he's going to show up? He's thirty minutes late," I say.

Caitlin laughs. "Don't be ridiculous, Taylor. You've known Chazy for five years. Of *course* he'll show. If Chase says eight thirty, he means nine. You know that." She's right. Chase does have a tendency to be late or, as he puts it, the rest of the world just has an obnoxious habit of being early. "See? I told you. There he is now."

Over at the entrance, Chase is already flirting with the hostess, and Annalee's chatting behind him with that John, or Jack, Buchanan, that gossip columnist from *Politik* who couldn't have been less interested in me two weeks ago. And the juxtaposition of Chase—all bulging bravado—against Jack—all withdrawn and calculated—makes for a fascinating anthropological diorama.

Caitlin waves to attract Chase's attention and he signals for us to meet him at the table.

"Hi gorgeous," he says when we're all seated. "And hi to you, too, Caitlin."

She smiles and blushes and I take the opportunity to note that Chase has been using this line since freshman year. Caitlin lifts her empty glass and points to it as the waiter walks by. "Rosé. The Les Domaniers Puits Mouret."

"Sorry we're late," Annalee says. "Chase got held up at work. And I had some things I needed to wrap up at the magazine."

"Dad needed some stuff taken care of." Chase reaches for the wine list. "Red okay with everyone?" Everyone nods except for Caitlin, who gives me a grin and then a condescending chuckle. "Jack, put that goddamn thing away." Jack looks up from his BlackBerry, which he hasn't ceased pounding on since we all sat down.

He finishes typing, sends the message, and puts the device back in its holster. "Sorry. Apparently some congresswoman from California made a scene on a dance floor at this fund-raiser. My editor's trying to get the scoop." Jack pauses for a moment. " 'Scoop.' Fuck. That's such a tacky word."

The waiter approaches the table and asks if we've made our decisions and before any of us can answer Chase puts in an order for a bottle of pinot noir and three appetizers.

"Which member?" I ask Jack once the waiter leaves.

"That's what I'm supposed to be finding out," Jack mutters, shooting a glance at Chase. Then, "I'd forgotten that you work in the California delegation. For Grayson, right? How's that going?" He removes his BlackBerry before I begin answering.

"It's all right," I say. "I'm kind of stuck doing the grunt work now, but I'm sure it'll pick up. My chief of staff says it's likely I'll be staffed on at least one issue by July."

"Have you met the missus yet?"

"Pardon?"

"Juliana. Grayson's wi—"

"No, not yet."

For a week after the Gold Cup, for seven long days, I thought about Juliana Grayson's warm breath on my neck an impossible number of times; and each incident concluded with heavy breathing, an increased heart rate, and a damp Kleenex. But by day eight, Judeo-Christian ethics and a sore forearm took over and one of God's commandments (the exact number's escaping me) managed to partially banish Juliana and her warm breath from my fantastic imagination.

"God. *That* whore?" This is Caitlin. Chase stops explaining the menu to Annalee and looks up.

"You guys talking about Juliana Grayson?" Chase asks.

"Grayson married her after his—God, what was it?—after his second term. That's right. Second term." Jack brings a water glass to his lips but doesn't drink. He just lets it rest there as he retells the story, which he seems bored with before he begins it. "People started speculating why a good-looking guy like Grayson hadn't tied the knot yet. Liberal media conspiracy or something." He finally takes a conservative sip. "Anyway, his parents introduced them. She's the daughter of some other land-developing mogul who worked with Grayson's father, I believe. Family friends, or something. From what I've heard from friends out West, she's never really had to do much with herself aside from socializing and getting herself into trouble. There's always some rumor flying around about her. A bit of an outsider who manages to find herself on the inside. Last year the Ladies That Lunch in Georgetown—God help them—started saying Juliana was sleeping with the son of the Argentine ambassador. No one ended up digging up any dirt on it, but pretty much everyone knew it was true. That's the thing about Washington—"

" '*That's the thing about Washington*'?" Caitlin interrupts his lecture and takes a large swallow of her rosé. "Did you *honestly* just say that, Jack? Did you *honestly say that*?"

He ignores her. "When people start whispering about something, it's usually true." He finally relinquishes the glass, which he's been using as a prop, and sets it on the table. "Anyway, she's attractive."

"Totally hot," Chase chimes in. Annalee elbows him in the ribs.

Caitlin rolls her eyes. "She's repulsive. Pathetic. A total *cougar*." Chase laughs and gives me a high five.

"And she knows it," Jack continues. "I remember last year, I

was at the Bloomberg after party for the White House correspondents' dinner—*a total fucking bore*. I mean, *Tila Tequila* was on the
guest list—but anyway, she was there chatting it up with some
young actor and seriously, it was like watching *The Graduate*. Mrs.
Robinson all over again."

"I'm sure it was nothing," I say.

"Right. Tell that to the actor's wife. She divorced him a month
later. Anyway, she's much more visible than Grayson is. Spends
very little time in California, from what I hear. I've got no clue
why, given this weather. Word is she whined until he traded that
studio apartment in for some town house in Georgetown. Courtesy of Daddy, I'm sure. I'm actually surprised you haven't met
her yet."

"Why would I have? It's not like I'm a dinner guest often."

"I think she was at Gold Cup, champ," Chase says. Jack and
Caitlin both look at me. An awkward pause. "But then again, it's
not like you were exactly coherent toward the end of the day."

The waiter returns with the wine and pours each of us a
healthy glass after Chase ceremoniously tastes it. He tells us our
appetizers will be out in a moment.

"Whatever. Just be careful of her. Or, don't be." Jack pauses.

Caitlin sighs. "Jack, stop being such a pig." Annalee giggles.
Chase signals for more wine.

An hour later and we're halfway through our third bottle of pinot
noir but we have eaten only a series of hors d'oeuvres. Twenty
minutes ago, I gave up hope on any formal sort of meal. Annalee,
who has remained quiet aside from the occasional snicker during
dinner, is now happily and drunkenly chatting about her afternoon,
which involved styling a fashion shoot featuring Middle Eastern
ambassadors' wives.

"It's called 'Glamorize World Peace.' You know, like 'visualize world peace,' but it's about fashion, so we're glamorizing it," Annalee says, forcing a proud smile. "It's nothing like New Guinea, but—"

"Sounds like a pretty standard *Capitol File* spread," Caitlin says, her voice toned down to that level of condescension that only two women could truly achieve.

"No, no," Annalee says. "*Capitol File* did something like this, but with Latin American ambassadors' wives. I think it was a year ago, or something. I guess the Bolivian and the Colombian women had some issues with one another. Something about a fight that friends of their husbands had over trade?"

"Sounds about right," Jack says under his breath.

"Anyway, it's going to be really great. In one shot, this princess from Jordan is dropping this huge gun in a big Dumpster. And she's wearing this Chanel gown that's *gorgeous*. The dichotomy of the images is just—"

"I don't know how many times *Cap File* or any of the other shitty glossies in this town are going to waste cash on spreads like this before they realize D.C.'s not New York," Jack says, cutting Annalee off and reaching for the bottle.

"I told you, it's not *Cap File.*"

"That's not the point. The point is Pennsylvania Avenue is not exactly Fifth Avenue, and people should stop trying to change that." Annalee looks down at the hors d'oeuvres, which she has yet to eat thus far.

"Well, I think it sounds great." Chase rubs her back. "God knows that if there's one thing D.C. needs it's a little style." We all sit in silence, moving food about our plates until Chase continues, "Caitlin, I heard about the big move to Baghdad. Dad told me this afternoon. Congratulations. Don't count on me visiting, but congratulations." Chase raises his glass.

"Thanks," Caitlin says, making every possible effort to remain cool, composed. "Taylor and I were talking about it all before the three of you got here. I'm absolutely *thrilled.*" The word lingers in the air. Everyone nods. *Thrilled. Baghdad* and *thrilled.* Judging from the looks of the group's reactions, I'm not the only one who's shocked to hear the two words together. But just as she did two hours ago at the bar, Caitlin doesn't let the reactions faze her; Baghdad, New York—what's the difference? One's got dangerous insurgents, the other dangerous socialites. She's likely already dealt with the latter and emerged victorious, so why not try her luck with the former? She stares straight into Jack's gaping mouth and sips her rosé (she'd said no thanks to the pinot). "Absolutely. Thrilled."

"Well, more power to . . ." Jack stops in midsentence and looks toward the bar. "Shit."

"What?" Chase and Caitlin say in unison.

"We've got a Halert." They both groan.

"A what?" I ask, thoroughly confused.

"A Hal Hastings Jr. alert. 'Hal' plus 'alert' equals Halert. It's something we've been saying since high school. In fact, we've copyrighted it." Caitlin laughs. "He graduated . . . what, Chase . . . three classes ahead of me? Which means he was five classes ahead of you. He worked in the Senate for a while. For some Republican from Texas, I think. God knows what he does now. Fuck, he's got to be pushing thirty. He's always around. Always drunk." I look at our table, which is littered with cocktail glasses and empty wine bottles and three shot glasses, and wonder if Jack—or the rest of us, for that matter—is in any place to be making such an accusation.

"He's just one of those on-the-scene boys," Caitlin chimes in, once again reaching into her bag to fetch the compact.

"An on-the-scene what?" I ask.

She sighs as she fishes around in her giant purse.

"You know the type, Taylor. Frat boys who can't grow up so they end up spending weeknights playing survivor flip cup and hitting on interns at Smith Point. And then they adopt these little protégés *they* train to fill *their* loafers once they get married. It's just this pattern. It's just the way things happen. I mean, it's pathetic. *Utterly pathetic.*" And she's applying lipstick now. "My friends have slept with half of them."

"He's on his way over," Chase says, trying not to look up from the dessert menu, which has been sitting on our table for the better part of the past half hour.

"You cowardly fucks owe me," Caitlin says with a kiss, rising from her chair.

"That's no way for a lady to talk," Jack says with a grin. She slips past him, allowing her purse to hit him square in the face in the process.

We all turn to watch as Caitlin—hair swooshing and hips swaying and lips pursing—works to diffuse Georgetown's equivalent of an improvised explosive device. A woman's smile has got to be more persuasive, more politically powerful than any standard stump speech, I think as I watch her work. The promise of sex and pleasure and procreation debases us to our most primal states, our most vulnerable. Cleopatra knew something about this when she was batting her eyelashes at those Romans, and so did Elizabeth when she was keeping her ankles crossed. Men, for all of their guns and testosterone and power ties, are the simpler of two political beasts.

"Real quick," Chase says when it looks as though Caitlin has successfully martyred herself for our own comfort, "before she comes back. Dad wants to throw a going-away party for Cate. Something over the Fourth of July weekend at the Chesapeake House." I had been to the Lathams' bay house once before (it has a name—"Right Side of the Bay," I think)—sometime during the spring of junior year for a party his mother was throwing. Most of the weekend was spent either drunk or high or hitting on the underage daughters of his mother's friends, but I remember it being

big. Maybe even sprawling. "Anyway, keep your calendars clear."
And then, "Shit, okay . . . they're coming back."

Aside from the fact that it'd be difficult to hide him on account of his inflated midsection, I honest to God wasn't exaggerating when I said that Hal Hastings was Georgetown's own IED.
Watching him give the other diners hearty slaps on the back as he
passes them on the way to our table, it's safe to say he's unpredict-
able at best. And then as he spills a glass of Syrah on the daughter
of the Latvian ambassador, there's no doubt he's destructive. I'm
beginning to see why the group was so determined to steer clear
of him. "I'm sorry," Caitlin mouths to us once they're both table-
side. She shrugs, as if to say, "I tried to stop it from detonating.
And I've got the lost limbs and stained dress to prove it."

"Holy shit," Hal slurs, and the stench of bourbon and beer
and sweat forms a toxic cloud over the table. "Ho-ly *shit*. Chase
Fuckin' Latham. How long has it been, man?"

Chase brushes aside a wisp of hair and rubs his right temple.
"Three days, Hal. I saw you Saturday night." People are beginning
to look up from their meals.

"Really? Fuck, man, I'm sorry, I must've been shit-faced."

"Yes. From what I remember you weren't exactly sober." Jack
pulls out his BlackBerry and starts typing. Annalee continues to
fuss with her portion of the hors d'oeuvres—not eating, just poking. Hal nods at Chase's retelling of Saturday night, then looks at
me and cocks his head.

"I don't think we've met. Hal Hastings Jr." He juts out a moist
hand.

"Taylor Mark." I stand as he grips and violently shakes my
hand. I think I hear the bones cracking.

"Real nice to meet you, Tyler, real, real nice."

"Actually, it's Taylor."

"You mind if I join you crazy fucks?" Hal doesn't wait for an
answer but instead he just steals a chair from the table next to

us. "Thanks. So, listen to this, man. I'm driving through Chevy Chase today after having lunch with my old lady and I pull up to this stoplight at Wisconsin and Willard, the one right by Cartier. My window's down and I'm blastin' Journey—you know, 'don't stop, belieeeeeeeevin' '"—and I'm just feelin' my fucking *vibe*, you know?" He laughs and sighs and takes a sip of Chase's wine. "So anyway, I'm stopped at this light and I see this chick, total babe, sitting on this bench near the sidewalk. I give her the nod, you know, the 'this Beemer's got room for one more' nod, and she stares back. I'm eye-fuckin' the *shit* out of her and she's totally giving the vibe back. So I figure there's about ten seconds till the light changes and I say, 'Hey, sweetheart, you'd look a lot better in this seven series,' but the bitch just keeps staring. Totally giving me the eyes, but just *staring*. And then, right before the light changes, this fucking fag comes out of Gucci and picks the bitch up—like, physically *lifts* her off the bench and the bitch doesn't even move. And then it fucking dawns on me, man: *the bitch is a goddamn mannequin!*" Hal shakes his head as if this is all Gucci's fault, as if the blood that was pumping in his groin this afternoon was the fault of those wily bastards back in Milan. Even Annalee looks up. "Anyway, man . . . what've you been up to?"

Chase has been rubbing his right temple the entire time. Now his eyes are shut. "Work, Hal. Just lots of work."

"You still working for your old man?"

"Yes, at the firm."

"Well, hell, man, That's great. Just great. I'd love to have Kip as a boss. I love that son of a bitch. What's he got you doing?"

"Golfing," Jack mumbles, his eyes and fingers still on the BlackBerry.

"Buchanan!" Hal says, eyeing Jack. "You still taking it up the ass at that newspaper?"

"Yup, Hal." Jack doesn't look up. "Still taking it up the ass at that newspaper."

"Dad has me assisting on a few different accounts," Chase says. "And what is it you're doing now, Hal?"

"Oh, you know me," Hal says, looking up at Caitlin, who is still standing, and then he wraps a thick arm around her waist. "I've got my fingers in a few different pots." She squirms out of his grip.

"Yes, Hal, we certainly do know you. You know, Caitlin here is moving to Baghdad in August, so that's going to be one less pot for you to have your finger in."

Caitlin shoots Chase a glare.

"Baghdad! Ho-ly *shit.*" Hal slaps his hand down on the table, which not only attracts the attention of the restaurant's other dinners, but also its maître d', who I've noticed has been eyeing Chase with the scorn of a man who wants to exert what little power he has, but isn't in a position to do so. "You gonna go find Osama for us, Cate?"

"Hal," Caitlin says with a sigh and sits back down. "You *know* I hate when people call me Cate. And Osama's in Afghanistan, not Iraq. But yes, I'm moving in August." Again, I can't help but conjure up the image: Caitlin with a cosmo and an M-16, standing over the lifeless body of a terrorist she's impaled with a stiletto.

"Sorry, babe, *sorry.* You know I love you." He takes a stab at a wink, but ends up just contorting his entire face. "Hey, you guys hear about the LNS party on Friday night?" Hal asks, referring to Late Night Shots—a D.C.-based, invitation-only social networking website that, over the past few years, has turned into somewhat of a Schindler's List in reverse: its unspoken goal is to save the city's WASPy elite from intermixing with the blacks, Hispanics, Asians, Jews, gays, Indians, and otherwise undesirables who fester in the regions outside of Georgetown. In addition to featuring discussion forums (e.g., "There are black people in Adams Morgan. STAY AWAY"), LNS informs its members of sponsored parties and other social functions where they can meet without fear of infiltration and heterogeneity and interbreeding. Chase invited me to join a few days ago. And after a few brief moments of hesitation, I did. My number (you're given an identification number on LNS—just another uncomfortable similarity to one of mankind's greater tragedies) is 1013—which, while not in the triple digits, is still low enough to be acceptable, so says Chase. *Anything below 2000 and you're golden, champ. Once you've hit 2001, though, you're fucked. You're trash.*

"Kind of," Caitlin says. "I just scanned the e-mail. What's the deal with it?"

"Smith Point. Celebrating this year's class of summer skinterns. You fucks better come, I'm helping promote it." Hal's cell phone vibrates and starts to sing. "Don't Stop Believin'" is the ring tone. "I gotta take this. Beer pong tourney at Wilkonson's place tonight. He's calling about the bracket." He springs up from the chair with speed and determination that are surprising for a man of his girth, almost tackling our waiter in the process. Before flipping open his phone, he snaps his right hand into the shape of a gun and shoots us. "See y'all on Friday night."

The waiter, shaking from his brush with near-injury, asks us if we'd like anything else. Chase says no, and hands the man an American Express card, to the protest of the rest of the table.

"We'll expense it," he says coolly. "Whatever. We talked about Baghdad. That's work, right?" Everyone nods. And then,

"Hal Hastings. Ugh. He's *horrible.* Just absolutely *disgusting.* I can't believe Abby Walker was sleeping with him for such an inappropriate amount of time," Caitlin says, running a hand over her dark hair.

"I can. Abby's a whore." This is Jack.

"And 'skinterns'? Why the hell is *everyone* saying that? It's demeaning."

Jack rolls his eyes. "Come off it, Caitlin. It's funny. Albeit unoriginal, but funny. That party's going to be worthless, though. Anything Hal touches turns to shit. Total, utter shit."

"*Totally.* Can you imagine the people who are going to be there? The whole thing'll turn into some drunken orgy by midnight."

"Likely."

"Are you guys going to go?" I ask once I'm able to get a word in edgewise.

And then, together, "Probably."

IV

May 6, 2006;
8:31 P.M.

O *r maybe it starts like this:*
 I know something's off when Nathaniel orders a double vodka before we've even been given the menus. Nathaniel rarely drinks. In college, he attributed his monklike behavior to his obligations on the swim team; he was the captain, and he held the school's record for the hundred-meter butterfly. Truly, though, he's just that type of person: he extracts more pleasure in watching other people drink and reminding them of the foolish things they've done once they've come to the next morning.

"To celebrate your graduation," he says, giving me a shifty smile, when I ask him why he's indulging. He looks at his watch—a Rolex given to him by our father upon his own graduation (summa cum laude) from Princeton four years ago. "You've been a college graduate for about eight hours now. How do you feel?"

"Unemployed," I say.

He moves uncomfortably in his chair and looks toward the entrance of the restaurant, onto Walnut Street—one of Philadelphia's main arteries of commerce and culture. Our parents were supposed to have met us here. "Yeah, well, employment's over-rated."

This is a lie. Nathaniel takes pride in his position at Gold-man Sachs like most parents take pride in their daughters' first ballet recitals. It's his baby, an infant whose DNA is comprised of spreadsheets and IPOs and market shifts. A week ago he was calling me twice a day to remind me that idealism didn't pay bills, and that while Camus may have been known for his bold philoso-phies, his investment portfolio left something to be desired. By the third day of the harassment, I turned off my phone.

"How's the vodka?" I ask as I watch him grimace through a second sip.

"Delicious. I'd forgotten how much I love this stuff."

"Thanks again for coming down from Manhattan. I know it's a hassle."

"Don't be ridiculous. It's my little brother's graduation. I wouldn't miss it for the world."

Another lie. On the second day of last week's harassment—a day before I shut off my phone—Nathaniel had asked me if I knew how much work would pile up in twenty-fours hours of his absence. Spending a day in Philadelphia, he had told me, would surely mean that he'd have to forgo his Sunday morning run around the reservoir (he did four laps) in Central Park, not to mention the reservation he'd made a month ago for dinner at Babbo on Saturday night. It was an inconvenience—no, worse: an *imposition* on his precious time.

"Right . . . well, thank you. I really appreciate it." He's not lis-tening. He's smiling through another toxic sip and looking toward the door.

"There's Mom and Dad. I'll go get them."

And here's when I know something else is wrong.

I turn and watch as Nathaniel sets his napkin on the table and hastily rises to retrieve my parents. But even now, even as

Nathaniel kisses my mother on the cheek and shakes my father's hand, I can tell that they're not the same people I've known for the past twenty-two years. For starters, they're standing at least a foot apart. My mother, a woman who was raised to believe that it's always more polite to smile now and gossip later, has her arms folded snugly across her chest. As Nathaniel whispers to her, she turns her head away, and even though her eyes are being covered by an enormous set of black Gucci sunglasses, I can tell they're rolling back in their sockets.

Why is my mother wearing her sunglasses at night?

My father, Frank Mark, looks equally uncomfortable. He pulls at the collar of his shirt and scuffs his loafers against the floor and maintains a safe distance from my mother. He nods as Nathaniel barks directives at him and then he scolds Mom as she teeters on her high heels. Is she . . . *drunk?* I'm not sure what to make of any of it, I think, as they smile at the hostess and begin making their way toward me. The mood had been entirely different this morning. I saw them briefly—right after the ceremony—but everyone seemed to be getting along perfectly fine. We're not a family that fights. We never have been. Problems are swept neatly under a large, imported rug, where, in time, they're recycled or forgotten. And when one of us dares to lift a corner to peek under that giant Persian mat that so elegantly graces the floor of the Mark genealogy, Nathaniel is always there to slap a wrist.

But this is confusing. Nathaniel and the vodka. Katie and her sunglasses. I'm watching a silent foreign film. I can't read the subtitles quickly enough as the reel jumps to the next frame, and reds and blues and yellows are draining from Technicolor faces until everything's in varying shades of gray.

"Hi, honey," Mom says as she sits down without removing her glasses. "Sorry we're late. Your father was busy combing his hair. Doesn't it look nice?" Dad sighs and shakes his head.

"Mom," Nathaniel starts. It does look different, though. *Lighter.*

The streaks of gray that used to flank his temples are no longer there. I hadn't noticed this morning.

"Well, Nate, it *does*. It's lighter, Taylor, in case you couldn't see in this light."

"Mom," Nathaniel tries again, "take off your sunglasses."

"No way, José," she says, adjusting the frames with perfectly manicured fingers. "Not until this restaurant learns the meaning of a little *mood lighting*." She leans over and whispers to me loud enough for the rest of the table to hear. "Sorry, sweetie. I know you wanted to go to Le Bec Fin for dinner on your big day. But your father hasn't had a secretary in a few months, and planning ahead has never exactly been his forte."

"What happened to Christine?" I ask. My father has had the same secretary for fourteen years. Christine Salvo remembered every detail of my father's life—both inconsequential and paramount—that he tended to forget. How had he been functioning without her?

"Katie," Dad says, giving a look to my mother that, in more words or less, reminds her that he still pays the bills, "that's enough." After a brief skirmish, Katie obliges Nathaniel and Frank's wishes that she quiet down, just as long as she doesn't have to remove her glasses.

"Mr. College Graduate." Dad smiles, but there's something behind it; something that's not quite happiness. Something else. And what's that on his earlobe? Is that an *earring*? "Your mom and I are so proud of you."

"Me, too. So proud." Nathaniel flags down the waiter and asks for menus and another double vodka, light on the ice.

By the time I take the last bite of my filet (good, but no Le Bec), the air has become so thick, so laden with a palpable discomfort that even the busboys are avoiding our table. The sound track of the past ten minutes hasn't been one of conversation and dialogue, but rather one of silverware scraping against china, punctured occasionally with Katie's pregnant sighs. If the upper crust of America could devise its own form of torture, this would surely be employed more frequently than elementary techniques created by professionals, like waterboarding. It's the worst kind of abuse: watching a familial squall gather its brute force as you're left with no nails to board up the windows. And even though this position, this lack of knowledge, is familiar to me (when I was eight and my grandmother passed away, the news was kept from me until the following Christmas, after I inquired as to why I hadn't received a present from Nana), it's no less uncomfortable than it's ever been. The clinking and the clanking of the forks and knives start aching in my eardrums. Finally I decide that—boarded windows or not—I can't take it anymore.

"Is there something wrong?" I say, laying down my fork. *Is something wrong?* What sort of question is that? And shouldn't I be insulted that my own family has put me in a position in which I should feel the need to ask it? My mother's three sheets to the wind, my brother's glancing around the room like a mobster expecting a hit, and my father may or may not have a pierced ear. Of *course* something's wrong.

"No, not at all, why do you say tha—"

"Oh, knock it off, Nate. He's a graduate, not a moron." My mother nips Nathaniel's prepared response—one that he undoubtedly practiced countless times in front of the mirror before dinner—in the bud. "Your father's leaving me, Taylor. We're getting a divorce. I'm a divorcée. Which, if you ask me, has a certain ring to it, wouldn't you say, Frank?" Dad shakes his head before putting it in his hands. I turn to Nathaniel.

"How long have you known about this?"

"For about three months. I told them not to tell you so that you wouldn't lose your focus before your finals."

"I graduated .02 of a grade point short of magna."

"Well, at least you had your focus, I suppose." Nathaniel moves the remainder of some duck confit around his plate.

"I called Nathaniel once your father said he was moving to Belize."

"Belize?" As in the country, Belize? Or was there some town named Belize in California? Somewhere north of L.A. but, say, south of Fresno, maybe? I look to my father, who is still shaking his head in his hands. It's lighter, his hair. It's definitely lighter.

"Yes, Taylor, Belize. As in the banana republic. Belize *is* a banana republic, isn't it, Frank? Anyway, dear, perhaps you've heard of it. Right by Guatemala. Your father's decided that it's the right time he looked for his lost shaker of salt south of the border." I think I see a dark streak of mascara emerging from under the lower rim of my mother's glasses as she signals for the waiter. "Another vodka, Nate?"

"Absolutely."

After dinner, Nathaniel escorts my mother back to the Ritz on Broad Street, where she'll raid the hotel room's minibar and will demand that he go to the nearest convenience store to buy her a pack of pepperoni pizza–flavored Combos. Being Nathaniel, he'll agree, under the condition that she never mention this evening at family gatherings for as long as she is physically in control of her functions. My father and I, meanwhile, walk from the restaurant to Rittenhouse Square, where we take a seat on an empty bench as the warm May night swells around us.

"So what do you think of the hair?" my father asks once we've both endured two minutes of a painful, awkward silence.

"Looks good," I say, which I don't expect him to believe because I barely believe it myself. "It's subtle. I didn't really notice it this afternoon."

"Well, pal, I've been making a lot of subtle changes lately." *Divorce* isn't exactly subtle. And *Belize* most certainly is not. My father reaches into the pocket on the inside lining of his sports coat. "Cigarette?" I shrug and accept and resolve that my feelings upon seeing my parents enter the restaurant were frighteningly accurate: these people have become strangers. Somewhere along that uniform path between a cap and a gown and some foie gras, Katie and Frank Mark ceased to be my parents.

But maybe this is what maturation is, I consider, as I watch my father strike a match and bring the flame to the tip of his Marlboro Red ("go big or go home," he's always said). Maybe it's watching the people who've shaped you and the people who've molded you be stripped of their ethics and influence and morals until they're nothing more than a messy pile of words and exclamations; a heap that—only in the best of lights—can be discerned as human beings.

"So . . . Belize?" I take a drag off the cigarette, which is harsh and burns my throat.

"That's right, pal. *Belize*." If I didn't know any better, I'd say he was happy—proud, even—of this most sudden development.

"Can you tell me what happened between you and Mom? I mean . . . whose decision was this?"

He exhales a cloud of smoke and rubs his head. "Well, Taylor . . . that's not really the way this works. Sometimes these things just happen. It's never really just one person's *decision*."

More, more, more lies. My relationship with Caroline, the doomed and dramatic nature of which had caused much of my experience at Penn to seem like a prolonged Dashboard Confessional ballad, taught me better than this. Sure, these things *happen*, they transpire. But at the end of the day, when all's been said and done, one person decides to jump ship. One person decides that the vessel's got too many holes, too many leaking cracks to be in the realm of reasonable repair. One person decides there's something that's better suited to his or her needs. There's always a decision.

"Then how does it work?" I ask.

My father transfers his weight back and forth on the bench as if he's trying to find a comfortable position from which to deliver a story that he already knows will sit disagreeably with me. It all started with a fishing trip, he says. One to—you guessed it—Belize, that he and Sam Jackson, his best friend from high school, had planned more than a year and a half ago. ("Actually, it was fishing and hunting. A cast-and-blast. But don't tell your mother that. You know how she feels about guns. Then again . . . I guess none of that really matters now.") Before the trip, there had been problems between him and my mother; nothing of the romantic nature, per se, but simply the minutiae that come along with middle age. A friend of theirs had suggested therapy, a little help to get over the hump, but neither of my parents proved to be malleable in the capable hands of cognitive psychology, so the sessions turned into a boring, one-hour drama that was promptly canceled after four episodes. And so, at the beginning of February, Frank left for Belize, in search of some temporary rejuvenation, but secretly open to something more.

I find myself fighting the urge to become sick once my father starts discussing the way the open ocean air can change a man. He can't expect me to understand, he says, at least not yet. Fifty-six years down the road, he was feeling trapped, *emasculated*. His job—private equity—which he used to view as a seven-figures-per-year drug—was now stale and draining. He had kissed every cheek and had shaken every hand in southern Orange County more times than he could count. He had funded the same school for kids with autism through the same charitable program for more than a decade. It was an impossible race whose only finish line was death. And he was tired. He'd had enough. Then there was Katie.

Three years ago, he noticed difficulty becoming aroused.

I watch a young couple wander down Walnut Street and wonder, silently, if either of them have ever experienced this nightmare, this torture of having to sit, unmoving, unflinching, on the verge of *fainting* at the thought of one's father's erectile dysfunction. Sadly I conclude that at least one of the two of them has; that this, as much as I'd like to believe otherwise, is not a unique experience.

At first he blamed a faulty prostate, he says—he didn't want to admit, and indeed often refused to—yet he was getting older. His runs took longer and his bones were starting to ache. But then there were the looks, just these brief and sporadic glances during which he could recognize the woman lying in the bed next to him but couldn't pin down a reason as to why he'd married her in the first place. And here's another thing they don't tell you: sharing, as it turns out, is a hell of a lot harder than giving. But people change, he says, they *grow,* Taylor. Truth is, though, he'd grown on a different trajectory than my mother. He'd fallen out of love, and he'd hit the ground with a deafening thud. Now each time he saw his wife of twenty-four years, each time he saw a framed picture or watched a home video (he'd thrown half of them away), he was reminded of what he'd given up to ensure someone else's happiness.

"But you kids," he says, stubbing out his cigarette, "you kids make it all worth it." And I suddenly feel guilty.

So, back to Belize and its majestic salt air, he says, reaching for another cigarette. He and Sam (whom my mother never liked, and whom I was beginning to like less and less) had chartered a small fishing boat for the day, a single-engine vessel called *The Little Whore* that was captained by a man named Paco who sported a tattoo that was a mermaid but bore closer resemblance to a malnourished Chinese dragon. In the eight hours they were at sea, there were three bites and three fewer catches. But it didn't matter. The boat riding the sea's mild rolling current, coupled with a cooler packed to the brim with Belikin, Belize's local beer, were all that my father needed. Sometime after lunch, as Sam and Paco spoke in a Spanish-English hybrid about the differences between Central American *chicas* and North American women, my father got to thinking about his childhood; an activity that, he should know by now, is a dangerous journey on which one should rarely embark.

"There was this day when I was about twelve years old—about ten years younger than you are now," he says. "My dad drove me down from Encino to Huntington Beach for the day. This was right before the cancer got real bad." My grandfather—a man, a *legend* I never met—passed away when Dad was thirteen. Since then, his existence had been aggrandized into a modern mythology of a hardworking hero who had passed on after saving his family, his town, and the future of American values. "After spending the day on the beach, my father pointed out to the ocean and said, 'Frankie, that's where your dreams are. Don't you ever settle for less. Because you're worth more than that, Frankie. You're worth more than that." He starts tearing up, which, I suppose, I should find touching, but it hits me more along the lines of offensive. The small gold stud in his ear reflects the yellow light emitting from a nearby streetlamp. "So, I'm sitting there on this boat, and this Belize air is *talking* to me, Taylor. Honest to God, it's *talking* to me. It's saying, 'Have you forgotten Dad?' And I'm saying, 'Goddamn it, I *have*.' And then I see everything just passing in front of me: more work in that goddamn office, your mother draining the life out of me, you kids moving away. And you know what I said to myself, Taylor?"

"No."

"I said, 'Fuck it.' I got mad. I said, 'It's time to start thinking about *me* for a change.' Life hasn't been the same since, pal. I feel *free*. I went and grabbed Sammy by the collar and said, 'We're not leaving this place.' And he said he'd been thinking the *same god-damn thing*." Of course, my father's actions surprise me, but Sammy's don't. He's been married three times. The last escape was to a woman sixteen years his junior, making her four years older than his eldest daughter. He was, as my mother put it, a perpetual child who hadn't learned the true purpose of a zipper.

"So . . . that's it?"

"Well, no, There's also the bar."

"The bar?"

"Sammy and I have got to have something to keep ourselves busy, pal!" Dad slaps my back. "So we bought this bar—this great little dive—in Fort George. It'll be a great place to vacation with your buds. Honest to God, you'll love it. We're going to call it *Exit Strategy*."

Indeed.

The plan has always been to go home, anyway; spend a month or two in Laguna Beach, regroup, and figure out my next steps. I'll take advantage of the lack of responsibility to decompress, I told myself, as unemployment loomed through the second semester of my senior year. Then I'd look for something in New York, or Chicago maybe—put that education to good use. But now with Dad's sudden departure, and with Mom left to her own devices, my temporary vacation is threatening to become an extended sentence.

"I can't take time off work," Nathaniel pleads the next day, two hours before he's scheduled to take the Acela Express back to Penn Station. "You were planning on going home for a month or two, anyway. Just stay for a month or two longer, until she's back on her feet and everything's been finalized. Jesus, I've never seen her like this. The glasses haven't come off since last night."

"It's called a hangover, Nate."

"That's not the point. The point is that this is *family*." And he shakes his head and he gets in the cab and I can't decide to be angry at him for eliciting my fears of feeling dispensable or to thank him for providing me with a role.

For the first two months, Katie keeps it together. She's angry, understandably, and without doubt bitter—but she's functioning. She maintains her obligations to her numerous charitable endeavors (Meals On Wheels, the autistic school, bidding at fund-raising auctions, etc., etc., etc.), and continues to socialize with her countless acquaintances. Slowly, family pictures that contain my father start disappearing from our home's walls. She clears out his office. She befriends the Internet and sells his golf clubs on eBay a day before he asks her to ship them down to Belize. I consider these to be normal symptoms of a divorce.

Almost immediately, we schedule a meeting with her divorce lawyer, a shiny man named Richard Yale, Esq., who insists on maintaining the esquire in his name with the same vehemence with which he insists on bleaching his monstrous teeth. His office includes a fifty-gallon fish tank that holds a miniature piranha (and nothing else) and is adorned with Le Corbusier chairs and white walls and plaques from Stanford Law and the University of San Diego. I sit next to my mother in the painful leather creations of modernism—which, at least by my accounts, sacrificed something in the way of comfort in the name of utility—and wait as she adjusts her sunglasses and he riffles through paper. Finally, Yale, Esq., leans back and folds his hands behind his bleached blond hair (parted, *glued* in a wave) and sighs.

"Katie, doll, you know I love you, and you know I work hard for you."

"You certainly charge me like you do."

"Mom," I say, "take off your sunglasses. Please." Katie doesn't budge but rather crosses her legs and sets her purse on her lap.

"But there's not a lot I can do for you here. It's California law—everything's split right down the middle. His assets are pretty liquid . . . he's transferred them all to offshore accounts. Your half includes the house, the art, some investments in a few mutual funds." He looks at another paper. "There's alimony, of course, which he'll pay. His lawyers have agreed to that. But your current lifestyle, Katie—"

"Who's his lawyer?"

"Dale Sampson, but that's not important."

"Taylor, write that down."

"Katie, what are you going to do? Egg his house?"

She sets her fingers on each side of the glasses and carefully adjusts them. "I'd be lying if I said the thought hadn't crossed my mind."

Yale removes his hands from the back of his head and rubs his face. "Why don't you try getting a job?"

She finally rips off her glasses and I start rubbing my temples and I put my head between my knees. "A *job*, Richard? Is that what I'm paying you for? To parent me? To tell me to *get a job*?"

Yale, Esq., sighs again and moves some papers around his Herman Miller desk. "Well, you've got the house. And it's paid for. So that's formidable. If you set yourself up with an experienced agent, you could sell it for at least four and a half million dollars. I could help you find a solid financial adviser, and we can work from there."

"That house was in *Architectural Digest,* Richard." Katie slams her fist on the desk and I jump. "Twice. I'll be damned if I have to sell it to some family from . . . from *Arizona.*"

Yale, Esq., throws his head against his desk, on the papers he's spread out in front of him. Legal snowflakes, I think, no two scribed with the same complaint. "I don't know what to tell you, Katherine. I'll go through all this again, but I'm not promising anything. You've got my hands tied."

I keep rubbing my temples in small circles and the sun reflecting off the Pacific is starting to burn my eyes and then Katie turns to look at me.

"What?" I say, stopping.

She turns back to face Richard. "What about child support?"

"Your sons are twenty-two and twenty-eight, Katherine."

"Aren't those just technicalities?"

A week after the meeting with Richard Yale, Esq., I get a job waiting tables at the Coyote Grill, a small but popular restaurant that's a stone's throw from my house. I work double shifts and befriend the eatery's small army of cooks—an amicable group of Mexicans who teach me Spanish slang and fix me dinner and occasionally supply me with low-grade weed for free. Katie agrees to "make attempts at cutting costs." And so about once a week, my mother has a piece of art appraised, after which she watches an old romance on AMC, cries, and fixes herself a scotch and soda before falling asleep on the couch at 9:00 P.M. Three months or so into the routine, after much coaxing, I convince her to jump-start sessions with another psychiatrist, one who came highly recommended by our next-door neighbor, an elderly widow who boasts about nervous breakdowns like Boy Scouts boast about merit badges. Nathaniel calls and praises me for my efforts.

"I cannot *believe* that I've agreed to this," Katie says as we drive along PCH to her first therapist appointment. "I'm perfectly fine, Taylor. Perfectly fine."

"I know you are, Mom," I say, turning the white Mercedes SLK into a small office center with palm trees and ocean views. "But this will help you to be *more* perfectly fine."

"Just missed magna, hmmm?" she says, flipping open the overhead visor and applying lipstick. I'm relieved as she exits the car and slams the passenger door shut.

For the next hour and a half, I sit in the parked car under a monstrous palm and exchange text messages with Chase while halfheartedly reading the editorial page of the *Los Angeles Times*. Someone, I quickly learn, has an opinion about what's to be done in Baghdad. Another person, though, disagrees. And so on. And so forth.

"What r u up to?" Chase writes.

"Nada. Katie therapy appt." Five minutes later, my cell phone vibrates again.

"How is drving ms daisy?"

"Har har. Fine."

"U should move 2 DC. Would b a blast."

"We'll see."

"Pussy."

I put the phone on the empty passenger seat and return to the editorial page. I had never considered Washington. Even with a politics major, it had never crossed my mind. My idealism, I told myself, was above politics. I viewed my personal philosophies to be above the two-party system, above petty partisan lines. When I get to the sports section, the right-hand door of the Mercedes swings open and Katie ducks into the car. She sets her purse on the floor and then puts on her sunglasses and turns to me.

"You know, Taylor, I'd like to thank you." I'm caught off guard.

"Really?"

"Yes. I was being too judgmental of this whole 'therapy' venture." She says the word like it hurts her lips. "I think that Dr. Thompkins—*Charles*—is going to be very helpful."

"Well, Mom, that's great. I'm glad."

"Now"—she opens three folded prescriptions she's had clutched in her hand since entering the car—"we have some things we need to pick up at the pharmacy."

Dr. Thompkins's pharmaceutical regimen is an ambitious routine for which I'm initially grateful: Prozac for depression (she hadn't noticed the signs), Klonopin for anxiety (her increased drinking had masked it), and Ambien for sleep (just in case). In terms of cognitive therapy, Thompkins (a Stanford Med grad who has published three books, including *If Men Are from Mars, Then Nuke the Damn Place*) focuses on my mother's own liberation. Frank is following his own dreams (however irresponsible and erratic), so why not pursue hers? Art classes? Gourmet cooking? Fencing? The world is still her oyster; age, after all, is nothing but a number.

The SSRI–benzodiazepine–zolpidem cocktail softens my mother's edge and, when combined with alcohol, takes away the edge completely. I remind her constantly that Charles has, in fact, warned *against* the consumption of alcohol while she's taking her meds (and, indeed, the warning labels on her pill bottles emphatically support my case). Katie, though, waves her painted fingernails in my general direction at such remarks. "Those labels are there for legal reasons," she says, slurring. "To protect the drug companies from people who can't hold their liquor."

Per Thompkins's advice, however, she does start something new—tap classes at the Laguna Beach community center—to which I drive her dutifully for two weeks. Tap, though, doesn't prove to be the escape Katie was looking for. The other women (and the one man) in the class aren't her people, she claims. The instructor—a sixty-five-year-old, off-off-off-off-Broadway veteran named Eileen—talks incessantly about her cats (there are seven of them, each one named for one of Snow White's loyal dwarfs). And instructions such as "kick ball change" inspire feelings that are more along the lines of revenge than forgiveness.

So she stops attending classes, despite my desperate pleading to give the sessions just a few more tries ("but your calves are looking fantastic, Mom"). She's a stubborn one, though, Katie Mark, and flattery of vanities do little to move her.

"Cats, Taylor," she says over margaritas at the Coyote Grill. "Seven of them. And you know how I feel about quadrupeds named after people."

It's true. As a child, Nathaniel and I had attempted to name our black Lab Henry. My mother had found it grossly inappropriate.

Daily I'm forced to remind myself that Katie Mark is a good person who was recently dealt a bad hand. She's never been one for warmth, and this recent upheaval certainly hasn't done much to melt that arctic layer that envelops her heart. But she means well, and she always has. I watch her as she examines her reflection in her compact, fixing the collar on her Lacroix blouse before signaling to the bartender for another round of margaritas. There was this time during first grade when I must have been no more than six years old. I had always been small for my age, and never particularly athletic. And in that cruel and anarchic world of childhood, those two dreaded qualities equate to nothing less than a death sentence. Recess was torturous, and the playground became a level of hell that even Dante would have difficulty imagining. One boy in particular, Michael Garrick, took particular pleasure in turning my lunchtime into thirty-five minutes of psychological and—at times—physical abuse. Multiple times a week, I'd walk home from the bus stop, bruised, bloody, and often crying. My father, who had never spent time in the crowded trenches of the pathetic and the unpopular, gave me suggestions that only further pointed to his tragic misunderstanding of the World of the Uncool. "Hit 'em back," he'd say. "These punks, if they get popped good once—just *once*—they'll leave you alone." I'd tried that, I told him. Thing was, Michael Garrick had about thirty pounds on me, so my featherweight swing had elicited but two things: (1) a blink from Garrick; and (2) an even more brutal beating from his gang of other prepubescent thugs. My mother had largely stayed out of the affair—the world of boys and men, she figured. "Listen to your father," she'd say halfheartedly. "He understands these things. If you've got problems with your first bra, then we'll talk."

But one night—it was April, I think, a week after our spring recess (a brief reprieve) had ended—she walked by the closed door of my bedroom to hear me sobbing inside. She cracked the door open to find me crying into my blanket—a large, tattered piece of cloth that Nathaniel had given to me two days after my birth (a peace offering, most likely, his way of saying, "Look, we've got to share these people. Let's try to make as little fuss as possible").

"Taylor?" She sat on the edge of my bed. Normally, my mother avoided terms like "sweetie" and "darling." They felt unnatural, she said. "What's wrong?"

"I hate school. I don't want to go back there," I wailed, throwing my head into her lap.

"Why do you hate school, Taylor? School's important. You have to go."

"Because people are mean. They don't like me." I stopped making sense. "I hate it."

"Are you talking about that boy? Michael?" She began stroking my blond hair, strands of it damp with tears.

"Yes. Michael Garrick. I tried doing what Dad told me to do but he just hits me harder and makes fun of me more."

"Mhhm. Well, you can't let one person make you hate school, Taylor. That's letting him win." I lifted my head off her lap and looked at her desperately.

"But I don't know how to beat him!"

"We'll figure something out," she said, continuing to stroke my hair. "We'll figure something out." And then she put my head back in her lap and told me a story—one about a boy who grew up shining a prince's shoes until he found out he was a prince himself—and I fell asleep in her arms.

The next morning, as she poured me a glass of orange juice, my mother told me that she'd be picking me up at school, and so not to take the bus. My father, who was in the kitchen at the same time, asked her why, and she told him I had a doctor's appointment, which, even then, even with my childish instincts, I could tell was a lie.

At school, the day proceeded as usual: a black eye during the morning recess, lunch money stolen by noon, hiding in a bathroom stall during kickball. After the final bell rang, I went to the area of the school's parking lot reserved for those parents who had the free time to pick up their children. I saw Katie, dressed nicely in a St. John knit suit accessorized with lavish—but not gaudy—jewelry, laughing with a small group of other mothers gathered in a rectangle of grass that ran tangentially to the parking lot. As I approached her, Michael Garrick cut me off (he didn't get picked up, nor did he take the bus—he walked home, likely to a latchkey apartment where he was underloved and underappreciated, I liked to imagine). Katie took notice and excused herself from the group.

"Where you going, shorty?" he said, pushing my shoulder and knocking me a few steps back. "Isn't the bus for the retarded kids the other way?" I scuffed my feet against the concrete. "Or, what, is your mommy picking you up in your car seat?" He reached again to push me, but Katie caught his hand.

"Yes, Michael. His mommy is picking him up today." Michael kept on his defiant mask, but I could tell he was caught off guard. "And where, may I ask, is your mother?" Michael said that his mother was at work and then, after wiping some snot on his shirtsleeve, demanded to know why my mother wasn't at work. "Oh, Michael," Katie said, slowly and calculatingly replacing a strand of hair that had fallen out of place. "I am at work. I'm raising my children. A job that, from the looks of it, your mother's skipped out on." And then: "Taylor, would you excuse us?"

I'll never know what Katie Mark said to Michael Garrick—what she threatened, what maternal wiles and tricks and strategies she enacted. But as she gracefully crouched down in that red St. John suit, something happened to the little heathen's face. It softened. His jaw slacked. And as Katie leaned in to whisper something in his ear, Michael Garrick's eyes filled with an emotion I'm assuming he'd never felt before: terror. He looked back at me, his eyes welling with tears and his cheeks shaking, and then, as my mother stood and flattened her skirt, he exploded into a blubbering mess of water and salt and unconditional apologies.

"Come on, Taylor," Mom said, taking my hand. "Let's go get some ice cream."

In spite of the rolling eyes and the incessant judgment and the generally disagreeable behavior, one thing will always be true: Katie Mark loves her children. And although she won't admit it here, now, at the Coyote Grill over Cadillac margaritas, she also loved her (now former) husband. She'd melted that damned heart of hers, that muscular organ that'd experienced the deep freeze that accompanies a childhood in old Pasadena, as best she could for Frank. And now that it was thawed, and he had left, she was doing her best to keep it from bursting into flames entirely.

I lean my back against the wall at the Coyote Grill, silently, as she runs her finger along the glass's salted rim.

"I don't understand," she says with a choke, and a few grains of salt fall from the glass to the floor at her feet.

"I know," is the only thing I can think of to say.

At Katie's request, we up her appointments to twice a week, each session lasting for an hour and a half. In about February, though, sometime after Valentine's Day, I start noticing items she'd carelessly left around the house: pages of old love letters that Frank had written to her (they'd exchanged love letters?); yellowing pictures of the two of them—Frank in bell-bottoms and Katie with her hair tied casually in a gingham scarf—on vacation at Lake Havasu. And then, one night, as we drive back from a performance of an Arthur Miller play at the South Coast Repertory, we pass Cleo's Caribbean Bistro, a kitschy mom-and-pop restaurant in Corona del Mar where my parents had their first date—my father the ambitious banker, my mother a Pasadena princess and recent Stanford grad. The lights are off at Cleo's this night, and a large sign that reads "Closed for Good, Darlings" is taped over one of the windows.

"Pull over, Taylor," my mother says quietly.

"Huh?"

"I said 'Pull over,' goddamn it." The volume of her voice increases, and the tone becomes shrill. I bring the car to a halt along an empty space of curb on PCH and my mother kicks open the door before the wheels have stopped rolling. Slowly, she walks over to the darkened window, each stiletto heel hitting the ground along some imaginary line. I stay in the car for a minute or two as other vehicles fly by.

I get out of the car once I see her knees buckle and hit the ground. I put my hand on her shoulder and ask if she needs help getting up, but she tells me she'd prefer if I just sat down with her. She's sorry, she says, she's just frankly feeling a bit out of herself this evening. I tell her to stop apologizing as small rivers start streaming down her face. She's always hated them, she says, tears. They tell too much. And they're contagious. One person starts crying, and then the next person feels some need, some *obligation* to follow suit. I promise her I won't cry. Cleo's, she says with a laugh. *Cleo's, of all places.* The date hadn't gone well, and she hadn't meant to call him back. But something had compelled her to give this man Frank a second chance, and look where that ended up. The cars continue to whiz by on the highway and my mother starts aimlessly pulling at a hole in her stocking—a casualty from the fall. I think back to Caroline and my own naïveté in thinking that, at nineteen, I had the ability to comprehend what love was, aside from a mixing of chemicals and electrical signals in an already muddled brain. "I'll be honest with you, Taylor," she says once the tears have stopped and the traffic has temporarily quieted, "I didn't think this was how it was particularly supposed to end."

After that night, Katie refuses to spend much time alone. The world that was supposed to be her oyster, the one that Dr. Thompkins had described during her first therapy session, becomes confined to Klonopin; her best friend, Suzanne; and Neiman Marcus. That wound, the one that was ripped open outside Cleo's, doesn't heal as much as it hides itself from view—which, in Katie's mind, is equally convenient. By mid-March I begin fearing that I've lost control of the situation. I call Nathaniel, who tells me that things will be fine and that it'll just take a few more months and that he wished he could help, but that a deal's going public and he can't possibly take the time, and that that absolutely *breaks his heart*. On a separate occasion I phone Dr. Thompkins to explain my concerns. She's not forming intelligent sentences, I tell him. And I'm fearful that she's abusing the medication he's prescribed. A true champion of American psychiatry, he increases her dosage. The edgy depression's been traded for a constantly grinning divorcée who'd ask a quadriplegic to dance if given the opportunity.

Until now, my patience has been kept in check by a healthy degree of guilt. At nights, after working a double shift, exhausted, and smelling like fish burritos, I keep my selfish rage at bay by remembering the feelings that Nathaniel had impressed on me during that weekend in Philadelphia: I was needed. I was *wanted*. This was *family*. My head on my pillow, I think back to Michael Garrick and his sobbing, pathetic wails and my mother's face, proud and protecting, as she grabbed my hand

and led me to the family car that we then drove to Dairy Queen for banana splits.

I'm caught between a rock and a precariously hard place—a place that was diligently molded, and then even more diligently honed, by multiple generations of hardworking, naturally guilty Protestants. Nathaniel escaped it through work. My father couldn't take it, so he hightailed it to Belize. And me? I haven't yet found a way to excuse myself from that Great American Family Dinner. So, in the meantime, I continue along this standardized path, staring across the oak table, fearing all the while that the person sitting at the other end, the man, the *boy* whose face is worn for wear far beyond its years, the one that's looking back at me, is none other than my own.

By the beginning of April, after spending nearly a year in Katie's beachside prison, the final straw falls and my back, in a sense, breaks. On a whim—one that I suppose is inspired by a handful of Klonopin chased with a shot of Glenfiddich—my mother and Suzanne buy tickets to a White Stripes concert. Neither of them has heard of the band, and I imagine that if they had, they'd opt to attend some other musical function. But Suzanne persists. She tells my mother it'd be fun—*spontaneous*—and since Katie has been in no mental position to argue or oppose or do much of anything aside from smiling, she agrees.

"You're going to hate the music, Mom. It's loud. Really loud," I say to her as she prepares for the night out (slacks and a black silk blouse from Chanel—casual gear).

"You don't know that, Taylor. You don't know that." Actually, she's probably right, I think, as I watch her apply lipstick. Lately, after that night, I've become convinced that my mother can no longer distinguish between levels of volume. "Suzanne is driving."

"Good. You don't have a valid driver's license." She hasn't had one in years.

"Yes, well, my point is don't wait up."

And so I don't. I have the night off from the Coyote Grill, so I take the opportunity to watch three hours of *Law & Order: Special Victims Unit* reruns and hit the sack. At about midnight, the phone rings. Startled, I answer it.

"Hello?"

"Hello . . . hello, Taylor?" It's a woman's voice, not exactly panicked, but audibly concerned.

"Suzanne?"

"Yes, yes, it's Suzanne." I look at the clock beside my bed: 12:13 A.M.

"Where are you? Hasn't the concert ended?"

"Yes, it ended awhile ago."

"So . . . where are you?" I was not about to play this game with a drunk middle-aged woman at twelve-fifteen in the morning.

"Well, that's the funny thing, Taylor. We're at the emergency room at Mission Viejo Hospital."

Per Suzanne, this is what happened: "The concert had been a *blast*. An absolutely *fabulous* time. Katie was really enjoying herself; she was *laughing*, Taylor, truly *laughing*. And had I seen that boy Jack White? Adorable. *Priceless* smile. Anyway, they had met a nice group of young men near where their tickets had them located (near the front and on the floor, thanks to Suzanne's husband's American Express black card). The young men were charming, really they were. Not the hoodlums that Suzanne had initially expected. And then one of them—his name was Logan, perhaps?—offered us some marijuana. And you know me, Taylor, I said absolutely not. *Absolutely not.* They just offered it right there. *Right out in the open!* But Katie. You know Katie. She's just been so *relaxed* these past few weeks, so *unlike* her normal, composed self, and that, you know, given *everything* that's happened isn't necessarily a bad thing. *And so she smoked some.* She coughed, of course, and I obviously became worried about her. Is one *supposed* to cough? But she seemed fine, and she seemed like she was really enjoying herself, even though she had spilled a bit of beer (*we were drinking beer!*) on that gorgeous Chanel shirt. And I can't remember precisely what happened next but when I turned around Katie had disappeared—well, not *disappeared* but was certainly not standing next to me anymore; she was *making her way toward the stage* with Logan. I called and called and called but it just looked like she was having *such fun.* In any event, within moments I saw Katie onstage with her arms *wide open.* A security guard was screaming at her, and Jack White (so cute!) was laughing and laughing and the lights on that Chanel shirt just looked *fabulous* but—"

"Suzanne, I don't mean to be rude, but what happened?"

"Oh, right, of course, sorry, sorry. Katie, at Logan's bidding—*God,* what do people call it—stage diving? The thing is, though, the only person there to catch her was *Logan.* And of course Katie isn't heavy, but she has put on a few pounds since all of this has happened—and if you tell her I said that I will positively deny it—but Logan was a small boy, and his jeans were far too tight to be appropriate—and he couldn't *catch* her."

"So she fell."

"Yes, yes, yes. She fell. And she broke her wrist. But she's *fine.* She's absolutely *fine.* She actually said she couldn't feel *a thing.*"

This doesn't surprise me. I close my eyes and rub my face.

"Which hospital are you at? Mission Viejo?"

"Yes, that's right. Mission Viejo. The doctors are just setting the cast now. She should be ready to be released in about an hour."

"Okay. I'm on my way."

"Aren't you just so *proud,* though, Taylor? Stage diving? Your mother went *stage diving*! It's just so *unlike* that Stanford graduate from Pasadena who had refused to *dance* before the divorce. Aren't you *proud*?"

"No. Not really."

Mission Viejo Hospital's ER is virtually empty by the time I arrive. As I'm sure you can imagine, southern Orange County is not necessarily a locale plagued with early-morning gang fights and armed robberies. Suzanne, still looking surprisingly put-together given the eventful night, is sitting in the waiting room reading a month-old copy of *Us Weekly*.

"I just can't *believe* these young stars nowadays," she says as I take the seat next to hers. "I mean, look at this, Taylor. Just *look at this*." She raises the magazine and points to a headline that reads "LILO'S COCAINE EXTRAVAGANZA." Below the giant bolded script are pictures of who I presume to be Lindsay Lohan, droopy-eyed and wasted, skirt raised up like a tube top. "Absolutely no responsibility. *None what-so-ever*." I nod, all the while thinking of what the tabloids might say if they gave a rat's ass about an emotionally decrepit Orange County mother with a taste for antidepressants and scotch. "KATIE MARKS THE SPOT," maybe. Or "KLONO-FALLIN'." They'd be vicious, for sure, and debatably accurate.

When two male nurses roll my mother out in a wheelchair, she looks fragile and sedated. Not old—my mother's never looked old—just fragile. They'd given her a spot of morphine, the nurses explain, something to ease the pain. I tell them that that probably wasn't necessary, but thank them anyway for their efforts. Don't get the cast wet, they tell me, make sure she uses a large latex cover whenever it may be exposed to water. Then they ask me if she'd like it if they signed the plaster bandage.

"No, thank you," I tell them. "I don't think that'll be necessary."

She starts coming to about halfway along the quiet drive home. She smiles and tells me she had an enjoyable evening and that, despite my protests, she'd actually *enjoyed* the music, that it wasn't *that* loud at all.

"But this cast," she says, looking at her wrist. "This cast is such an atrocious color. It won't match anything that I own. We'll go to Neiman's tomorrow."

We reach a stoplight and I slow the car to a halt. The streets tonight are empty and quiet and dark. As the engine murmurs, a drop of rain lands on the windshield, causing a tiny explosion that fans outward in asymmetrical tributaries.

"I can't do this anymore, Mom."

"I know."

May 23, 2007;
8:15 A.M.

I wake up thirty minutes late and my mouth tastes like a vineyard facing foreclosure and my head feels like a Journey concert seen from the back row—just too many sounds and visions without anything in real focus. This is the reason, see, that I avoid Chase Latham on Tuesday nights. Wednesday mornings shouldn't be accompanied with headaches associated with glam rock and brief recollections of what might have been.

It's not that the night had been a complete failure (though, at this point, I'm still trying to decipher what constitutes success). After Café Milano, after I'd made a feeble and half-assed attempt to hail a cab home, I agreed to go with Chase and Co. to Smith Point, where, two more G&Ts later, I found myself listening to Caitlin's foolproof plans for curbing Sunni insurgents. The details are hazy, but from what I recall the brunt of her plan hinged on more threats, more guns, and more, more, more blood. I'd come home once she'd convinced me (enough) that the troubled country (Iraq, not America) was dodging disaster, despite countless reports that signaled the opposite. I'd promptly passed out—clothed, teeth unbrushed, alarm unset—by twelve thirty. So: vineyards on the lips and glam rock in my skull.

I shower and dress and surrender to the reality that for the first time in my two-week tenure, I'll be arriving late to 1224 Long-worth. At eight thirty-five, I leave the studio apartment with my shirt untucked and hair uncombed and I emerge, ever so slowly, into the morning's harsh light, which ups Journey's volume against my temples and to which I simply cannot adjust. Two blocks later, I'm thankful to submerge into the cool air of the Woodley Park–National Zoo/Adams Morgan Metro stop. The platform's crowded with other stragglers and a few of the season's first ambitious tour-ists and I have to fight my way onto the first train that arrives.

Nabbing a seat at this hour of the morning is, of course, wish-ful thinking. So I stand, smashed against one of the train's doors, and wonder when public transportation made the leap from modern convenience to daily hassle to inducer of claustropho-bia. Around me, the city's commuters are reading copies of the *Express,* Washington's free daily that's distributed throughout the District's sprawling Metro. It's a pop-culture synthesis of today's top stories, the *Express*; the only local publication that manages to run stories about opium in Kabul side by side with photo editori-als on the summer's hottest fashions ("Afghan Drug Trade Sky-rockets" and "Peek-a-boo! Big Glasses Make a Big Hit"). Normally I'd read it cover to cover before transferring to the Orange Line, but today, with this headache and this tardiness and whatnot, I pass on the opportunity.

At Metro Center, passengers from the system's multicolored tracks file from streams and into whirlpools in the station's under-ground tunnels. I push against traffic down to a lower level, to the Orange/Blue lines, which run with little to no security under the nation's Capitol building. As I wait for the second train, I take a free moment to tuck in my shirt, which elicits some looks of dis-dain and concern from a mother and her daughter, and so I stop halfway through and leave the other half of the oxford dangling lifeless to my side.

The Orange Line train isn't as crowded as the Red, so when the train arrives I manage to find an open seat in the middle of the car. Two interns outfitted in D.C.'s standard-issue summer soldier uniform—khakis, striped tie, navy blazer, scuffed penny loafers— file into the row of seats directly behind me. Proudly, they sport the badges distributed to each person working (paid or unpaid) in the U.S. Capitol. Large yellows letters that read "INTERN" grace the bottom of each one.

"Big day?" one of them asks. His friend sighs; a huff of defeat and exhaustion and overbearing *importance*.

"When is it not?" I can't see them but I know the other one's giving a tired nod. "I've got these committee hearings, a legislative meeting . . . but when does it ever stop, you know?"

"I hear you, pal, I hear you. It's a bitch, but it's worth it. I just hope we survive till August. Recess'll be a good break. I'll be able to catch up on some stuff."

Of course, what the two rising sophomores behind me have failed to disclose to one another is that "committee hearings" is a romantic translation for "filing," and that "legislative meeting" roughly equates to "discussing who got smashed at Front Page last Thursday night" while fetching coffee for office assistants like myself. These, though, are the inconsequential details that seem to get lost in the town's ever-thickening humidity. As the air gets heavy, so do the lies.

Or maybe these kids have just learned how to play this game better than I. Maybe they've just kept their cards closer to their chests. Maybe they've brought better masks to the ball, better costumes to the charade. Maybe an ill-conceived notion of self-worth is better than no self-worth at all.

"Goddamn it, Taylor, where the *hell* have you been?" This, apparently, was not the day to have a morning meeting with pinot and expressionism. Peter is standing next to my desk, pounding his fist against the wood. The rest of the staff is gathered in the lobby/meeting room/reception space.

"I'm really sorry. Really. My alarm. I just—I don't know—I just forgot to set it." No one believes this but frankly I don't blame them, what with only half my shirt tucked in and all. And they make me aware of their doubts by avoiding eye contact with me, with the exception of Janice, who shakes her head disapprovingly while finishing the late bites of a cheese Danish.

"And what about all those *goddamn* e-mails I sent you?"

"What e-mails?"

" '*What e-mails?*'! That's what they taught you at that goddamn Ivy League school? I've been e-mailing you since midnight. What the hell do you think a BlackBerry's for? Text messaging your goddamn fraternity brothers?" This elicits snickers from Janice and Kelly, whom I suspect were spurned by the judgmental gauntlets of Greek rush and are just now beginning to extract their malice.

"I . . . uh . . . Peter, I haven't gotten a BlackBerry yet."

"WELL, WHOSE FUCKING FAULT IS THAT?"

In all fairness, the oversight is Peter's—not my own. The second day of work, the chief of staff had told me that I'd be receiving the mobile leash, but, happily, had failed to follow through on his promise. I suppose I could have reminded him, I could have mentioned something about it, but between Googling my own name and answering phone calls from Florence Rivers, Bud Buckings, and other constituents concerned with Those Damned Mexicans, the expense hadn't seemed truly worthwhile. I decide, though, that the argument will be lost on Peter, given his current state, and take a seat on the two-person couch, the one that's currently playing host to three people. Peter knocks his fist lightly on the desk a few more times before removing his glasses and rubbing the bridge of his nose with the other hand.

"For those of you who *don't* know," he begins, and I start suspecting that I'm the only one he's addressing, "here is what we're dealing with.

"The panel at UCI was last evening. According to Sarah, it went well. Grayson hit all the necessary talking points: working with conservationists while not standing in the way of innovation; green, but business-friendly. You know, the same bullshit. He misquoted three statistics, which we can deal with later." Everyone nods. "And the Newport Charity League loved him." A pause. "But his father probably paid them to, so that doesn't really count." Peter's wrong on this point, I think. Katie, before adopting an SSRI diet, had been highly involved in the Newport Charity League, primarily for the lunches (three-martini by nature, at the Four Seasons near Fashion Island). According to her, the women had a strict policy when it came to philanthropic functions: our husbands earn it, and we give it away. Often the organization's events posed severe, offensive dichotomies that could only be conceived over tea spiked with imported rum: a leather and fur fashion show raising funds for PETA; an eight-course meal (with wine pairings) to garner monies for the hungry. You get the general idea. I wouldn't be surprised if Grayson's appearance on the panel ranked as one of the group's more intellectual functions.

"What stats did he misquote?" Janice asks, licking some frosting from a finger.

"He said that up to thirty-five birds use the bay at a single time."

"And?"

"And the correct number is thirty-five thousand."

"Oh. Whoops."

"Yeah. Whoops," he says with a sigh. "But like I said, that's not the problem. The problem is what happened after the panel. According to Sarah, immediately after the Q & A ended, Grayson was talking to Wyatt Keeler." The staff groans. Keeler, a political science professor at the University of California, Irvine, makes the Bolsheviks look like right-leaning centrists. His books, which include *God Is Dead and I Dug the Bastard's Grave*, are consistently perched atop the *New York Times*'s bestseller list, where they remain among the ranks of *Harry Potter* and Dan Brown books due to their popularity among a certain liberal elite. "Anyway, Keeler asked Grayson what he thought should be done to calm the situation over in Baghdad." Peter pauses and hangs his head.

"And?"

"And"—he looks at his BlackBerry—"and our fearless leader said, and I quote, 'I don't understand why we don't turn the whole goddamn city into high-rise condos and shopping districts. You know, a kind of Dubai for the sectarian-savvy.'" Kelly laughs.

"The man's got a sense of humor, Peter. And let's be honest, you think those housewives in Newport disagree? If you ask them, shopping centers could've saved six million Jews. The bigger deal we make about this, the worse off we are. Keeler's a raving lunatic anyway. Any mainstream reporter would say the same thing. Who cares what he heard?"

"The microphones were still on."

"Oh."

"And the *Orange County Register* was there. For once."

"Shit."

"And the *L.A. Times*."

"Fuck." Peter throws a copy of the paper's local section onto the table. Above the fold, there's a photo of Grayson, hair coiffed as if it were part of a Botticelli statue, smiling behind a table. The headline above the picture reads O. C. CONGRESSMAN: IRAQIS SHOULD SHOP TILL THEY DROP. Kelly snatches the print off the table and fumbles with a pair of glasses before sliding them on her face. "*Fuck*. Where else has this run?"

"I'm not sure," Peter says before eyeing me. "I haven't seen the clips yet."

"And the blogs?"

"They've all got it. *ThinkProgress, Daily Kos, Huffington Post.* Those rabid little eggheads . . . they're all over it. Crooks and Liars has the audio. Son of a bitch." Peter, who proudly admits to being one of the last political warriors to have come of age before the dot-coms and the dot-orgs managed to stage a hostile takeover inside the Beltway, has blocked off a special circle in hell for bloggers. Criminals, he calls them; the ugly, discarded spawns of an Internet boom gone awry. And the fact that they're starting to actually *matter*—well, that's just twisting the knife.

"What reporters have called?"

"Boltz from the *Register*. Vonovich from the *Times*. Those fucks wouldn't give us the time of day before. And now this happens and they want a statement within the hour."

"Well . . . at least we're getting coverage?" I'm not sure if it's the traces of alcohol in my blood or general foolhardiness that compels me to contribute to the conversation. But Peter's stare, one that tells me I've surpassed being in over my head and am now dragging my feet along the sea floor, shuts me up.

"We've gotten three requests from local drive-time radio shows in Orange County."

"We're not going to book him," Kelly says, removing her glasses and cooling her voice. "Not until he's got something to say. Something that's intelligent, for once. When does he land?"

"He got on a six A.M. flight out of LAX. That puts him on the ground at Dulles at two P.M. He's scheduled to head to his house to put on a fresh suit after he lands; then he'll be in the office. There are some votes set for this afternoon." Janice reaches into her purse and produces another Danish. Raspberry filling this time.

"Perfect." Kelly stands, flattens her khaki skirt, and begins pacing—sternly, focused; like some World War II general—around the front office. "That gives us a good six hours. What was the *Times* quote?"

Peter flips through the paper to a page that's covered in coffee stains, scribbled notes, and a small tear. "It calls him 'disconnected,' 'uncompassionate,' 'seemingly unknowledgeable,' and 'a perfect representation of southern Orange County.' "

" 'A perfect representation.' At least we know we won't have problems with our constituents. They didn't call him a hawk. So we're good there. I'll draw up a statement. An apology for the misunderstanding. And then something about Keeler spinning the truth."

"This doesn't have anything to do with Keeler."

"Sure it does. The man hasn't got a sense of humor and he doesn't understand the merits of capitalism." And I begin to see why Peter hired Kelly in the first place. "In the meantime, we've got to tackle this uncompassionate tag. If there's one thing Grayson's got, it's the guy-next-door allure. We'll work to keep that. What's coming up on the calendars? Any bills we can jump onto as a sponsor? Money to save some goddamn child soldiers in Myanmar or something?" The aides, notebooks flipped open, stare back. Kelly rolls her eyes. "Will someone *please* look into that?" She taps an acrylic nail against her moleskin journal. "Okay. That's a start." She turns to me. "You. The congressman's dry cleaning is hanging in his office. Take the suit over to the congressman's house in Georgetown. And do me a favor: try not to stop by any pubs on the way back." Janice snickers condescendingly as Kelly turns around and scribbles an address on a piece of paper.

"The house is on the corner of Thirtieth and P. Yellow door.

You can't miss it. I'll give you cash. Concepción, the maid, should be there to let you in." I nod and take the piece of paper and thirty dollars from Kelly. "And if she's not, then Juliana will be." She checks her watch. "She usually gets back from spin class around ten thirty. Sorry, Juliana is Grayson's wife. Should've explained that. Have you met h—"

"No. No, I haven't."

I roll and unroll one of the twenty-dollar bills that Kelly's given me as the cab veers down South Capitol and onto Pennsylvania. My left leg is shaking uncontrollably, and the driver, some Ethiopian guy with a wrinkled, sun-bleached picture of Jesus on his dashboard, keeps asking me what's wrong, and I tell him "absolutely nothing," which I suppose we both know is a lie.

It's not that I want to sleep with Juliana Grayson; it's not that I want her to transcend the world that I've created for her in my studio apartment into the land of the living and the possible. As far as I'm concerned, she should continue to be exactly what she is: the leftovers of a sexually depraved adolescence.

Desires are easy to handle, just so long as they don't materialize.

But as the taxi hauls past the White House, I start to worry that what I've suspected all along might actually be true: that conscience is, at the end of the day, just some construct of our imaginations. And then, as the cab pulls up to a big yellow door on Thirtieth and P, as the driver's picture of Jesus stares back at me, I wonder if Dustin Hoffman knew exactly what Anne Bancroft was doing that first time he dropped her off at her house in Beverly Hills. And if, as she poured a drink, put on some music, and opened up about her personal life, the very last thing he wanted her to do was stop.

I knock three times—two hard, one a bit softer—on the big

yellow door and wait for what seems like ages before I hear three bolts go "click" and see the handle turn.

"Is this the congressman's dry cleaning?" Concepción's thick accent is, at first, a bit difficult to understand. Each *r* sounds like rolling thunder—nothing like the cooks at the Coyote Grill. Concepción takes an unprecedented amount of pride in her job. You can tell by the way her light blue uniform is pressed and steamed just so.

"Yes, ma'am." She ushers me into the town house, which, while it's easily 150 years old, is decorated with a Scandinavian sparseness, a taste of interior design that's cultivated and honed in Los Angeles. The foyer's large and airy, featuring a single, simple table that hosts an abstract piece of sculpture of indeterminable worth. Two sets of curtainless French doors lead into the adjoining rooms: a dining room furnished in light oak, and a sitting area that appears to have gotten about as much use as Grayson's copy of *Robert's Rules of Order*. At the other end of the room, a curved staircase winds up to the second floor of the home. A Pollock print (an original?) is splayed along the wall above the case's rail.

"Sir, you can put the dry cleaning in the sitting room." Concepción motions to the left. "Can I get you anything to drink?" I suddenly remember my hangover that managed to elude my attention and tell her that a bottle of water would be fantastic. She tells me to make myself comfortable in the sitting room and that she'll be back shortly with the water.

Aside from a broad, full bookcase that flanks one of the sitting room's walls, the space is as empty as the foyer. Only one piece of abstract art adorns a cream-covered wall. I wander over to the bookshelf and read the titles along some of the volumes' spines: *Anna Karenina, Crime and Punishment, The Sun Also Rises, The Great Gatsby, The Beautiful and the Damned, Shakespeare's Complete Folio, The Collected Plays of Euripides,* a spattering of Tennessee Williams pieces.

Even at brief glance, it's safe to say that Grayson—or at least one of the Graysons—has a preoccupation with literary tragedy.

But it's the last title, a *livre poche* by Frédéric Beigbeder—a controversial French author whose celebrity has crossed the Atlantic with only limited success—that catches my attention. I read *Mémoires d'un jeune homme dérangé* during my sophomore year of college not by choice but rather by instruction handed down from a French woman with large hair and leather pants. She'd assigned it to the class as an example of how the literature of her country "had gone to *merde*."

"*Dérangé* means 'unsettled,' or, more colloquially, 'nuts,'" Madame de Maulthier told us. "Much like Beigbeder's attempt at writing." Like most of the reading in the course, it was completed in a hurried mess a night before the final. From what I recall, I hadn't thought it so much *merde* as I had thought it rather repetitive—just this unvarying path of action that dissolved and dissipated into nothingness: young man goes out, drinks, attempts to work, drinks (this time in Austria), goes out, makes some failed attempt at something that could be construed as love, works a bit more, drinks. I haven't thought about it until now.

"He doesn't read French. That's mine." Juliana's voice, low and smooth like steel, echoes behind me. I turn and see her holding my water, which has been poured into a glass with ice and a lemon slice.

"I'm sorry," I say, fumbling with the book and dropping it before returning it to its empty slot along the shelf. Her hair's still wet from the shower, and the damp brown waves are creating translucent windows on the white T-shirt she's wearing.

"It's fine." She sets the cup on a glass side table beside a neutral-colored couch. Her hair is the darkest thing in the room. "Here's your water. I assume you're my husband's new office assistant?" She moves over to the windows and opens three sets of giant curtains whose color matches that of the couch.

"Yes." I shove my fists back into my pockets. "Taylor Mark. I actually think we met at the Gold Cu—"

"And how do you like the office? Everyone treating you well?" She leans over and rearranges a stack of magazines set on a minimalist coffee table. Her father's picture is on the cover of one of them. I keep trying to rearrange the growing bulge in my pants.

"Yes. Everyone's been very accommodating." She moves over to the bookcase, from where I've since backed away, and picks up *Mémoires d'un jeune homme dérangé.*

"You've read this?" she asks, holding up the book.

"Yes. During my sophomore year of college. In Madame de Maulthier's class. She wore leather pants and was a total bitch."

Juliana cocks her head and looks at me. *I have no idea why I told you that, either.* "French professors usually are." Beat. "What'd you think of it?"

"*Très dérangé,* I guess."

She smiles. "*Dérangé,* indeed." She thumbs the pages and pauses on one in particular for a moment. "I'm impressed you read it."

"It was required for the final."

"I see." The sun, which has been flooding the room like some giant spotlight, is temporarily obscured by a cumulus cloud. She's reminded of herself. "I assume you brought my husband's dry cleaning?" She looks at her watch, a Movado whose face is almost as dark as her hair. "He'll be home in a few hours and will need a fresh suit before he heads back to the Capitol. Sounds like he made quite a stir with those liberal bloggers, hmm?"

"That's what it sounds like, Mrs. Grayson."

"I'm sure you're in for some long nights at the office."

"It wouldn't surprise me."

"I prefer them stiff."

"Pardon?"

"The shirts, Taylor. I prefer that they're stiff. And so does he. I'm assuming you asked for extra starch?"

"I didn't have them cleaned. I'm just the messenger, actually."

"Isn't that always the case?" The sun's rays once again bathe the room in a light that seems to be a little too warm, a little too harsh. She runs a manicured finger along one of the book's edges and I look down at my loafers, which are in desperate need of a proper polish. It's only now, as I look at the scuffs along the brown leather, that I realize that I've stopped breathing.

Concepción enters through the double doors carrying a bottle of Évian water. "Oh, Señorrrr Marrrrk, I see Señora got you your waterrrrrr."

"Thank you, Concepción. Mr. Mark was just leaving." Juliana turns to me. "Thank you for dropping off my husband's dry cleaning." The phone rings and Concepción leaves the room to answer it.

"You're welcome, ma'am." I turn to leave and make it to the front door, half-relieved, half-heartbroken when I hear Juliana say my name.

"I believe this belongs to you." She reaches out and hands me a pink, seersucker bow tie, still folded in a perfect square.

Back at the office, the phone is a constant and steady stream of harassing rings. It's a puzzling world, the media; one moment taking on the role of prey, evading phone calls and e-mails and any trace of contact, and the next descending upon you like a pack of wild beasts. I sit on the blue-green couch (I've been banished from my desk) and watch as Kelly adeptly handles each call: of course Grayson was joking, and it's so unfortunate that Keeler's (likely) altered state of mind (you do know he's extremely supportive of legalizing—completely!—marijuana, don't you?) couldn't pick up on that. The congressman's been to Baghdad. Twice, in fact. He supports our troops and the city's local merchants, alike. In fact, last time he was there, be bought a rug. No, Grayson and

Company is not considering buying real estate space in the Green Zone. That's not legal. Any other questions should be directed to the company's spokesperson at area code nine four nine, blah blah blah, blah blah blah blah.

"You're good," I say to Kelly once the phone quiets for a moment.

"I know." It rings again. The reporter who's calling is a friend of hers. They chat for a bit about the weather in San Francisco before one of them realizes that there's a purpose to the call and the conversation veers toward business and spin and tiny white lies. Kelly reaches into my desk for a piece of paper and a pen. When she's stopped scribbling she waves the white sheet at me.

It says: "Grande quad skim extra hot latte. Hold the whiskey."

Back downstairs, back in the basement, I wait in line and clench the bow tie in my pocket and can't help but think about how fucking *dérangé* this whole goddamn situation is. Three years ago, Caroline Hugo had dumped me in her room at the Delta Delta Delta house with Sarah McLachlan playing in the background (she had a thing for dramatics). She traded me in for a Wellbutrin prescription and a senior from Drexel, a hulking figure named Kyle, but who preferred to be called James and looked like someone out of MTV's *True Life: I'm from Staten Island*. The idea—the *fantasy*—of sharing a sweaty bed with the wife of a congressman is outrageous at best. And the suggestion that she—that Juliana Grayson—shares desires similar to my own is beyond outrageous. It's rapes and pillages and plunders outrageous. It's preposterous. It, in fact, runs directly contrary to the physics that have thus far defined my life. I twirl the bow tie once over through my fingers. But then, as she thumbed through those pages scrawled with French, and paused just so between her ambiguous answers, and—

"Sir, there is a line. Your order please." A small Asian man with an angry voice and angrier eyes yells at me from behind the Starbucks counter.

"Excuse me?" I ask, rather startled.

"*Your order*. You want coffee or not?"

"Yes, yes," I tell him. "I do want coffee, and I apologize for holding up the line."

"You move aside. More people need to order, sir."

I nod and apologize again and move down the counter to wait for Kelly's drink.

"That guy can be a real ass."

I keep fondling the bow tie but look up to see the nacho girl, the one from the cafeteria, the one I met yesterday.

"You've dealt with him before?"

She shakes her head. "Just today. Twice this morning, already. Usually there's this woman named Delores who works at this one. She's fantas—"

"I love Delores."

"Everyone loves Delores." She looks down at my right hand, which is moving about in my pocket. "What's in your pocket?"

I stop rubbing the cloth. "Nothing. Why?"

"It just looks like you're playing with keys or something. It's distracting."

"What—people don't do that in Spanish Harlem?"

"I'm actually from Boston."

"Oh." I scuff my loafers against the dirty floor. A man brushes between us to retrieve some blended frappuccino-something-or-other from the bar.

"You look like you've had a rough day. It's amazing what our bosses say sometimes, you know?"

I'd half forgotten about Grayson's gaffe at UCI. "Yeah. Rough day."

"To be honest, you look like you could use a drink."

This she's right about. I could use about nine of them, prefer-
ably with Juliana Grayson, who, even with wet hair and a pair
of sweats, looked like some creature from a thirteen-year-old's
modern mythology.

"You want to grab one after work?"

I look up uncomfortably.

"Like . . . a date?" I ask.

She laughs. "Easy on the self-flattery, tiger. I've got a boyfriend. Back in New York. I meant just to help you take the edge
off. But if you've seen *When Harry Met Sally* one too many times,
you know . . . I can appreciate that."

I look down and laugh.

"Sorry." I run a hand through my hair. "All this stuff about
Baghdad and condos and Dubai and stuff. It just has my mind
elsewhere. I'd love a drink."

"Great." She grabs her drink, a black coffee, that's been
placed on the counter. "I'm Vanessa, by the way." She extends a
hand.

"Taylor."

"Nice to meet you. I'm assuming you'll have some work to do.
So why don't we make it late. Eight, say?"

We agree to meet at Sonoma, a wine bar on Capitol Hill, at
eight thirty (just to be safe) and she goes left down the hall and
I go right, back to 1224 Longworth, which, during my short absence, has taken on the appearance of a war room, so many charts
and papers. It's hard not to get the feeling that these people, these
staffers, fear days such as these while secretly longing for them.
It'd be a disappointment if they never came.

"This better be hot, goddamn it," Kelly says, snatching the
Starbucks cup from my hand.

"You need anything else?"

Janice calls from behind the partition. "Yeah. How about a
muzzle." I laugh.

"For the congressman?"

"No, you little twerp. For you. Now sit down and get out of everyone's way."

And so I mouth "bitch" to myself and sit on the couch and pick up a copy of *Politik*—the newspaper for which Jack Buchanan writes and fancies itself as the Beltway's version of the *New York Post*, but has circulation statistics that tell a slightly different story. I thumb through the gray pages until I reach Jack's column—a small section of real estate by journalistic standards titled "Capital Capers" (not the cleverest of names, even Jack will tell you).

Nothin' but Net at Hoops for Hope
Jack A. Buchanan

It may not be basketball season, but Washingtonians don't seem to have a problem shooting three-point shots—especially when they're being backed up by Wizards MVPs at a black-tie event at Beltway posh spot Citronelle, and the proceeds head to needy children in Afghanistan.

The event, planned by lobbying powerhouse Latham, Scripps, Howard, raised nearly $60,000, and is already being considered one of D.C.'s social summer successes.

"We just couldn't be more pleased," Kip Latham remarked after snagging an autographed basketball for $3,000 during the event's silent auction. "It's always wonderful to see Washington come out to support such a worthy cause. I'm planning on shipping a crate of basketballs to Kabul."

Who else was on the guest list? Check out *Capital Capers*'s website for exclusive photos.

Guess who . . .

GUESS which California representative got a little tipsy at an ACLU dinner and made full use of her liberties on the dance floor?

GUESS which local news anchor was seen snogging a
young man a third his age near DuPont Circle?

Ten minutes later and the phone has temporarily quieted and Peter calls another all-staff meeting in the front office. The aides file in from the adjoining room with their sleeves rolled up and their shoes kicked off. It's only lunchtime but it looks like they've spent years in the trenches. Peter taps his fist on the desk.

"I've been on the phone with the district office for the past forty-five minutes," he begins. "Apparently four or five hippies— sorry, *protesters*—have gathered outside the office, but that's about it. The *Register* has snapped some shots of them. So has the local paper in Newport. But aside from that, things have been quiet." He reaches down and quickly types on my computer. "Those fucking blogs, on the other hand, are a different story." He turns the computer screen to face the staff. Splayed across the front page of the *Huffington Post* is JOHN GRAYSON (R-CA): HAIR TODAY, GONE TOMORROW?

"That'll die," Kelly says, once again drumming her acrylic nails. "Someone else will fuck up tomorrow, or the next day. We'll get a follow-up story this week; if the cycle's dead, we'll get another one next week, but that's it. Keeler may get high and write something for *TNR* online, which only four people read anyway."

"How are we on press, by the way?"

"The usual suspects called. Plus a few unexpected ones. He's booked on two drive-time shows this afternoon. Two ten-minute segments. I'll prep him on message before he goes down to the floor today, in case he's accosted in the halls. No calls for TV yet. We won't push him out unless he's excellent on radio. Which he won't be."

Peter nods and turns to the aides. "Where are we on the leg-islative front? I like this idea of keeping Grayson's boy-next-door image. We've got to get him on something good, but under the radar. Something that won't make ripples. I want the bicameral equivalent of vanilla ice cream."

The aides throw open their notebooks and start sounding off ideas, the product of their two-hour Big Think: Klemson from North Carolina is trying to label the Friday before Thanksgiving as "Fill Up America's Bellies Friday" (no—we don't want to offend any Native Americans—and did he actually use the word "bellies" in the bill?); Ilken from Colorado is pushing to expand Boulder's law that no one is a pet owner, merely a pet "minder" (no—those women at Fashion Island take their Chihuahuas very seriously; we don't want to upset our constituents); Willingham from Los Angeles is pushing a bill to provide "for the expeditious disclosure of records relevant to the life and death of Tupac Amaru Shakur" (no—are you kidding me? in Orange County?). Peter rubs the bridge of his nose.

"Anything else?"

"Well . . ." Anna unfolds a piece of paper that's jutting out of her notebook. "I found this on Thomas.gov . . . but it just seemed a little too ridiculous."

"And Tupac isn't?"

"Point taken."

"What is it?"

"It's bullying."

"What?"

"Bullying—you know, like on school playgr—"

"Yes, yes." Peter's voice's irritation index increases with each syllable. "I know what it is. What about it?"

"Johnson from New York—"

"The Democrat or the Republican?"

"The Democrat."

"Bipartisan. Good, good. Go on."

"He's introducing a campaign to outlaw bullying on school

playgrounds. Basically he wants the Department of Education to help states to create programs to combat harassment or something. He's desperately looking for sponsors." She reads from the folded piece of paper. "The law 'requires states to protect all students against bullying, regardless of race, creed, religion, disability, gender, sexual orientation, or gender identity.' I don't know. Like I said, it's ridiculous."

"Get them to strike sexual orientation and gender identity and it's perfect."

Under Peter's orders, I've been researching the pervasiveness and rate of recurrence and effects of playground terror since lunch and here's what I've come up with and really what you should know: the jungle gym is nothing short of a combat zone; Nam, but with kickballs and Frisbees and taunts beginning with "you're so fat that . . ." They say that war is hell, and evidently so is elementary school. Moreover, through my research—which, I'll admit, likely hits a little too close to home with regard to my own childhood—I find that the outlook is equally as grim for the offender as it is for the offended. The bullies, in other words, are the ones who are likely to end up behind bars. And while I suppose this shouldn't surprise me and while I'm certain there are more pressing matters in which I should be engaged, I can't help but to think back to Michael Garrick, with his dirty hands and unkempt hair, and I wonder what infractions he's committed of late. Robbery, I'd wager. Armed, maybe. If there's any justice in this world, he's behind bars somewhere, tucked far away, out of striking distance from the fragile self-esteems of underdeveloped six-year-olds.

The screaming phone jolts me from these visions of Michael Garrick's chubby hands grasping a set of iron bars.

"Mr. Mark!" Kip Latham's voice sings loud and seductive and clear on the other end of the line. "Kip Lath—"

"Hello Mr. Latham." I wait for him to request—ever so politely—to call him Kip. But he doesn't.

"I'd love to chat, Taylor. I've been hearing absolutely the best
things about your work there. And Chase tells me he couldn't be
happier that you're in D.C. Patricia and I will have you over for
dinner soon."

"That sounds great, Mr. Lath—"

"But I've got to speak to Peter quickly. He's there, I'm assuming?"

I turn around and look to Peter, who glances up from his
computer and mouths "Who is it?" I cover the receiver with
one hand and whisper "Kip Latham" in return. Peter buries his
head in his hands, which initially strikes me as odd, until I remember the many times that I've buried my head in my hands
after having navigated Chase's antics. Peter finally looks up and
says "voice mail," and I tell Kip that Peter's stepped out for some
coffee.

"I'm sure he has," Kip says and I can sense, even through the
jumbled wires of telecommunications, that he's starting to smile.
"Do me a favor, Taylor. Instead of patching me through to his
voice mail, would you mind just relaying a message to your boss
for me?"

"Sure," I say, "absolutely. That sounds fine."

"Let him know that I won't be at dinner tonight, but that I'm
sure he'll find Paul Howard's proposal very convincing." I scribble
the note on a piece of scratch paper.

"Anything else?"

"That's it. But make sure he gets it."

"Absolutely," I say, and I start taking the receiver away from
my ear when I hear him coo, "And Taylor, Patricia and I are *so*
looking forward to seeing you soon."

It's eight o'clock when I finally pull myself away from the computer. The light sneaking in from the window next to Peter's desk

is just starting to soften, though it's safe to say the heat's still there. He's the only one left in the front office, with Janice at dinner, and Kelly at the congressman's home. Grayson had foregone his trip to the office and the Capitol to prep for his two radio interviews.

"Taylor." I turn and see Peter, tattered leather bag slung over one hunched shoulder, standing next to my desk. "You can take off. There's really no need for you to be here this late."

"It's okay, I'm just finishing up on these numbers. I'm meeting someone at eight-thirty, anyway."

He punches me lightly on the shoulder. "You got a hot date?"

"No, no," I correct him. "Just a friend." He lingers awkwardly for a bit longer, rubbing the bald spot on the crown of his head. "What about you? Big plans?"

"Just dinner." I remember Kip's call from an hour or so ago.

"Right. I almost forgot. That's what Kip Latham called about."

Peter looks up. "Oh?"

"Yes." I reach for the piece of scratch paper and struggle to read my own writing. "He said that he wasn't going to make it—"

"Typical."

"—but that you'd find Paul Howard's proposal 'very convincing.'" He readjusts the leather strap of his bag and shakes his head. "Is it just you and Paul?" I ask.

"No . . . no, the congressman will be joining us." He lingers awkwardly.

"My friend Chase works at Latham, Scripps, Howard," I say, and Peter shifts his weight from foot to foot.

"Yes, I know. Kip's son."

"Right," I tell him. "That's right."

I think of the Pauls, staring at me like two giant ancient carvings, chipped around the edges, at the Gold Cup. "I met Mr. Howard and his wife when I first moved to D.C. They seem like nice people."

Peter chuckles and sighs. "Right. Nice people." He looks at his watch and twists it around on his wrist. "I should get going. I'm already late." He walks toward the door but pauses before he exits into the echoing hall. "Look, I'm sorry for coming down hard on you this morning. That wasn't fair."

"It's fine. I was late. I deserved it."

"You get enough crap from the two of them." He gives a nod over to Janice's corner of the office. "I know how they seem, but they're good at their jobs. I know you're working hard. There's a learning curve. Some institutional knowledge that's got to be learned. That's all." And then, "How old are you, Taylor?"

"I'm twenty-three. I'll be twenty-four next February." Peter loosens his tie and runs a hand once more over his bald spot.

"Christ. Twenty-three years old. I wish I could remember what this town looked like when I was that age."

May 23, 2007;
8:35 P.M.

Bullying!?" Vanessa manages to choke back a swallow of white wine before erupting in raucous laughter. "You've got to be kidding me."

I shake my head. "No, I'm not kidding you. Bullying's a big deal. Did you know that thirty percent of kids report being involved in some kind of harassment at school?"

She rolls her eyes. "I can't believe you're buying this—"

"And try to keep it down, all right?" We're on the second floor of Sonoma, the wine bar a few steps from the Capitol that—thanks to exposed brick walls and hardwood floors—has managed to maintain a sleek, sophisticated vibe despite its IKEA furniture. "I don't want to lose my job two weeks into it because I leaked some goddamn information."

"Yeah," she says, crossing her legs, "it sounds like you're working with some real geniuses. I'd want to hold on to that job, too."

I take the wine list from her and quickly scan over the white section. The thought of having any more pinot noir after last night still makes my stomach churn, even this late in the day. "Look, if I wanted to be berated, I would've stayed in my office. Can we just talk about something else?"

"Sorry," she says. "I didn't mean to bully you."

"Very funny. What are you drinking?" She reaches across the small table that separates us and takes the wine list from me.

"I don't know. A chardonnay, I think?"

"Which one?"

"The second-to-cheapest one."

"You shouldn't do that."

"Do what?"

"Order the second-to-cheapest wine on the menu. They trick you with them. It's a scam."

"Excuse me?"

"They trick you. The second-to-cheapest wine on the menu isn't any better than the cheapest wine on the menu. They expect people like—"

" 'People like'—"

"Just, you know, people *in general* to order it. So it's not really any better. It's just more expensive. If you're going to order some wine, you may as well have a nice glass."

"I'm not sure I'm following."

I laugh and rub my temples. Frankly I'm not following, either. "Forget it. It's just something this friend of mine from school always says. 'Life's too short to drink cheap wine.'"

She looks unimpressed.

"Is your friend aware that you sort mail on the American taxpayers' dime for a living?"

"Actually, he's the one who helped me get the job."

"Damn," she says with a smile. "Fine merlots, getting people jobs. Who is this guy, Jesus?"

Well, kind of. It depends on whom you're asking, I reason.

"No. Chase Latham."

"Of, like, the Latham, Scripps, Howard Lathams?"

I signal to the waiter to come back to our table.

"Oh, so you've heard of them?"

She signals to the waiter, too.

"Yeah," she says with a smile and leans back in her chair, cross-ing her arms. "From what I know, they gave money to Reyes's op-ponent during the last election cycle. Haven't they been in some hot water before? Something about a dead puppy?"

"Hearsay." The waiter arrives and I tell him that I'll have a glass of the pinot gris (sixteen dollars per) and that Vanessa will have a glass of the second-to-cheapest chardonnay, unless, of course, she'd like to try something else.

"No," she says to the waiter, "the chardonnay will be fine, thanks."

The waiter returns with our wine and, over the course of the next hour, the conversation drifts and wanders from pend-ing House legislation to the Thievery Corporation to the Gypsy Kings to Dave Eggers to the Coen Brothers' last movie. About half of her references are too obscure, too under-the-radar. She al-ludes to highbrow concepts with proper punctuation and foreign accents that I can't place. She's above me, this girl, I think, but in a way that makes me feel comfortable; a way that makes me want to understand these foreign tongues and fascinating topics that have eluded my knowledge for the past twenty-plus years.

I'm self-conscious for spending sixteen dollars on a goblet of fermented grape juice that's been given a fancy name.

Two more glasses in I ask her about her boyfriend. She tells me that his name is Alvaro, and that they're both from Venezuela and met while going to school at Columbia (not *in* Colombia), and that he's finishing up his second year at NYU Law.

"We've decided to hold off on any marriage plans until he's done with school."

Marriage. Mar-riage. *Marriage*. Christ. I'm going home with fanfares of how Juliana's diaphanous T-shirt this morning revealed the tan, soft blush of her skin, and Vanessa is going home with thoughts of solidarity and white dresses and something that probably flirts with normality. I lean back in my chair and finish a glass of pinot gris in a giant swig, trying to flush away the traces of Belize and a bar called Exit Strategy and Prozac and Jack White and all the other tastes—sour, bitter, or otherwise—that marriage has left in my mouth.

"What about you?" she says, trying to make eye contact with me, noticing that my mind has started drifting somewhere unpleasant. "Are you dating anyone?" I laugh and reach into my pocket and feel the bow tie that has started to become yellow with the oils and sweat from my hand.

"No, no," I say, "I haven't dated anyone since college. And that didn't exactly end well."

"How so?"

"Let's just say the last stages of the relationship were highly medicated."

She smiles awkwardly, because she probably doesn't know what else to do.

I tell her about Caroline, and how no one had necessarily wronged the other, and how that, really, that's the worst possible way something can end.

She agrees. "The most humane thing someone can do when he leaves you is to give you a reason to hate him," she says. "Or, I guess in your case, her."

I tell her I don't understand.

"Well, it's just like you said: the worst way something can end is when there's no justification for the end at all. If the person gives you a justification, you can focus on that. In a twisted sense—and I'm not saying I'm endorsing philandering—but in a twisted sense cheating's the most humane thing you can do to a person that you expect to desert."

I tell her that it sounds like she has experience in this department. She shakes her head slightly and slowly and drinks some wine.

"There was this guy before Alvaro. During my freshman year at Columbia. My first real relationship, I guess. I'm still trying to decide if I was in love with him or with the concept of having him." Even with Alvaro there now? "Yes, even with Alvaro." Her voice becomes shaded with defensive tones. "People don't just vanish." She sets down her glass and gathers her thoughts. "I don't know where we all got this idea that we should be immune to the pain of losing someone; that, like, it shouldn't happen to us, that we're all such *good* people that we should be protected from hurt or something. Because we're not. No one is. At the end of the day, being deserted is probably one of the few things we've all got in common."

She asks me how I ended up here. I ask her how far Belize is from Venezuela and she laughs and tells me that they're far apart—Belize is near the tip of Central America, and Venezuela is at the tip of South America. I apologize for my ignorance when it comes to geography and tell her that I'm here because of Belize.

"Belize?"

Yeah, I say, Belize. Specifically, because of a particular fishing trip and a newly opened dive bar called Exit Strategy. And then it all comes out, like some flood of too many words: everything about that Last Supper in Philadelphia, about Nathaniel and his goddamn job with Goldman Sachs, about deep sea fishing, about Dr. Thompkins and the Coyote Grill and those love letters—yellowed and torn and smudged. About eight hundred different things that I haven't heard myself discussing until really this instant.

I tell her about Katie, and how if wondering how this all happened wasn't so futile, if doing so would actually produce a different result when all of this inevitably reaches its climax, I'd give it a try. I'd give it a shot. But that I had this feeling in my gut that I was learning the hard way that a person can't will something to happen; that some of fate's traitors act out of our control, without a trace of our interests in mind.

Dérangé, really.

"What about you?"

She sighs and tells me her story isn't really all that interesting, that it epitomizes that Modern Immigrant Experience that's been written about in so much of today's fiction and that's been depicted in so many of today's films.

I laugh. "Come on," I say. "I'm a straight white guy from Orange County whose parents are divorced thanks to a midlife crisis. If anyone here is a cliché, it's me."

She tells me she's not so sure about that, that if you look at the stats and the figures and the graphs and the charts, more and more counties in the United States have a majority of minorities, and that maybe my experience is the new American journey.

I tell her I doubt it.

"Anyway," she says before asking our waiter for the check. I tell her that I've got it as I reach to my back pocket for my wallet. She puts up a fight—valiant, sincere for sure—but eventually gives in, allowing me to pay. "Like I said, it's all pretty typical. My father was a teacher in Venezuela. History and literature. For some reason or another, he thought there'd be more opportunities—you know, educationally—for my brother and me in the States. At first we moved to Ohio. My mother had family in Toledo. My father planned on getting his credentials there. Halfway through the program, though"—the waiter returns with our check and she thanks him—"halfway through the program he died from a burst appendix." I add a final *swoosh* to my signature and I set down the pen.

I tell her I'm sorry.

"It's fine. I was young." Then: "Thanks for paying."

She tells me she remembers holding her brother's hand at the funeral and that, for some reason, she couldn't cry. "My mother moved the three of us to Boston." She laughs. "Funny, right? Three South Americans living in one of the coldest cities in the United States. She became a custodian at Tufts."

I ask her what she does now.

"The same thing. She's still there." She hands the bill back to the waiter. "Anyway, I wanted to do something. Enact some change, you know? So when I was studying at Columbia, I started a program that helped women in Spanish Harlem register to vote. Then, after graduation, I ended up here." She pauses. "I told you: same old story. You ready to go? This place looks like it's clearing out."

I turn around and see two people—a man and a woman, not together, but sitting two seats apart—at the bar. We walk downstairs and out into the heavy May night.

"Bullying." She shakes her head as we walk down Pennsylvania. "I'll give it to you, Mark, the more I think about it, the more it's got a kind of ironic brilliance."

I tell her thanks, but that brilliance might be pushing it a little bit.

"Really?" She gives me a playful push. "This coming from the guy who, two hours ago, was telling me how many kids are terrorized on the handball courts?"

I shove her back and ask her what she's doing for America's children when my phone starts vibrating next to the bow tie in my pocket.

"Hello?" I signal an apology to Vanessa and she shrugs and starts mindlessly walking along the curb like it's a balance beam.

"Champ. What's your status?"

"Hey, man. I'm just leaving Sonoma."

Chase snorts on the other end of the phone.

"On the Hill? I hate that place. Way too nouveau. Who you there with?"

"Just a friend from work."

"Look at you, Mr. Social, making friends left and right. Who's the lucky man?"

Vanessa loses her balance but temporarily regains it before forgoing her footing and stepping into the street.

"I told you. She's just a friend from work."

"*She,* Casanova?"

"It's not like that. She's just a friend."

"Sure it is, pal." He loses interest and moves to the next topic. In the background, I hear Annalee ask him something about which DVD he wants to watch— *The Notebook* or *Talladega Nights.* "Anyway, you're coming on Friday, right?"

"What's on Friday?" He sighs.

"Hal's party. At Smith Point. I put you on the list, so you're coming. Bring your new piece of ass, too. It'll be a blast." He tells her—Annalee—that he can't believe she has to ask, and that they'll be watching *Talladega Nights.*

"I thought Jack and Caitlin said it was going to be lame."

Chase starts getting frustrated. "We'll make it fun. Lathams don't *do* lame. It's not in our genes."

"We'll see."

"Don't give me that 'we'll see' bullshit. You've got nothing better to do. I know that for a fact. We're pregaming at my place beforehand. Just me and you. A little bonding time. Get to my place at nine o'clock." Then the line goes dead.

"Who was that?" Vanessa asks, stumbling back onto the sidewalk.

"My friend Chase," I say, sighing and putting the phone back into my pocket.

"It sounded like you were talking to your dad, or something."

"Yeah, well . . ."

" 'Yeah, well . . . ' " She laughs and walks a few steps ahead of me. I'll give it to her—her impersonation of how words constantly desert me is discerning.

"Hey."

She turns around.

"What are you doing on Friday night?"

She shakes her head and grins. "Taylor, I told you. I've got a boyfr—"

"Easy on the self-flattery, tiger. And besides, I don't date Democrats."

"Socialists," she says, nodding.

"Goddamn Commies, I say."

She laughs. "Nothing. I'm doing nothing on Friday night. Alvaro gets down here Saturday morning."

A taxi flies by us, heading past the lit dome of the Capitol and down Pennsylvania.

"You want to go to this party at Smith Point?"

She howls and readjusts her purse—brown and simple with no visible designer labels—on her shoulder. "They'd mistake me for a member of the cleaning staff," she says, still laughing. "Have you ever been to that place? It's like walking into Sweden or something. I think they actively despise Latinos more than gays, and that's only because all those ex-frat boys end up getting wasted and hooking up with each other, anyway."

"So that's a no?"

She rolls her brown eyes and pulls her raven hair back off her face and into a bun on the back of her head that she fastens with a pen that she takes out of her purse. "It's just not really my scene, Taylor. One of those girls' outfits costs more than I pay for six months' rent. Trust me, I'd just embarrass you."

"No. No, you wouldn't."

We both stop moving for an instant and I honestly can't tell if she's just being nice or she can tell that I rarely have conversations like this or, if on some hidden level, my face is betraying a certain vulnerability that I've always worked so hard to mask, to conceal, and that in that moment, in that *very second,* she's making the grave mistake of planting that dangerous seed of the idea that she might be the one to save me from what's ahead.

"Okay," she says, nodding, "I'll tag along."

She reaches out an arm and hails a cab, and asks if I'd like to share it. She lives at Ninth and U, which can be on the way to Woodley Park. I tell her thanks, but that I'm going to walk.

"That's a long way, Taylor."

"I don't mind." I put my hands in my pockets. She nods and gets in the cab and rolls down the window.

"Friday?"

"Friday."

VII

May 25, 2007;
9:00 P.M.

You're early," Chase says before buzzing me up to his apartment—the penthouse of a converted town house at Thirty-sixth and Prospect.

"I thought you said to be here at nine o'clock," I say into the intercom. It screeches back at me until the screeches turn into Chase's laughter.

"Jesus, who actually gets *anywhere* on time? It's bourgeois. Tonight's first lesson: always come about ten minutes late. It's more polite. Come on up, though; you can make us some drinks. Door's unlocked."

The door buzzes and I enter and climb the four flights of stairs to Chase's apartment, which, with its dark, Brazilian hickory floors, its overstuffed leather couches, and its seventy-one-inch flat-panel plasma TV, truly is a sight to behold. In Chase's bedroom, behind a closed door on the other end of the sprawling living room, I hear a faucet turn off and a stereo cue up. Music— French hip-hop—starts thumping across the cold, stark panels along the floor. A spattering of magazines—a selection ranging from *Foreign Policy* to *Playboy* is fanned out across a bi-level cof-

fee table that spans the length of the couch. I reach for a three-
month-old copy of *Maxim* with Jessica Alba on the cover and flip
through the pages ("Make Her Go Whacko While You Jacko!")
as I try to discern the lyrics of the rhymes pulsating from Chase's
room: something about being born in Senegal, about the *banlieu*
of Paris, about *des flics.*

It should be pointed out, I suppose, that Chase took a semester of Spanish during his freshman year. Not an ounce of French.

The door to his room swings open and the music gets louder,
and Chase, standing in the doorway wearing only a pair of jeans
and still drying himself off from a shower, tells me to get the Goose
out of the fridge and to make him a vodka, neat. I steal one envi-
ous glance at the lean muscles that create deep, shadowed creases
along his stomach before obliging and moving into the kitchen.
The freezer—one of those Sub-Zero numbers—may as well be a
top-shelf bar. Grey Goose, Patron, Bombay, an unmarked bottle
that could be absinthe (the real kind, the kind from Amsterdam,
not the nonhallucinogenic stuff from Spain).

"Have whatever you want!" I hear him yell from his room,
over the din of rap *français.* "Except stay away from that unmarked
bottle, unless you want to get really fucked up. And if you do, be
my guest." I tell him thanks and pour myself a Bombay and tonic
that's erring on the strong side.

"So where's your flavor of the week?" Chase says as he walks
into the kitchen while fastening the final button of a Thomas Pink
shirt tucked into his jeans. I hand him his drink.

"Who?"

He takes a hearty swig of the vodka and smiles as his Adam's
apple bulges. "C'mon, bud. You don't have to play it cool. The
'she' from the other night."

"Vanessa?"

"So 'she' has a name!" He raises his glass and clinks it against
my own.

"Chase, honestly, she's just a friend. She said she'd meet us there." Chase reaches into the back pocket for his BlackBerry and begins typing. "What are you doing?"

"She's got to be on the list, champ. What's her last name?"

"Ramírez." Chase looks up and raises an eyebrow.

"Look at you, Ambassador Mark, befriending the United Nations."

"Whatever. I just met her at work. Someone to have lunch with, you know? We'll see." I sip my G&T and start wondering if Vanessa was right, if this was a bad idea.

Chase reaches past me for the Grey Goose.

"Speaking of work," he says, pouring himself another full glass, "how are things in the Pantene model's office?" I pour myself another drink as well.

"Interesting," I say. *What is it about gin that tastes like pinecones?* "I'm assuming you heard about Grayson's fuck-up on his panel at UCI?"

Chase moves into his bedroom, where the stereo is, and I call my question after him though I'm fairly certain he doesn't hear me.

"Sorry," he yells back. "Jack's been trying to get me into this French hip-hop shit and I can't fucking *stand* it, you know? It's just fucking *gay*. I'm telling you, sometimes that kid can be the biggest queer." The music cuts out for a moment and is then replaced by something safer, a little more mainstream, Gym Class Heroes, I think. Chase comes back into the kitchen.

"So much better. Anyway, what'd you say about Grayson?" he asks.

"You hear what he said at UCI?"

Chase shakes his head.

"Really?"

"Yeah, really. There're four hundred thirty-five of those fuckers. You can't expect a guy to keep track of all of them. Christ, all you Hill rats are the same. You all think your boss is the center of the goddamn universe."

"I've worked on the Hill for a grand total of three weeks."

He reaches and opens up the freezer and takes out the bottle of Patron and laughs. "It'll happen, it'll happen. Pretty soon you'll be banging some chick from the office down the hall and shotgunning PBR at Politiki or some shit." He holds up the bottle. "Shots?" I shrug. "Anyway, what'd Grayson say at UC-Whatever?"

I throw back the ounce of the cool, clear liquid and even though it's practically frozen it still burns my throat in a hot kind of way. I tell him about how Grayson told Keeler that Baghdad should be developed like some Los Angeles suburb, or Reston, Virginia, or something, and Chase tells me that, building conditions aside, he doesn't think that'd be a completely bad thing.

"Right, anyway," I say, refilling the two shot glasses. "On Wednesday, Peter—he's our chief of staff—"

"Yeah, I've met him."

"He decided he wanted to make sure Grayson keeps that boy-next-door image or whatever—"

"Gay."

"So he told the staff that he wants Grayson to cosponsor this bill that Johnson from New York—"

"The Republican or the Democrat?"

"The Democrat. Bipartisanship, you know."

"Even gayer."

"He told us he wants Grayson to cosponsor this bill to outlaw bullying on school playgrounds. So he'll look compassionate, despite what he said at UCI."

"Bullying?" Chase picks up his shot glass off the granite counter.

"It's kind of a big deal, dude."

" 'Dude.' "

"Save it. Seriously, though. Did you know that bullies are more likely to become criminals later on in life?"

Chase throws his head back and swallows the tequila without the slightest sign of discomfort or disgust.

"Whatever, champ. I came out fine." He holds up his arms as if I'm supposed to be inspecting him for flaws. "You poured that shot, you going to drink it or stare at it?" I put the glass to my lips and choke through another agonizing gulp that I chase with the gin. "So, what happened? You guys become a sponsor?"

I nod. "Yeah. Grayson signed on to the bill yesterday." I raise my glass. "He became the first official cosponsor of HR 273. He's headed back to California this weekend to do some local television appearances."

Chase laughs and shakes his head and slaps my back. "*God,* I love this town," he says. "Can't fucking get enough of it." Then, "You ready to meet some skinterns tonight?"

I tell him yeah, sure, why not, should be a blast, and it's been awhile since I've slept with someone (though I leave this last part out in fear of judgment and retribution). My head's starting to get light and airy and my vision isn't quite catching up with the movements of my eyes and I can feel the gin and tequila start working their way through the microwaveable mac'n'cheese I had for dinner. "What time are we taking off?"

"Soon." He checks his BlackBerry. "Caitlin and Annalee are having dinner at Hook. Their reservations were at eight o'clock, so they should be finishing up soon. I told Caitlin that we'd just meet her at Smith Point."

"Since when are the two of them hanging out alone, together?"

"I told Annalee she needed to reach out and make some more friends in the city." He looks up from the BlackBerry and raises an eyebrow. "You're her cousin, Taylor. I don't see you calling her much."

"I know," I say, looking down, remembering the extent to which Annalee and I used to correspond before she met Chase. "I need to change that."

Truth be told, this is the first time that Annalee and I haven't been close. During Frank's departure, during Katie's downfall, during *Belize,* it was Annalee who would often pick up the phone when I needed support. While the rest of our extended family, on the other hand, managed to distance themselves a bit from Katie and Nathaniel and me. As Nate describes it, it's almost as if some message, some telegram, was sent out along the Mark wireless to let the others know that we've been tainted, *damaged* by some socially unacceptable ailment. Annalee, though, either didn't get the memo, or chose simply to ignore it.

"Okay." Chase puts the device into the back pocket of his Seven jeans. "Caitlin says they've just paid. I gave Annalee my AmEx. Told her to chalk it up as a business expense for LSH."

I give him a confused look.

"You know Caitlin. Baghdad. Whatever."

So I'm standing between these two blond interns who are wearing BeBe halter tops and who are grinding against me, but not because they're meaning to, but rather because the three of us are all trying to get the bartender's attention, and I can't tell if the sweat that's beginning to drench my shirt is theirs or my own and I think my loafers are starting to stick to the floor, which is hypersaturated with gallons and gallons of beer and one thing's for certain: I'm definitely drunk.

As a destination, Smith Point isn't particularly impressive. On the contrary, the watering hole leaves much to be desired. It's a cheap dive bar at best, a few blocks up from M Street in Georgetown. But at some point somewhere in its sordid history, the Powers That Be decided that getting in required being on a list, and being on the list required a membership that required that one be recommended by X number of individuals who had already been *graced* with a membership, etc., etc., etc. I suppose you could spend time wondering *why* the city's young and beautiful and privileged opt to spend their free evenings in a venue rank with the stench of stale booze, but in a capital where one's character is defined by one's access, the answer's self-evident. And if it's not, as Chase says, you shouldn't be here in the first place.

I smile at one of the girls, the one standing to my left, and I ask her what she's drinking.

"Whatever you're not drinking," she says, grabbing the arm of a brunette girl standing next to her. *Ah, yes, the arm grab. The international symbol for "get me the fuck away from him."* The other one taps my arm and tells me she's drinking a cosmo, if I'm interested in what people are drinking, and I notice a little baby fat around her cheeks as she smiles and I decide that the only girl who would order a cosmopolitan at a place like this is one who's underage and not accustomed to drinking and has probably seen one too many episodes of *Sex and the City*. I tell her that's wonderful, her penchant for cranberry and vodka and all, but that I'm not one to support underage drinking, despite my presence at the party. She rolls her eyes and shoves her way past me to the bar. *One strike, one ball.*

The bartender passes by me without asking for my order once again so I reach into my pocket and check my cell phone. One new text message from Vanessa: "Be there in 10. Running late. Find you inside." I snap the phone shut and look around for Chase or Annalee or Caitlin or Jack or *someone* I know at least *vaguely*, but my search only turns up a sea of shifting eyes and upturned collars. My shoes are definitely sticking to the floor.

"She did *what*?!" The blond girl, the one to my left who shot me down moments ago, is speaking to the brunette in a frantic tone. She brings a manicured hand to her mouth.

"You heard me." The brunette nods mischievously.

"Wait. You're telling me she *slept* with him? As in—"

"As in *sex*." The brunette takes a sip of her drink through a candy-colored straw.

"*No.*"

"*Yes.*" She nods slowly, as if each movement of her head is spelling out s-e-x.

The blonde takes a moment to gather her thoughts and carefully and lightly passes a hand through her hair. "Don't get me wrong. I love Jerome. I absolutely *adore* him. Did he go on scholarship to Potomac? Because isn't he from Prince George's County? Anyway—"

"Right, *anyway.*"

"It's just that I can't believe she slept with him."

"Right. That's my point." *For Christ's sake, won't one of them just say it already?*

"I mean, he's—"

"He's *black.*"

There.

Outside and I've finally gotten my drink from that clusterfuck of a bar and I just received a garbled voice mail from Vanessa telling me that she's waiting in line, but that it's quite long and that it might take her awhile. Still no Chase, but Caitlin sent me a text saying that she and Annalee are outside. Next to me, three men, all wearing button-down oxfords, loose khakis, and boat shoes stand in a huddled group. One of them I identify as Hal Hastings Jr. and he instantly recognizes me, too, and slaps me on the back.

"Tyler!" His Bud Light foams at the mouth as the contents of the bottle slosh and spill down its neck.

"Taylor," I correct him, again.

"Right, right. You having a good time?" The other men in the group turn their backs and continue their conversation. Yes, of course, I say, an excellent time. "*Awesome,* man. You find any skin-tern ass yet?" I tell him that no, I haven't, not yet at least, but that it's still early and that, really, I just got here.

"Nice, man, nice." He swigs his beer and his belly bulges. "I like your style. Play it cool. Look at 'em, though." Hal surveys the crowd. "There's a fuckload of 'em out there. Just make sure they're legal, eh, comrade?" He laughs and snorts and punches me in the ribs. Over in the distance, I see Caitlin and Annalee emerge from the bathroom, giggling.

"Good luck with all that, Hal," I say and excuse myself.

After much trial and tribulation I make my way through the crowd over to the two girls, whose eyes are looking fresh and shiny and wild and who are discreetly wiping their noses and talking at accelerated speeds. Annalee's sipping a Redbull/vodka through a straw and Caitlin's drinking vodka on the rocks.

"Lover!" Caitlin throws her arms around my neck and kisses me on the cheek. "*Fabulous* to see you. *Totally* fabulous."

Annalee smiles and looks past me.

"Tell me *immediately*, like right this very *second,* where you've been!" Caitlin keeps her arms around my neck and I peel one of them off.

"I've been at the bar," I say, holding up my gin as evidence. "It took forever to get a drink. I should've texted you guys to see if you wanted anything."

Caitlin shoos her hand at me. "Don't be *ridiculous.* We're fine. Us gals are *fine,* aren't we, Annalee?" Caitlin clutches Annalee's hand.

"Mmhmm," Annalee says, dabbing her nose with her free hand. "*Totally* fine." She runs her tongue over her gums. "Chase said you had a friend coming. Where is she?"

"*She?*" Caitlin says.

"Yes, *she.*" Annalee giggles and punches Caitlin lightly on the shoulder. "I already told you he wasn't gay."

I pretend to be oblivious to the comment. "She's in line. Outside." Caitlin reaches into the Fendi Spy bag and frenetically digs out her compact and holds it under her nose and looks up and wipes something white from the side of one of her nostrils.

"Well." I take a sip of my drink and put my other hand in my pocket. "It looks like you guys are having a great time. Glad that dinner went so well." They both smile and their eyes dart this way and that and they keep holding hands.

Fifteen minutes later and I've managed to get myself another drink and find Vanessa, who was being preyed upon by Hal and his friends and who is drinking whiskey, straight. I ask her if she's having a good time, and she gives me a look, then laughs and says sure, why not—those guys ("Was his name Hal? I couldn't understand him") were just *great*.

"Yeah, sorry about that," I say, and I think my speech is starting to slur and I'm sort of wobbly on my feet, "thanks again for stopping by." Journey starts playing in the background and the drunken chorus starts.

"Don't worry about it!" she yells over the first verse. "Sorry I'm late. I had this dinner thing to go to for the CHC."

"The what?"

"The Congressional Hispanic Caucus. My chief of staff invited me."

I nod and wish that my interest lasted beyond the word "Congressional." "Ah. Cool." I bob my head to the music. "So, you ever been here before?"

"Once." A blond girl in a pink Polo shirt bumps against Vanessa's shoulder and glares. "I told myself I'd never come back."

I laugh and put my arm around her shoulder. "Oh, come on, Ramírez. You don't mean that. This place is a blast."

"You don't believe that."

I look down and grin and swirl the ice around the small glass cup. "You're right, I don't." I finish my gin and tonic in another swig and order another.

Hal Hastings stands on the bar above me and belts out the second verse of Journey's "Don't Stop Believin'," which is currently playing for the fourth time this evening. He misses the higher notes by entire octaves but his singing is still deafening, even over the din of the bar.

"Where are your friends?" she asks.

"No clue."

The song ends and Vanessa says she needs to get some air and that the crowds and the sticky floor and the tang of alcohol are overwhelming her, so we snake our way through the throngs of high-fiving men and hair-flipping women and make our way outside.

"Much better," she says, though, really, it's not. The outside's practically as crowded as the inside—there's just better circulation. I point out Caitlin and Annalee, who are still standing suspiciously close to the outside bathroom, and I tell her that I'd like to introduce her. Vanessa shrugs and says "Sure," but I can tell that she's nervous even though she's trying to hide it from me.

When we reach them, Caitlin and Annalee are looking more alive and wide-eyed and just so *into it* than before, though they've stopped holding hands. Caitlin strokes my arm before linking it with her own. Vanessa crosses her arms against her chest.

"Hellllllllo my favorite Californian," Caitlin coos. "Annalee and I were just talking about Chazy's absolutely *spectacular* house out on the bay and how we all must—*must*—take a trip out there for a long weekend at some point this summer." The space, the time, between the individual words of her sentences have decreased. Annalee nods and sips a full Redbull/vodka.

"Speaking of whom," she says after she's swallowed, "have you seen Chase?"

I tell her that, no, I hadn't seen him in the past—well, come to think of it, since we got to the party, really, but that I'd like to introduce them both to a friend of mine. Vanessa uncrosses her arms and flattens her skirt and smiles. Caitlin polishes off her vodka, smiles, and hands the empty glass to Annalee, who then quietly places it on a nearby table.

"Sweetie," she says, taking Vanessa's hand, but she doesn't really shake it so much as she just holds it. "How *wonderful* to meet you. It's just *great* to meet one of Taylor's friends from work." Then, with a slight cock of her head, "Are you enjoying yourself?"

Vanessa shrugs, and before she can answer, Caitlin grips her hand tighter and smiles wider. "I know, I know. This place can be a *bit* overwhelming. Not like those *adorable* dive bars on the Hill. But you'll have a fantastic time. *Fantastic.*"

Annalee cuts between them and pries Vanessa's hand away from Caitlin's white-knuckle grasp.

"I'm Annalee," she says, kissing her cheek with a vigor that I can't decide whether I should attribute to overall friendliness or some of Colombia's finest. "I'm Taylor's cousin."

Vanessa tells her that it's very nice to meet both of them, and then smiles back at Caitlin, who brushes her hair to one side instead and purses her lips in return.

"Caitlin's moving to Baghdad in two months," I say, trying to diffuse what, with my limited male instinct, I read to be an explosive situation. "She'll be working for the Treasury Department there."

Vanessa finishes her whiskey and squints. "What a shame," she says. "I hear the Green Zone's just *not* the place it used to be."

An hour later, at one thirty, I'm standing by myself outside and the crowd has started to thin out, but only slightly. Vanessa left about forty-five minutes ago, and though I can't really blame her, I'm still disappointed—not due to any sort of sexual chemistry between us, but rather due to the fact that she seemed to be the one thing sober and sane in this sea of overpriced madness. After her departure, I rejoined Caitlin and Annalee, but we had unfortunately reached that awkward point in the evening where it had become painfully obvious that they had had help sustaining their energy, and I—well, I hadn't. My mind slugged through gin and tequila to keep up with their conversations, which I was unable to understand both on a contextual and a phonetic level, and all of it eventually just ended up giving me a headache so I excused myself to the bathroom (the inside one). I found Jack, whom I hadn't seen yet this evening, and talked with him briefly about work, the paper (*his* paper), the bar's crowd, and the like, but then a young man with clear blue eyes and jet-black hair who was of *very* ambiguous sexuality walked by and Jack abandoned our conversation and followed him to the bar.

I can tell that the night—or at least my night—is coming to a close because, truthfully, the only people who are out past 2:00 A.M. in this town are the sort of folks that you don't want to be out with anyway. Against sounder judgment I decide to give this skin-tern thing, this s-e-x thing, a final shot, so I drink my gin and scan the crowd until I find a target: a thin, blond girl, maybe southern, probably nineteen, definitely drunk, sipping a clear beverage and leaning against a wall about ten feet from me.

"Having a good night?" I say, leaning against the wall next to her. She shrugs and stirs her drink.

"It's okay."

"Yeah, nothing to write home about. You look like you're running on empty there," I say, nodding to her drink. "Can I get you another one?" She smiles and says thanks, but she should probably pass, because she's "totally wasted already." *Check.*

I tell her that she's much more responsible than I am, which is admirable, and she tells me that I'm cute, and I wonder when we can just get past this bullshit and go home already, because I honestly can't feel my face anymore. She asks me where I live, and I tell her Woodley Park, and she smiles and flips her hair to expose more of her neck, which is tan and slender, and she tells me she *loves* that area. *Check.* Sir Mix-A-Lot's "Baby Got Back" starts pumping over the bar's speakers.

"Great song," I say.

She smiles wider. "Yeah. You know who *loves* this song?"

"Who?" I slip my arm around her waist and she squeals and giggles.

"My dad." I remove my arm.

"How old is your dad?"

"In his early forties." I take a step back.

"How old are *you?*"

She starts biting on a fingernail and grinning. "I'm seventeen."

I take a giant step back and stumble.

She stops grinning. "Please don't tell anyone, though. I told my cousin Hal that I'd lie and tell everyone that I was twenty-one if he let me in. If my parents found out that I came here and that I'm not at Kimmy Calvert's house I'll be totally busted. Like, *grounded.*"

I run my hand through my hair and tell her not to worry, that her secret's safe with me, and she sighs and says thanks and asks me when we're going to Woodley Park. I tell her to get ahold of me after her eighteenth birthday, and I start making my long way to the bar's front entrance.

Seventeen fucking years old.

I make it halfway to the door and I literally have to peel the soles of my loafers off the soggy floor each time I take a step, when I come across a roadblock that's comprised of a group of people—

both men and women—clustered together, laughing, and pointing toward a corner of the room. I stop, allowing my feet to sink into the ground, and follow their gaze to a corner of the room where I see the broad back of a young man turned toward the crowd. His head is lifted upward, in an overaffected pose that's reminiscent of the seventies porn clips that Chase and I used to download for free during freshman year of college. Between his legs (which are spread—again, I think as I roll my eyes, rather affected) is a young woman, whose blond head is awkwardly pushed—*shoved*—into the man's crotch. One of her hands (manicured—French) is gripping the man's left thigh, while the other is grasping a string of pearls dangling from her neck in an attempt to keep them—the pearls, those white orbs—from bouncing against her chest. The whole operation—this whole expedition into the often complicated world of oral sex—looks uncomfortable at best, and is sickening at worst. They're knotted into an uncomfortable position, this couple, in what looks like a broom closet whose door has been casually flung open. The girl's shirt has been unbuttoned, and the man is thrusting his pelvis against her face at some sloppy beat that's not in time with the music bouncing off the walls. Both of them seem unaware that the door, their shield of privacy, is now ajar, and has thus turned their tryst into one of the evening's many forms of aspirational entertainment.

"What a whore," a girl next to me says, and I see that it's the same blond girl from earlier in the evening. "I mean, she's practically *raping* him."

"Oh, please, that bitch is lucky and you know it," the brunette friend says, giggling.

The blonde laughs and says, "You're so *bad*." She wraps her tongue around a straw.

"Like you wouldn't go down on Chase Latham in a broom closet."

I squint my eyes and look closer. *That girl isn't Annalee.*

"I mean, have you seen his abs? He's a god."

"Isn't he dating someone?"

"Some Duke chick. Heard she's a total idiot. I think she works for, like, *Capitol File* or something." The brunette rolls her eyes. "But whatever, you know? Like that's stopped him before."

"I don't see you calling her" comes to mind.

The girls laugh and sip their drinks and reapply their lipstick and I want to slug them both in their forged, counterfeit faces.

"You look surprised."

I turn and see Jack, who's alone and who is looking disappointed and dissatisfied.

"I guess I just didn't have any idea," I manage to say.

"Yeah, you did." He lowers his head but keeps his eyes on Chase, who is now moving one hand to cup the girl's left breast.

May 26, 2007;
1:55 A.M.

I sit down on the corner of Dumbarton and Wisconsin and light a cigarette that I've bummed from some barely conscious guy who was speaking—mumbling—on a cell phone outside the bar. It takes me four matches to light the damned thing, and with each strike comes another ill-conceived solution to the calamitous mess to which I've just borne witness. Once the embers on the end of the rolling paper are lit, though, I stumble across the conclusion that gin, tequila, and tobacco do not a solution make, and I just let the smoke waft up and hover above my head.

The bar's door opens periodically like a gaping mouth, spilling its contents—drunk and rich and happy—out onto O Street. I watch the horde amass and gather and decide what to do next. In one of the groups I see Hal's cousin—the seventeen-year-old—being propped up by a man a few years older than I. She sways and swoons and he whispers into her ear and kisses her neck and she gives him this silly look and nods.

A clump of ash falls off the cigarette and wafts into the gutter. *The crowd's doing the waltz, see, and I'm tripping through a tango.*

Moments later, the door opens again and Caitlin struts out onto the street with a confidence that seems unfitting—taste-less—for this hour of night. Behind her, Chase is typing on his BlackBerry with one hand and holding Annalee in the other. She kisses his cheek and I take the final drag of my cigarette and he puts the phone away and Caitlin gives someone a digital camera to take a picture of the three of them. Once the flash has fleetingly lit up their faces, Hal Hastings saddles up to Caitlin's side and she allows him to until she realizes that people are watching. He laughs when she shoves him away, and then he says something to Chase, who relays the message to Annalee and Caitlin, who look at each other, nod, and then follow Hal down O Street toward Thirtieth, away from Wisconsin.

But before he turns his back, before he walks away, Chase squints as if he recognizes someone sitting on the corner of Dumbarton Street, smoking a cigarette. And he lets the rest of the group, the rest of his pride, move a few steps ahead of him before he nods and smiles, and then spins to join them.

The first drop of rain has already fallen by the time I get up from the curb. But the sky hasn't opened up yet—there's just a light mist that I frequently forget is there—so I decide to keep walking, stopping at CVS to buy a pack of cigarettes, and then heading up Wisconsin and turning onto P Street, which, with its tree-lined sidewalks and proper homes in ancient brick, seems worlds away from the clamor and circus of Wisconsin and M Street. It's empty, P Street, and for the first time this evening I can hear each of my steps as my feet hit the aging sidewalk.

I suppose I could tell myself that it was aimless intoxicated wandering that took me on this current trajectory; that after what I witnessed at Smith Point, I need some air, some *peace,* and that my desperate search simply happened to lead me to this particu-lar street where I dropped a particular *livre de poche* at the feet of a particular married woman.

But from what I can tell, this city's got enough deceit.

It's the way we work: upon seeing another man's transgression, the ostensible part of our psyche condemns and berates and tsk-tsks his sins. But that other part, that other voice—the one that gets louder with gin—enrages us with taunts that he's having something we'll never have the courage to touch. And so: P Street, with the full knowledge of Congressman Grayson's absence, and with even greater awareness of his wife's presence.

At the corner of Thirty-first, I stop under a giant oak and light another cigarette, this time with only three matches. High above me, drops of rain tap lightly on the tree's leaves. I inhale hard on the orange filter and try to suffocate Jack's comment: *I had always known.* I had thought at the time that the declaration was directed at me, at my own denial. But now under this monstrous oak, as I recall the look in his—in Jack's—eyes, this blend of lust and hunger and jealousy and desperation that terrified me with both its foreignness and its familiarity, I'm starting to think otherwise.

But still. I had always known.

"No, champ, no." Chase looks at what I'm wearing—a white shirt, freshly starched, open collar, no tie, jeans, black blazer, and Converse sneakers—and shakes his head. "You've got to change."

"What are you talking about?" I move to the mirror on the other side of our dorm room. "I wore this outfit to the Homecoming dance during my senior year." Chase laughs.

"Exactly. And therein lies our problem." He reaches into his closet and pulls out a Thomas Pink tie. Thomas Pink. What the hell kind of name is that? Without doubt, he had his head flushed in a toilet more than one time as a child. "And kick off those shoes." I look down at my pair of black All Stars, a pair that I've worked to break in to that perfect convergence of comfort and personality.

"Dude, what's wrong with my shoes?"

" 'Dude.' " Chase throws his head back and howls. "Do me a favor, champ: try to keep the 'dude' bombs to a minimum tonight. My pops knows my roommate is from Laguna Beach, but I don't want him to think I'm living with someone from that goddamn MTV show or something." I sit down on the edge of my bed and remove each of the shoes and ask him if he's got any better suggestions. He turns back to his closet.

"Of course I do, Taylor. I've got every suggestion in the book." He shows me two pairs of shoes—both black loafers with metals clasps across them. "You want Ferragamo or Magli?" I shrug and tell him I couldn't tell the difference if he paid me and he tells me to go with the Ferragamo. "I'll probably wear the Maglis," he says.

I slip one of the leather shoes onto my right foot. The shoe is still and unsupportive and feels foreign. Chase throws me the tie. "Throw that on," he instructs. "You're not in L.A. anymore, champ. We're going to Striped Bass. Not In 'n' Out Burger." I look into the mirror and button my shirt's top button, and then wrap the silk around my neck and tie it in a half Windsor, the only knot that Frank, my father, had ever taught me. Chase sighs when he sees the tie job, but checks his watch and says we're already late and that really we don't have time for a proper tie-tying seminar at the moment, but that at some point ("and at some point soon, champ") I really need to learn these things—especially how to tie a bow tie. It's a dying art. He grabs my shoulders and spins me to face a mirror.

"So? What do you think? Much better, eh?"

I see my Converse sitting limp and dejected littering the floor next to my bed. "Yeah. Much better."

The cigarette doesn't last as long as I expect and the rain's starting to come down harder against the protective leaves of that giant oak. I walk out from under the massive shield and the water starts dampening my hair and running down my face. I stop there, between Thirtieth and Thirty-first, and I stare across the street at the bright yellow door as the drops polka-dot my shirt and cool my face against the hot May night and I'm alone on this dark, quiet street.

And I'm ready to leave, I'm ready to admit that I'll never have the courage to do what Jack and I have always known Chase takes as second nature, when I see the lighter flicker and I hear:

"Taylor?" The voice, melodic and sad, with traces of smoke and booze. I look harder across the street, though I already know who it is, and I squint through the rain, which is slowing to a drizzle.

"Mrs. Grayson?" I hear the wood and the chains of an old porch swing creak as she rises and crosses to the railing at the edge of the porch.

"Yes, it's Juliana." She leans her bare, tan arms against the wet railing and smiles. Her dark hair, which looks like it was once pulled back into a tight knot off her face, has loosened, a few of its shadowy strands framing her brown eyes. She's dressed simply: white tank top, jeans, no shoes. I take a step from the sidewalk and onto the street. "You look like you're getting soaked, Taylor."

I shade my eyes and look up into the sky. "Yes, but it looks like it's letting up. I'm apparently not the best judge of Washington weather."

She laughs. "But who is?" A pause and then, "Why don't you come and dry off on the porch until it stops?" I run a hand through my wet hair and rain runs off in every which way and I think about that bow tie, crumpled and soiled and yellowed, sitting on the nightstand next to my bed.

"I'm not sure if that's the best idea. I should probably just head home. I really am very tired, and"—the rain stops falling against my shoulders—"and I'm not in the best state."

"Taylor"—she stops laughing—"don't be ridiculous. At least come up here and dry off and let's call you a cab."

I hesitate for a moment—a courtesy, if anything—and then I cross the street.

⤫

"Just do me a favor tonight, okay?" Chase tells the cabbie to take us to the Striped Bass, and to step on it, because we're already late.

"Sure," I say, pulling at the tie, which has started cutting off circulation to my neck. "What's up?"

"Just don't bring up the lacrosse thing." Chase examines his reflection in the driver's rearview mirror. "I haven't had the chance to tell my dad about it yet, and I'm not sure how he'll react."

Chase had quit the team weeks before. He had been anticipated as one of the team's most talented recruits. But it had gotten in the way, Chase said, had gotten in the way of girls and parties and booze and drugs and, like, college, *you know?*

"Yeah," I say. "Sure, of course."

Chase squeezes my shoulder but keeps looking at his own reflection. "Good, champ. Good."

⤫

Juliana hands me a towel for my hair and tells me to please take a seat on the swing.

"Can I get you something to drink?"

"No thanks. I've had a bit to drink tonight already."

She unpins the bun sitting on the back of her head, and midnight waves collapse onto her shoulders. "Don't be ridiculous. What do you prefer? Scotch? Vodka?" She pauses. "Gin. You drink gin."

"Mrs. Grayson, honestly—"

"*Not another word*, Taylor. It'd be rude of me not to ask, and ruder of you not to accept. Sit here for a moment, I'll be back with your drink and a phone number for a cab company."

I tell her thank you as she opens the big yellow door and disappears behind it. It really is coming down harder now, the rain, turning the asphalt of P Street into some silver river, its puddles reflecting the garish glares of streetlights. The swing creaks and moans as I shift my weight. Next to me there's a small side table containing a pack of Dunhill cigarettes, a silver lighter, and a copy of *Mémoires d'un jeune homme dérangé*, the pages of which are beginning to curl and bend and yellow.

The yellow door swings open again and Juliana hands me a tall tumbler with gin, tonic, and a slice of lime. She sits next to me on the swing, which creaks under the additional weight. She reaches for the Dunhills and the lighter.

"So where have you been this evening? Out and about?"

The Zippo flicks and flashes and throws orange light on her face.

"Yeah." I drink the gin and tonic and she crosses her legs. "Out and about. Were you able to find the number of a cab company?"

She exhales long streams of smoke. "No, Taylor; to be honest, I forgot. I'll have to remember when I go back inside to refill your drink."

"Thanks. That'd be a huge help."

The taxi pulls up to the corner of Fifteenth and Walnut and Chase pays the fare. I object momentarily, but he waves away the five-dollar bill I offer him. We walk through the restaurant's monstrous double doors and are greeted by the maître d', who calls Chase "Mr. Latham" and tells him that it's so nice to see him again, and that his father and mother are waiting for us at the bar.

We move past the entrance and aside to the bar, where Kip, with a smile like I've never seen before, greets us, and Patricia, obedient and silent and quietly matronly, smiles and kisses her son on the cheek.

"Taylor!" Kip grabs my hand and shakes it enthusiastically. "We've heard so much about you."

Patricia nods and smiles.

"It's so great to finally meet you," he says. "I took the liberty of order-
ing you a Bombay and tonic." He hands me a sweating glass. "You do
like gin, I hope."

I tell him thank you and that, of course, I like gin, though really I
haven't drunk it all that much before, that usually, in Orange County,
I've stuck to beer and vodka. "By the way. Love your tie."

"Really. It's gorgeous," Patricia agrees with her husband.

Chase nudges me in the side.

"Thanks," I say. "It's one of my favorites."

"So"—Juliana takes a deep drag off the Dunhill and lets
the contents fill her lungs, which makes her voice that much
smokier—"where did you have 'a bit to drink' tonight?" She
reclines on the swing and it sways backward.

"This party. At Smith Point." I clutch my drink with both
hands and look down.

"Smith Point? That's the bar off of O Street, with the list,
right?"

I tell her that yes, that's correct, the one with the list.

She smiles and lets smoke drift from the corners of her mouth.
"I've never been there."

I tell her that doesn't surprise me and she gives me a look and
asks me what's that supposed to mean.

"Oh, nothing," I say. "Or, nothing derogatory. I just can't imagine, you know, the wife of a *congressman* stepping into a dive bar
like Smith Point."

She rolls her eyes and stubs out the Dunhill. "Right. 'The wife
of a *congressman*.' Such fabulous parties and wonderful social events
afforded by *that* position." She reaches for my drink. "I'm assuming
you don't mind if I have a taste? I'm not sure how much gin I put
in." She brings the glass to her lips. "Enough. I put in enough."

She sets the drink down, on top of the copy of *Mémoires d'un jeune homme dérangé*.

We sit in silence as the rain starts to drum again on the leaves of the giant oaks. It's coming down harder now, sweeping across the street in violent sheets. A cab pulls slowly by the house and I tell Juliana that I should probably hail it, but she tells me to stay on the swing, that she can call one in a few minutes. The car stops briefly at the corner and then continues on its way, leaving small waves in its wake.

"Did you have a nice evening, Mrs. Grayson?"

She laughs and reaches for the Dunhill. "Define 'nice' for me, Mr. Mark. I had dinner with Mrs. Scripps and Mrs. Howard. At Galileo. You met them at the Gold Cup, I believe. They went to an event at the British embassy."

"Why didn't you go with them?"

"Because, strangely, my invitation must have been lost in the mail."

"Does that happen often?"

"Quite."

I think back to Bunny Howard's melodic voice. *That's his wife.*

"I did meet Mrs. Howard and Mrs. Scripps. They seem like nice ladies."

"You should ask their husbands." She ashes the cigarette onto the porch. "From the sounds of it, they know more about each other's spouses than they do about each other."

"Pardon?"

"They're atrocious."

"I'm not sure I'm following."

"More gin?"

"I think I've hit my limit."

"And I think you need more gin." She stands up and walks behind the swing, and then right across the porch, back to the big yellow door, and I'm not sure if it's the alcohol coupled with my preposterous imagination, or if it's reality, but I think she brushes a hand across my shoulders as she passes behind.

I've lit a cigarette and am staring at the rain, which is pouring down as hard as ever, when she returns with a drink that's stronger than the last.

"So tell me about your night at Smith Point." She slips another Dunhill between her lips. "Was it all you hoped for and more?"

I laugh and look into my drink. "To be honest with you, I've had better evenings, I think. Much better, as it turns out."

"Oh?"

"Yes."

I lean back against the swing and stare at the ice—fractured and irregular—slowly melting inside the glass.

She runs a hand through her hair and throws her cigarette into the flooded sidewalk. "So what exactly occurred at Smith Point that's inspired this existential crisis of yours?"

"I never said I was going through an existential crisis, Jul— Mrs. Grayson."

"A person doesn't drink Bombay and tonics and smoke Camel Lights with their boss's wife at two forty-five A.M. unless he's experiencing some sort of existential crisis." I sigh and slump deeper on the bench.

"Chase—do you know Chase?"

She nods and says "Who doesn't?" and I continue, "Anyway, Chase is dating my cousin, or has been dating my cousin. For the past two years."

"And?"

"And tonight I think I saw something that wasn't meant for my eyes." She nods.

I tell her about Caitlin and Vanessa, and how I hadn't known that Annalee still did cocaine, though I'm trying to convince myself that this was a rare relapse, a moral blip on my cousin's radar. And I tell her how my shoes—these goddamn loafers that Chase told me to buy for $425.00—kept sticking to the bar's floor. I tell her about the seventeen-year-old, and how I saw her leave with a man who was at the very least a decade older than she and at the very best had horrible intentions. And then last I tell her about Chase, about how I had met him at his apartment but how I hadn't seen him the entire night, not until the end, not until the door to the broom closet swung open to reveal him with some girl's mouth shoved between his khaki-clad thighs while his head was thrown back in this Ron Jeremy–type way that even I found to be embarrassing—for him, for everyone—and how that girl wasn't Annalee, and then I tell her about that look in Jack's eyes, that look he didn't want me to see, so dejected and damned.

Juliana arches her back and rolls her neck. Rainwater is starting to run down her arms. "Was she pretty?" she asks once she's stopped stretching.

"I don't think that's really the point."

"Who knows if it is or not, but just grant me this favor and answer the question. Was she pretty?" I think back to the girl's blond hair and lithe, tan shoulders.

"Yes, I guess. Yes, she was pretty." Juliana smiles.

"Of course she was." The sky opens up farther and a couple, huddled under a coat, run past the house. I look down at my loafers.

"There was this night in L.A.," she begins, "when I was sixteen years old. My parents had been invited to a dinner party at the home of this famous banker whose name I can't remember for the life of me, and I'm sure you wouldn't know it even if I did. Normally, my brother—he was older than I, by two years, but we were close. Very close. Anyway, normally my brother and I weren't invited to join my parents. They didn't want us to be exposed to—God, to *anything* really. My father hates Los Angeles. He says it destroys people's souls. He's a bit dramatic, I tell him. Which, of course, is never anything a father wants to hear."

I laugh, but she doesn't notice and she just continues speaking, still staring at nothing in particular.

"But my father liked this banker. He was a family man himself, so he allowed my brother and me to join them. God, that house was *gorgeous*," she says, looking up and smiling. "One of those ultramodern places in the Hollywood hills. It had a manmade stream running through the damned thing, Taylor. With koi. My brother thought it was ostentatious, which, of course, it was. He was always saying things like that—calling things ostentatious, saying my clothes cost too much. He wanted to be a documentary filmmaker. But I don't know, I liked it all. I liked the glamour of it.

"I don't remember what was served for dinner, I just remember my father telling my brother and me over and over and over again that we weren't to have any champagne. I suppose when you think about it, it's really no wonder he sent me away . . ." She trails off here and realizes that she may have hit upon a topic she's not fully prepared to discuss. And so, "Anyway, we didn't have any champagne. For a while, Jackson and I were both surprisingly well-behaved kids, which"—and she laughs here—"was a hard thing to be during the eighties in Los Angeles.

"We left the dinner party in two separate cars. I was riding with my parents, and Jackson had driven himself." Juliana stops and watches the smoke rise from her cigarette, and I wonder how I've ended up here. "I saw the accident coming from a mile away, literally." She chuckles and this makes me sad. "We were out of the hills and were driving along Santa Monica Boulevard. Jackson had a green light to cross Wilshire, but this guy—they say he was drunk, but who knows? I'm not sure that matters, anyway—

this guy in a pickup went sailing through the intersection. And I just remember it being the strangest feeling, watching this pickup truck fly down Wilshire, knowing that he was going to hit my brother and kill him. Do you understand what I'm saying?"

I tell her yes, but only sort of yes.

"I don't know," she finally says with a sigh. "I suppose it's just a matter of not being able to prevent these tragedies, even after you've seen them coming from miles away."

"I shouldn't have brought this up," I eventually say to her once she's finished and enough silence has passed between us to be considered appropriate. "Did you manage to find that phone number for the cab company?"

"No, Taylor, I'm sorry. I must've forgotten again," she says.

I start to get up from the swing. "I can find one. Is the phone book in the kitchen?"

"I told you I'd get it. I'll get it."

The water's starting to creep across Juliana's shirt, creating translucent, flesh-colored streaks.

"So what happened next?"

"After Jackson died?"

"Yes."

She rolls her eyes and gives a dismissive wave of a hand. "I'm sure you've heard most of it. It seems to be the topic of conversation in Georgetown whenever a bored housewife has allotted for too much time between hair and nail appointments."

I tell her that I had heard things—just whisperings, really, but nothing specific.

"Well," she says, her voice getting edgier, tainted with more gravel, "for starters, my good behavior went to shit, which caused my father to put me on a shorter leash, which caused me to act out more, which—" and she stops herself. "Jesus, Taylor, you know this story by now. I won't bore you with clichés. When all was said and done, I calmed down for an instant—a horrible decision that I'm thinking was influenced by sobriety—but it was just long enough for me to be convinced to accept a proposal I had been preparing for three years to reject, and I ended up here"—she points to the house—"with him." She points to the Capitol.

"Are they true?"

"Pardon?"

"The things they say about you. Are they true?"

"No." She stops. "Yes. Probably. I don't know. By this point I've lost track of what they've said."

I tell her that I'm sure there are worse sentences than being married to a congressman with famous hair, and she says that yes, yes, I'm right, there are, and they often involve having to endure meals with women named things like Bunny and Kitty. And then speaking of bearing witness to the unfolding of clichéd catastrophes, what—she begs my pardon—do I plan on doing about this current situation? I tell her that I'm not sure, but rather how I felt as I watched Chase cheat on Annalee, how I felt as though someone were pummeling my stomach, how I felt as though he were cheating on me.

"That's touching, Taylor." Juliana lights another cigarette. "Really, *really* touching."

"I should go." I stand up.

"So what are you going to do?"

"I'm going to walk down to M Street and find a cab on my own."

She laughs. "That's not what I'm talking about."

I sigh and run a hand through my hair. "I'm not sure," I tell her. "I haven't thought that far ahead."

Juliana's blocking the staircase leading down from the porch.

I stop before I reach her and ask her if she enjoys being the wife of a public official.

"Do I enjoy being married to a public official? Or do I enjoy being married?"

I tell her to choose to answer whichever question she prefers.

"Either one is quite audacious, particularly considering it's coming from an office assistant, wouldn't you say?" She brushes her hair behind and takes a step toward me.

I look down. "I'm sorry, Juliana. It must be the gin."

"I suppose at the end of the day you've got to come at the subject from a cost-benefit perspective."

"Pardon?"

"Marriage. You asked me if I enjoyed being married to John. And I'm telling you that it has its costs and its benefits."

"I got a C in econ."

"I'm sure you understand what I'm saying, though, right?"

"Yes, I think I do." Then, "So what are they? What are the costs?"

"Ask me that at the end of the summer."

"What are the benefits?"

She doesn't answer but rather just smokes and runs her hand through her dark hair and stares off at nothing in particular.

And then—and I suppose you could blame this on personal velocity, or on fate, or on gin, on Chase, or on my own misguided indiscretions—but then, as the rain falls like silver ribbons from those thunderous clouds and the street is asleep and silent, I reach my hand behind Juliana's wet neck and kiss her long and hard and deep.

IX

October 19, 2002, 9:00 P.M.;
May 26, 2007, 9:00 A.M.

splash cool water in my face and look into the gold-framed mirror in the bathroom at Striped Bass. My tie—Chase's tie—has started to come loose, so I pinch the silk at the knot and tighten the half Windsor and then brush some lint off my blazer. Even after the oysters and the smoked salmon terrine my mouth is still flavored with traces of gin, which is still new and foreign, and I'm starting to equate with pinecones. In a stall behind me, a toilet flushes.

"How you doing, champ?" Chase yells over the gargle of water.

I dry my face off with a hand towel. "Fine. I'm fine."

The stall door swings open and I see Chase in the mirror tucking in his shirt. I turn to face him and lean against the cold marble of the bathroom sink.

"I can't believe we've had three drinks and we're only on appetizers. I should probably have some bread or something."

Chase laughs and pats my shoulder a few times. "Don't be ridiculous, bud." He looks in the mirror and straightens his tie, which is knotted in a full Windsor and doesn't need tightening. "Who eats bread anymore, anyway?"

Well, a lot of people, I think. The French, for starters. And me. I eat bread. I had a sandwich for lunch. Chase continues to straighten his tie.

"Kip's a huge fan of yours." I look up from my—Chase's—loafers, which have become no more comfortable during the past hour.

"How can you tell?"

"He's my dad, Taylor. I know these things."

I smile and start feeling something in my chest that's somewhere between pride and something else. Acceptance, maybe?

"And Patricia." Chase smiles. "Patricia. Christ, if that woman wasn't married, she'd be all over that blond mop of yours in no time flat." He puts me in a headlock and ruffles my blond hair until, for a moment, it's standing straight up and I laugh. "So you're feeling a little buzz, eh?" he says once he lets me go.

"Yeah, man," I say, flattening my hair, "I'm getting there."

"Well, we got a long way to go, Casanova. A long. Way. To. Go." Chase enunciates each syllable as if life and death hung in the balance of my ability to exhibit some stamina, some umph, during the Striped Bass dinner. "What'd you order for dinner?" he asks.

I look up and think about it for a moment. It seems like ages ago when the waiter, white linen draped over one arm, came to our table. "Jesus, champ, are you that *drunk that you can't even remember what you ordered?"*

"No, no," I say. "I remember. I got the pistachio-crusted halibut."

"Perfect." Chase nods and reaches into the smallest, fifth pocket of his jeans. "Perfecto, really." He kisses the tips of his fingers like an Italian.

"Why is that 'perfecto'?"

"Because." He struggles a bit pulling the contents of the pocket—a small dime bag filled halfway with fine white powder—out into the open. "Last time I checked, pistachio-crusted halibut was complemented perfectly by South America's finest."

"South America's finest what?"

Chase gives a defeated sigh and looks up into the bathroom's lights.

"South America's finest cocaine." *This time he gives a Bolivian accent, which is spot-on.*

I shake my head.

My history with illicit substances is neither exciting nor extensive. The first time I smelled marijuana—at a Bon Jovi concert in the third grade—I asked my father, who was accompanying me, who was burning cardboard. Ten years later, in high school, I occasionally smoked pot, but only on the beach and only when there was nothing else to do (which, as the years in Laguna Beach dragged on, became an increasingly frequent phenomenon). Stronger, sexier, and more dangerous concoctions—speed, meth, acid, and the like—had been, and continue to be, confined to the stuff of local news. A meth lab blows up in a trailer park here. A teenager in Oklahoma overdoses on speed there. Cocaine—blow, Colombian gold, snow—I had seen it once before, during my sophomore year of high school when I paid a visit to Princeton to see Nate over a long weekend. His girlfriend at the time—a train wreck of a specimen named Cecile, who thought she could loosen my brother up a bit—railed eight and a quarter lines in front of me during a pregame for one of their eating club's parties. Nate promptly dumped her (which, depending on whom you ask, played a large role in her failing out of the famed university and her subsequent enrollment in Le Cirque rehabilitation clinic in Sundance, Utah) and told me we would not be attending the gathering.

"I don't know, Chase."

"What," he says, shaking the bag so the contents clump at its bottom, "you've never done a little blow before?"

"Oh, I mean, of course *I have." I laugh nervously. "I mean, I'm from* fucking Orange County. *Stuff runs like water there."*

Chase eyes me suspiciously and laughs. "Right, bud. Whatever you say."

I think back to the local news. "Freshman at Penn Dead after First Line of Cocaine"; "Mother Devastated, Father Drunk, Older Brother Disappointed"; "Escobar Weeps at Loss of Potential Client." The possibilities, per usual, are endless.

"Buddy, can you lock the door?" Chase nods to the bathroom's main door, which has no lock.

"There's no lock," I tell him, hoping that'll stop his latest attempt at the illicit and dangerous and—yes, I'll admit—thrilling.

"Fucking A," he says. "It's like these places try to pretend *like this doesn't go on, or something. I'm heading into a stall. Can you just keep watch?"*

Yeah, sure, I tell him. I'll keep watch. Whatever he needs. Just get the goddamn thing over with.

He disappears behind the stall once again and I hear the wooden door go "click" and then a fumbling of keys and various whisperings of "shit" and "goddamn bag" and "finally."

I turn on one of the faucets lining the sink.

"What the hell are you doing?" I hear him say.

"I don't know . . . I just thought that, you know . . . it'd, like, cover the sound or something." I hear a loud snort, followed by a violent, almost painful, sigh.

"Yeah, whatever." Another snort, another sigh. And then, "Get in here, champ."

"Excuse me?"

"Your turn, bud. I'll keep the faucet running." Chase opens the door and hands me a set of keys and the little clear bag. "Use the silver key," he says as he looks in the mirror and inspects the contents of his right nostril. "It scoops better than the brass ones."

I stare at the set of keys and tick my way through them until I find the silver one that is already encrusted in white powder. And then I look at Chase wiping his nose and the glitter in his eyes and the last thought to cross my mind before I unequivocally decide to enter the stall is, What would Nathaniel think?

                         ⌒⊃

A dog barks loudly outside and I wake up, half-naked, in an unfamiliar bed in an unfamiliar room. There's no one lying on the mattress next to me, just an indent in the white bamboo sheets of where someone used to be. Sunlight, brash and dazzling and offensive, streams through an open window to my right and I cover my face with both hands as I start to piece together the events that concluded last night. In the far corner of the room I see my loafers, scuffed and dirty, and my jeans and my shirt piled in a clumsy, hurried heap. Aside from this blotch, this smear, the room is stark and clean and empty.

I sit up slowly and I can feel the outer layers of my brain thump—pained and dehydrated—against my temples. That god-damn dog continues its desperate whining and I'd give anything in the world for it to stop, for it to just *shut the fuck up* so I can stop my brain from throbbing and give myself a moment to *think*. So I sit there for a moment, wearing only my boxers, in Juliana Gray-son's bed, and I look at my left bicep, which has a faint scratch mark on it—as if it were left by a fingernail or something—and then I look past my arm to a bedside table upon which sits John Grayson's photo, postinauguration, and I decide that it's time for me to leave.

Quietly and carefully, as if not to make too much noise (Does Concepción come on Saturdays? Or worse, does she live in the house?), I slip on my jeans and button up my shirt while I look into a full-length mirror that's adjacent to the bed. My hair, which has gotten too long anyway, is a mess of blond knots and clumps and waves. I run a hand over one of my cheeks. I need to shave. And my eyes have these dark circles that drown out the blue irises that, honestly, I feel like I haven't seen in months. Outside, the dog keeps barking, which makes my head feel like it's absolutely going to *explode,* so I forgo tucking in my shirt and I slip on the loafers and carefully open the bedroom door.

After waiting and listening for a moment, I decide that, thank you, Jesus, the house is empty, so I move quickly down this short, bright hallway and then to the curved staircase and then, finally,

out the big yellow door. The porch is littered with Dunhill cigarette butts that I briefly consider cleaning up before deciding that
a young man picking up cigarette butts on the Graysons' porch
might appear on the side of suspicious, so I jog down the steps
and turn right onto P Street instead.

The night and the rain have done nothing to offset the heat,
which is becoming more unbearable and oppressive and saturated
with humidity each day. Even so I walk faster and faster and faster
away from that yellow door because I just want to get as far from
that goddamn house as humanly possible. Once I'm two blocks
away, I reach into my right pocket for my cell phone, which tells
me that I have two text messages and one voice mail:

Text message one, from Chase, sent at 3:30 A.M.: "Where'd u
go? Come 2 Hals. Still partying."

Text message two, from Vanessa, sent at 9:00 A.M.: "Hope your
night ended well. Sorry I left early. Give me a call today."

Voice mail one, from Katie Mark: "Hi, Taylor, it's me . . . sorry,
I know you hate it when I say that. It's, um, it's Mom. I'm just
checking in. Nathaniel said this would be the best time to call.
I feel as though I haven't talked to you in forever, and I'd like to
hear all about the job when you have a chance. I have an appointment with Dr. Thompkins on Monday, and then on Wednesday
Suzanne and I are going to see another concert. The Killers? Have
you heard of them? In any event, my wrist is almost healed. And
I promise, no more marijuana or stage diving this time." I think
I hear a wave crash. "Laguna really is beautiful right now. The
weather on the beach is perfect. Jennifer stopped by with a few of
your other high school friends last weekend, and they said they
miss you." An awkward pause. "And I miss you, too, Taylor. I really, *really* do." She sighs into the phone. "All right. I suppose just
give me a ring when you have a second. I love you. And I'm so
very, *very* prou—" Her phone cuts out.

I close my phone and put it away and quicken my pace down

P Street. I keep my head bowed and out of sight because I'm feeling like a bit of a criminal, just a little bit *off,* but it doesn't do me any good because three blocks later I run directly into the seventeen-year-old blond girl from last night.

"Hi," I say, once the initial shock of encountering her on the street, after all this, has worn off.

"Hi . . . we met last night, right?" Her hair is pulled back, but she's still wearing a cocktail dress and her heels are off her feet and are in one hand and, when I look a bit more closely, it looks like her mascara has run a bit in the past few hours.

"Yeah, that's right." She looks down and to the side.

"You're still wearing the same clothes from last night," I say. She crosses her arms and fidgets and I notice a small tear on one of the spaghetti straps of her dress. She readjusts it on her shoulder. "Are you okay?"

"You're still wearing the same clothes from last night, too, you know," she says, getting defensive.

"I know. Rough night. Seriously, though—are you okay?"

"Yes," she says, almost yelling now. A woman walking her dog across the street looks across at us and I can't imagine how we appear, these two walking catastrophes screaming and fidgeting and looking—or at least one of us looking—like we've committed a crime. "Why do you keep asking me that? I'm fine, okay? *I'm fucking fine.*"

Back at the table and I'm feeling a little better, a little lighter on my feet, a little more on top of my game, *so I tell Patricia that we're sorry to have kept her waiting, that beautiful women shouldn't have to wait. And Chase and Kip laugh, and Kip tells me that, by God, gin is* my *drink, and fuck: I'm just so* goddamn *personable and funny. Chase winks at me from across the table, and I flash him a smile.*

"So Taylor, tell me," Patricia says after the sommelier has arrived

with our wine, a bottle of 1998 Châteauneuf, "what will you be study-
ing at Penn?"

"That's undecided, Mrs. Latham." *I lean back and allow the som-*
melier to fill my glass. "I've always enjoyed foreign languages, though.
So I'm leaning toward something like comparative literature. Maybe
French."

"How romantic."

"Oui, madame." *I see Kip give Chase a look of disapproval.* "Of
course, that will be paired with something more practical. Like poli-
sci." *Kip nods and Patricia smiles.* I'm just so goddamn quick on my
feet.

*"Well, it sounds like you've got it all figured out, son." Kip nods his
approval of the wine to the sommelier and the man proceeds to fill the
rest of our glasses. Kip rests his right arm on the back of his son's chair.
"Chase'll be studying finance. And I'll be damned if there's not a better
place to do it than Wharton. Isn't that right, son?" Chase rubs his nose
and nods.*

"That's right, Dad."

*Kip smiles happily and Patricia flattens her napkin across her lap
and looks down.*

*Our entrées arrive and even though my mouth is a little bit numb,
I can tell that the pistachio-crusted halibut is absolutely* out of this
world. *As a table, we power through two more bottles of Châteauneuf
("baptism by vino," Kip says, to which Chase echoes, "in vino, veritas,
eh, champ?") and I'm feeling perfect and priceless and my shoes—those
loafers—feel like they're barely there at all.*

*"Have you given any thought to going Greek, Taylor?" Kip polishes
off the last piece of his striped bass. "Penn's got a great system. And it's
the best way to meet the girls, isn't it, honey? Everyone loves a Tridelt."
Kip grips Patricia's hand and she looks down shyly and laughs.*

"Oh, Kip . . ."

"To be honest, I haven't given it much thought."

"Well, you should. You definitely, should." His voice gets earnest.

"Chase will be rushing Phi Delta Theta. I'm sure that neither of you would have problems getting bids. I can assure you of that." He gives me a wink. "I'm very close with the house still . . . if you know what I mean." He chuckles and shakes his head. "I had some great times in that house." He looks at his son, who is looking down, and he slugs him on the shoulder again. "And you will too, son. When I was at Penn, it's where most of the lacrosse players pledged. I'm not sure if it's the same now. These things change, you know. But regardless, Chase, I'm sure you'll be with some of your teammates." He looks at me. "Have you seen this boy with a stick? It's a thing of beauty, Taylor. A thing of beauty."

There's this awkward moment when the table goes silent and I start catching sectioned-off pieces of dialogue from the tables surrounding us and I remember Chase's instructions from the cab ride to Center City so I wrap my lips around my wineglass and wait for the instant to pass.

"Actually, Dad," Chase begins, "that's something I wanted to discuss with you."

Kip starts laughing and he nudges Patricia in the side.

"What, son—is 'beauty' not the right word?" He raises both hands. "Okay, okay . . . how about 'powerful'? You're a force to be reckoned with when you've got that stick."

Chase begins fidgeting and his voice softens. "No, no, that's not it."

Kip laughs again. "You're embarrassed that they've named the new training room after the Latham clan? C'mon, kiddo, a little family pride!"

The waiter arrives with four dessert menus and recommends the crème brûlée.

"No, that's not it, either, Dad." Chase runs a napkin across his mouth, and as I watch his hand I notice it's shaking. "Thing is, Dad . . . thing is, I've decided not to play anymore."

Patricia tells the waiter that we'll have two crèmes brûlées and Kip tells Chase that he'd like to speak to him outside.

᪤

I unlock the door to the studio in Woodley Park and step into the apartment's small entry, which, while only six feet long, is dark and muddled with clumps of gray dust. The curtains of the window on the far edge of the room are drawn, and I keep them drawn, in an effort to keep the room cool and dark and subdued. My head can't handle light right now.

I lazily toss my blazer, the one I was wearing last night, onto my bed (a queen-size one that seems too garish, too immense for such a meager space), and collapse next to the blazer. And then I slowly turn my head, as if to prevent my brain from contracting and expanding more than it already is, and I see the corner of a ragged piece of paper peeking out from the jacket's inside pocket. Upon closer inspection I see that it's a note, written in handwriting that, at one glance, could be called feminine, but at another could be called aggressive. It reads:

> *Taylor,*
>   *So glad I could induct you into this gorgeous disaster.*
> *Until it happens again.*
>
>   *J.*

᪤

The cab ride back to campus from Center City is mostly silent, with the exception of the car's wheels dipping into and out of the potholes along Walnut Street. It's mid-October, and the trees surrounding Rittenhouse Square have exploded into these vibrant shades of orange and red and yellow that even in this dark night manage to maintain their intensity and integrity of color.

    "My halibut was amazing," I say as the cab turns right on Thirty-second Street and heads toward the Quad, Penn's largely freshman dormitory. "How was the salmon?"

Chase mumbles something and puts his head in his hands.

We pass Irvine Auditorium, with its giant gothic steeple and then the university and the entrance to the lower Quad and then, with a screech of rubber against asphalt, the cab halts at Thirty-seventh and Spruce, across the street from the entrance to the upper Quad. Chase reaches into his back pocket for his wallet but I tell him not to worry about it, that I've got it this time.

"Thanks," he says and I hand the driver ten dollars and slam the door shut behind Chase.

"No problem."

Inside the Quad, on the compound's massive lawn, other freshmen have started to huddle in small groups of jackets and hoods and scarves, which will soon disperse to a myriad of fraternity parties around campus, the only locations that provide a surefire bet for underage drinking. We wind into and out of the groups—Chase's head down the entire time—until we're stopped by Joanna, a girl from our hall who's holding a red Solo cup and already smells like Captain Morgan rum and Diet Coke.

"Where've you guys been?" she asks, tightening her Burberry scarf with a free hand. "We've all been pregaming in Loren's room."

"We were at dinner with Chase's parents," I say, once it becomes obvious that Chase has no intention of answering.

"Nice. Where'd you guys go?"

"Striped Bass."

She smiles and hits Chase on the shoulder. "Verrrrrrrry nice. You guys were rolling high class tonight, huh?" She teeters on her heels.

"You know us," I say, giving her a high five.

She takes an impressive swig of her drink, which, from the looks of it, is mostly rum.

"So what's the plan for tonight?"

She winces through another sip. "Russell's older brother's fraternity—I think it's Beta—is having that Heaven and Hell party. I think the plan is to get over there pretty early. Apparently it fills up fast."

"Sounds like a plan."

She tightens her scarf again. "Jesus, how'd it get cold so fast?"

"I have no idea." I rub my hands together. "I'm rethinking this whole East Coast thing."

"I bet you are, Laguna. Last October wasn't even this cold in Greenwich." Since day one of school, Laguna has become my nickname—official in some circles, unofficial in others. "And, um, P.S., Taylor. That tie totally isn't *yours. My dad has that tie. It's Thomas Pink."*

I laugh and look at the tie. "I know, I know, it's Chase's. But hey—a step up from the Converse, right?" I strike a model's pose like I'm checking my watch or some bullshit.

She takes another sip of her drink. "Indeed, indeed." She looks at Chase, then she looks at me, and she mouths "What's wrong" and I shrug and she shrugs. "All right, well, whatever. Come meet us in Loren's room. I just came out here to smoke a 'rette." She reaches into her purse for a pack of Parliament Lights and a book of matches.

"Sounds good."

<hr />

For the next three weeks I avoid Chase's calls and texts and e-mails. At first he's harassing; he leaves me frustrated voice mails asking me if I've died—or, if worse, I've become a Democrat. I respond to none of them and eventually their frequency subsides until all communication is limited to forwarded invitations and links to collegehumor.com. In the office, Peter becomes progressively more impressed with my research regarding the war on playground terror. Even Janice, typically prone to calling me "You" and demanding extra cheese on those repulsive nachos, tells me one afternoon that I seem to be picking up on the game plan; *getting* it and all.

"I didn't say I was impressed," she qualifies her statement. "I just said you're starting to get it."

Personal experience, I tell them both, is the keystone of proper investigation.

HR 273, the Johnson/Grayson bullying law, languishes in the legislative process. After Johnson introduced the bill on the House floor, it was referred to the House Committee on Education and Labor, though, really, I told Peter, it should have been given to National Security, it being such a fantastically important matter and all. This got a good laugh and he told me to keep up the solid work on the research but to stay away from the politics.

As expected, after the initial flood and barrage of phone calls and press requests post Grayson's gaffe, the flow trickles until the only questions being asked are in regard to what type of condominiums, precisely, would the congressman like to see—square footage if possible—built along the banks of the Tigris? And then someone else, some member from Missouri, mistakenly says "segregation" when he indeed meant the opposite, and the calls from reporters, much to Kelly's disappointment, halt completely. Regardless, Peter keeps the bullying drumbeat alive and strong, and in the moments and hours between his impassioned speeches about political messaging and reelections I realize that it's nearly impossible to tell if his words are motivated by a sincere interest in Grayson's legislative future or by a fear of returning to the boring and banal that had conquered his days prior to the incident at UCI.

⚬⚬⚬

We get inside our room and Chase slowly and deliberately takes off his sports coat and hangs it on the back of his desk chair. I open our miniature refrigerator that's sitting on two cinder blocks and take out two Yuenglings and I give one of them to Chase. He mutters thanks and takes a massive swig from the bottle. From a room three doors down, David Bowie's "Young Americans" echoes through the hall. Chase moves over to an open space of wall next to our television and starts lightly tapping his fist against it.

"You all right, dude?"

He nods and doesn't say anything and just continues to tap his clenched knuckles against the white wall. I keep sipping my beer and tell myself that if this is what cocaine does to people, it's a damn good thing Nathaniel never got his hands on any.

Five minutes later "Young Americans" has changed to the Cure's "Six Different Ways" and I've changed out of the Ferragmo loafers (which started to become uncomfortable again) and back into my tattered black All Stars, and Chase is still lightly tapping on the wall.

"Chase," I say, this time louder, "man, what's wrong?" Again he doesn't answer, but the tap tap tap turns into a thud thud thud and I notice his elbow pull back a bit farther each time he cocks his fist.

Down the hall, Robert Smith is crooning about the lies we tell and the six different ways we tell them.

I watch as the tap becomes a thud, which becomes a legitimate punch. He's yelling things now, Chase, things I can't entirely discern but are at the same time angry and violent and sad. The tenth time he punches the wall the plaster gives way and his fist goes sailing into darkness but this doesn't stop him and he keeps punching punching punching. Around the hole, on the white space, I see flecks of red blood that have started streaming from his knuckles. I leap up from my bed, from where I've been sitting, and tackle him and he collapses to the ground. I pin his shoulders, even though he's not putting up a fight. His right hand is bloody and mangled and his second knuckle is gleaming with the grayish-white of exposed bone.

Still pinned, he turns his face to look at me and his eyes are streaming with furious tears, and I look down at his hand and tell him we need to go to the hospital.

⁓

On a few occasions, after spending extended days in the yawning halls of the Capitol, I go out with the legislative aides to Tapatinis or Fin McCool's or any number of the faceless bars on the Hill where conversation wafts directionless but is limited mostly to gossip regarding those who run the country. Off and on I'll make feeble contributions to the dialogue. Most of the attempts are efforts to steer the banter away from subjects regarding carnal relationships existing between bosses and workers.

And then, on three separate occasions, I accompany Jack to Local 16, a bar on U Street, away from the ever-seeing eyes of G-town. Prior to our first meeting, he e-mails me a message that is cryptic and enigmatic and vaguely haunting in a way that only Jack can be: "A friend will be joining us."

I arrive at the bar—all drenched in low red lighting—early and order a Bombay and tonic. The crowd's different from what you'd find at Smith Point—sleeker, more urbane, but still maintaining that air of having something to prove that I've found to characterize this town. While the conversation at SP is thunderous and belligerent, here it's calculated and hushed.

Ten minutes later Jack slips through the bar's entrance wearing a pair of rigid dark jeans and a gray shirt unbuttoned to about there and black Gucci loafers, no socks. Behind him, a young man who is barely twenty-one—if that—sporting an Abercrombie and Fitch shirt and slightly baggy jeans, clings to Jack nervously. He's good-looking, this kid, in the type of way you'd expect to see in college catalogs, advertising universities in the Midwest. Jack orders Oban on the rocks, and the kid orders a rum and Coke.

"Taylor, this is Scott." I shake his hand. "He's studying sociology at George Washington University." I nod and ask Scott what year he is at GW, and he looks uneasily at Jack, who is looking toward the other end of the bar.

"Um . . . a senior?"

"Anyway," Jack changes the subject and finishes half his scotch in a solitary swig. "Chase said you've been out of pocket lately. Where've you been?" I briefly consider explaining—or, at least, giving some vague explanation before I remind myself that Jack edits a gossip column for a Washington newspaper that, as its advertisers have disintegrated, has become increasingly hungry for content—both important and banal. And so I shrug.

"Working. It's been busy. Everyone wants to get things done before recess."

"Right."

The conversation—self-conscious and overwrought and purposeless—decays like this for nearly twenty minutes until Scott, whose cheeks have become flush after two rum and Cokes, announces that he has to use the men's room. We both watch him leave, and Jack turns to me.

"Cute kid."

"I guess? Where'd you meet him?"

"Online."

"Cool." *This is foreign territory to me.*

We both sip our drinks and put our hands in our pockets and recognize that, in so many unspoken words, Jack has laid naked a facet of himself with which he's not wholly comfortable, and which, if exposed, would likely cause earthquakes in his social sphere that he's not fully prepared to handle.

"Do me a favor," he says as Scott emerges from the bathroom on the second floor of the bar.

"What's that?"

"Don't tell Chase. Or Caitlin."

"Jack . . . of course."

Scott's halfway to us when I ask, "Can I ask why you feel comfortable telling me?"

Jack looks down at me. "Because people who are out of their league aren't in a position to judge."

So over the course of the month it goes on like this twice more, and each time Jack is accompanied by a different young man, and each time he reminds me that these outings, that these exploratory jaunts, never took place. And after the third meeting, during which Jack's date—a sophomore from Georgetown named Chris who has large triceps but that's really about it—gets so drunk off Long Island Iced Teas that he gets sick *right there at the bar,* I think about what Jack said—about being out of my league—and I settle on the fact that he's right. Because every time I leave Local 16, inertia and alcohol pull me to that big yellow door, to that gorgeous disaster, at Thirtieth and P.

The waiting room of the university hospital's emergency room is half-occupied with a motley crew of students and local West Philadelphians. I tell Chase to take a seat and then I tell the nurse working the reception desk what the situation is and she gives Chase a look and shakes her head and tells me that he needs to fill out these three papers and sign this one and hand over his Penn Card so that she can make a copy of it. After looking over each paper I ask her how long the wait will be and she tells me that, well, sweetheart, that just depends on how quickly my friend Mike Tyson fills out his paperwork and on how many stomachs the doctors have to pump—it is Friday night, you know. I nod and tell her thank you and take a seat next to Chase, who has his hand wrapped in a St. Albans Lacrosse sweatshirt. A few seats down from us, two blond juniors are alternating between copies of People *and* The New Yorker *and are thus intermittently discussing articles by Hendrik Hertzberg and photos of an emaciated Nicole Richie.*

"Cynthia!" one of them—the one with the People *magazine—cries out, folding the publication in half, "Look!" She points to a picture of an extraterrestrial-looking Ms. Richie whose tiny face is obscured by oversize glasses. "It says 'Miss Richie was admitted to Cedars-Sinai last week due to extreme exhaustion, says her publicist.'" The girl sighs and uncrosses her legs, which are thin and fragile and skeletal. "See? I'm not alone in this. I mean, that's exactly why I'm here." Cynthia flips through the "Talk of the Town" section and fails to feign even the slightest bit of sympathy.*

*"You're here because your glucose levels are low. Your glucose levels are low because you subsist on a diet of mustard, lettuce, and cigarettes."
The other girl lets out a wounded huff.*

*"I knew I should have asked Lindsay to come with me." Cynthia
closes the magazine and irritably sets it on the table next to her.*

*"No. You should have had a hamburger for dinner. That's what
you should have done, Lisa. In fact, you should have had about eight
of them." Lisa gasps. "Now can you please go ask the nurse how long
we've got to wait for the doctor to call you back there, just so he can tell
you that same goddamn thing?" She looks at her watch. "Because the
Oktoberfest party at St. A's is tonight, and we're already going to be getting there on the tail end of it, which means it's going to be packed with
fucking freshmen." Lisa crosses her legs again.*

"I can't," she says, picking up the copy of People *again. "I'm exhausted."*

*Cynthia snatches her purse off the ground. "Unfucking-believable,"
she stands, flips open her cell phone, and starts heading toward the door.
"Call me when they feed you something."*

*I turn my gaze from Cynthia, who is now spinning through the re-
volving door, to Chase, who is silent and looking down and hasn't even
picked up the paperwork yet, to Lisa, who is gawking at her friend's
effrontery. A moment passes and the triage nurse calls back an elderly
African-American man who has been coughing and looks faint, and
Lisa, broken from her offended gaze, dials numbers on her cell phone
until someone finally answers.*

*"Olivia?" she says. "It's Lisa. I'm at the hospital." She waits. "Oh, you
are soooooo sweet. No, I feel like shit, and Cynthia just walked out on me."
She waits again. "I know. Such a bitch. She left me here to go to that fucking A's party." Waiting again. "To be honest, I think it might be an ovarian
cyst." Waiting, and a little grin. "Please, please, please don't tell anyone."
Lisa looks over at me and she notices that I'm listening in on her conversation, which, I'll admit, is rude and inappropriate but nearly impossible not
to do. She brusquely stands up and moves to the other corner of the room.*

"So why'd you pick me?" I ask Juliana one morning after the sun has once again invaded the empty space of the bedroom, which no longer seems so clean or so proper. My clothes, a chaotic pile of cotton and denim and leather, are in their designated space in the corner.

"Pardon?" she says, propping herself up on a tan elbow and covering her breasts with the white sheets.

"That day at the horse races, and then that night when I was standing outside on the porch—"

"Yes? What about them?"

"I don't know." I smile at her and she answers me with this hesitant bewilderment. "Why'd you come up to talk to me in the first place?"

"Your bow tie."

I laugh, a little nervous, a little disappointed. "What about it?" And this is one of these moments—one of those instants where I recognize the inherent flaws in my question as soon as it's asked.

She sighs and in a flare of raven hair and perfect skin, she turns her bare back to me.

It was coming undone. "As someone who isn't from around here, either, it was obvious to me that you weren't from around here." The whole thing was unraveling.

I move closer to her and put a hand on her shoulder. "I told you"—I smile harder—"it was Chase's, anyway."

In a move that could be characterized by both anger or annoyance or maybe a little of both, she tosses her legs over the side of the bed and wraps the sheet around her and stands up, which leaves me lying there, on the bottom sheet, naked. Juliana walks over to the freestanding mirror on the opposite side of the room.

"Well," she says, lightly touching the few lines that do exist on her face while examining her reflection, "it *showed*."

I reach down under the bed to find my boxers. Once I've slipped them on, I swing my own legs over the edge of the bed and rest my elbows on my knees and stare at Juliana staring at herself in the mirror.

"I think it's nice," I finally say, quietly.

She adjusts the top sheet around her breasts and looks at me in the mirror's reflection. "You think what's nice?"

I begin wringing my hands and I look down and I wish I could just go back to the night before, back when there was just skin and hair and sweat and indiscretions that, frankly, the evening didn't have time to consider. "I guess I just think it's nice to have someone I can connect with."

She doesn't answer, but rather pulls the sheet up tighter around her.

"It's just . . . do you remember that first night on the porch when you said that relationships were—"

"I thought we could avoid all this," Juliana suddenly says.

"All of what?"

"All of *this*." She lets out an exasperated sigh and reaches for a pack of Dunhills on the nightstand. "I went through this same *horrible, god-awful* catastrophe last year with Fernando. It just"— she lights a cigarette and inhales a large drag—"it just ruined the whole, how shall I put this?, the whole *spirit of things*."

"Who's Fernando?" I take my elbows off my knees and sit up on the bed as she exhales.

"That's not the point." She strides over to the window and throws open the curtains and I shield my eyes against the brassy light. I watch her smoke the cigarette until I stand up and she turns from the window and looks at me with that cool, glassy gaze.

"Well . . ." The sentence is awkward and cumbersome and un-romantic at its very best. "Going back to what I was saying. Back when you said that relationships were a cost-benefit analysis."

"What about it?"

"I see you as a benefit."

She stops for a moment, and then she tilts her head and smiles and she puts a hand—the one holding the cigarette—on my cheek. "That's sweet," she says, and from behind her that picture of John Grayson, postinauguration, smiling wildly and bewilderedly, gawks back at me. "I see you as a benefit, too." And then, as something happens behind the sad, knowing glossiness of Juliana's eyes, as something *dies,* her hand, the one that's on my cheek, falls to her side and ash tumbles from her cigarette to the bare floor. "Just one with diminishing returns."

I turn back to Chase, who is still looking down and who still hasn't touched the paperwork I've laid before him. "How you feeling, bud?" I say after watching him for a moment.

"My hand is fucking killing me." It takes him a minute to reply.

"Yeah. I can imagine. But I bet that wall is feeling a hell of a lot worse."

He doesn't laugh. Behind us, the revolving door spins and two students who look like freshmen drag in one of their classmates, whose shirt is covered in vomit and whose eyes are only half-open.

"Let me see your hand."

"Since when did you become a doctor?"

"Just let me see, it, Chase."

He slowly unwraps the gray cotton, which has become spotted and browned with blood. It's a mess, but not as bad as I had expected. The thin flesh on the first two knuckles has been ripped open, exposing various levels of tissue and bone. It was one of nature's or God's or chance's or whomever designed us, flaws, I think: leaving so little protection over our only defenses against our attackers. Beneath the knuckles is bruised and swollen. "Pretty gnarly."

He smiles. "Do people really say that where you're from? Do people really say gnarly?"

"Sometimes, unfortunately." I laugh and he laughs and that makes me feel a little bit more at ease with this whole situation.

He wraps his hand back up.

"Sorry I ruined dinner," he says.

"You didn't ruin dinner."

"My dad would probably beg to differ."

The kids behind us, the drunk ones, are laughing and kicking and poking their friend, whom they have splayed out across four chairs.

"We all get into fights with our parents and shit," I tell him. "Honestly, it's not that big a deal. I still had a great time."

He shakes his head. "That's not the point." He continues shaking his head. "That's not the fucking point."

"Chase," I start, "I get it, okay? The whole deal about expectations, and not being able to live up to them. I mean, I've told you about Nathaniel and how perfect he is, I get all of—"

"No," he says, looking up for the first time. "You don't."

And so we sit in silence for the next thirty minutes as the drunk kid behind us is called back to get his stomach pumped and as a stabbing victim is wheeled in on a gurney and then, right after the triage nurse emerges once again through those swinging doors to call Chase's name, he looks at me and says:

"Do you think I'll ever be able to play lacrosse again?"

Later that evening, at home, I gather a load of laundry (whites, with some grays) and carry it in a large plastic basket to my floor's laundry room, which is three doors down from my efficiency. I pour detergent in the machine and start adding the clothes, piece by piece, checking each shirt for stains or marks. And it's as I do so that flashed images of the seventeen-year-old's face, that one from a month ago—dark with mascara—and the torn strap on her dress start and these memories of Chase's hand caked with dried blood wrapped in that goddamn sweatshirt and of Juliana's hair fanning out like Medusa's snakes against those bamboo sheets start defiling my mind. I close my eyes straightaway each time one of the reflections manifests and wait impatiently for it to pass. Which it does.

After I've loaded the laundry and paid the $1.75 that's necessary to start the machine, I go back to my apartment and collapse on the small futon that's set perpendicular to my bed and look at the texts I received earlier in the day—three from Vanessa, asking me where I've been, and that she doesn't hear from me like she used to, and to please call her, and one from Chase—emblematically casual. I have nothing to say to Chase. Or, rather, I suppose I do, I suppose I have dissertations and accusations and terminations that all need to be proclaimed, that all need to be articulated. And as for Vanessa.

I'd wanted to call her, I'd wanted to see her—this much is true. I've thought about her enough, occasionally at times that I'm sure could be labeled as inappropriate; these moments that could be called wrong. But see, it's been one of those matters of a person slipping away and another person taking his place, and truth be told, I'm not fully certain as to who this person is, or what he wants, or who this girl—really the only one who makes sense—is to him.

I look at the screen on my phone and move the device's cursor back and forth across her name, and then expand its range to encompass those names falling between "C" and "V" in my address book. I find myself stopping somewhere in the middle.

And so. As for Vanessa.

"Nathaniel Mark." In the background, I hear Nate typing figures and projections furiously into the spreadsheets that keep places like Goldman Sachs alive and maneuvering the world's finances. It's early on Saturday afternoon, so I know better than to try him at home, or even on his cell phone. Nate always works on Saturday afternoons.

"Hey . . . hey, Nate, it's me." The typing continues.

"Hey, bud. Hold on one second. I've just . . . got . . . to . . ." The typing gets faster. "There. Done." He sighs. "Sorry. This IPO is absolutely *killing* me. You know how much money is at stake here?" I tell him that no, I don't, and that actually I'm not sure I even understand what an IPO *is*. "We're helping this company go public and we've got to advise them on—" He stops himself. "Never mind. Anyway, what's up?"

"Nothing, really," I say, pulling at a loose thread on my jeans. "I just wanted to call and say hi."

Nathaniel pauses and I can hear his chair creak as he leans back in it. "Okay . . . well . . . hi." He pauses and I keep pulling at the thread on my jeans. "How's Washington? Hot?"

"It's getting hot," I say. "Pretty humid, actually."

"I bet."

Another awkward pause.

"How's New York?"

"It's good. We finally got a reservation at Babbo. Remember that place? The one that I canceled over your graduation?" I tell him yes, yes, I remember, and that I know that Babbo was a Mario Batali place and that I had heard good things.

"Chase has actually been there," I say.

"Chase from Penn?" I tell him yes, Chase from Penn.

"I never liked that kid. You live with him for four years and you come back telling me that you're embarrassed that you've never wintered in Gstad," Nathaniel says offhandedly. "I mean, forget Gstad. You started using 'winter' as a verb after knowing him. I knew kids like that at Princeton, and I work with half of them now. No good, no good. How's Annalee?"

"She's fine."

And then, briefly, I consider telling him the truth, and how, really, I hadn't spoken to Chase, not properly, in a month, and how the one sane companion I had in the city, Vanessa, was slipping through my fingers and that it was likely my fault but that I had no

clue how to tighten my grip; but the rate of return on eliciting advice from Nathaniel is not always high—just words, words, words.

Another awkward silence. And then:

"Taylor?"

"Yeah?"

"Are you okay?" I have to think about it for a moment.

"Yeah, I'm fine. Why?"

"I don't know." I hear the chair creak again. "Your voice sounds
different, or something. And . . . and I don't know, you never call."
And that causes me to think about why I'm calling him, because
he's right, because I don't ever call, and because I can conceive
a million reasons but no explanations as to why I've decided to
phone my brother—at work—on this particular Saturday in May.

"What, I can't call to say hi?" I laugh nervously.

"Of course you can. I mean, try not to call during the week,
you know, because God only knows how busy I am, but of course
you can call. It's just that I wrote that e-mail to you earlier this
week and I hadn't heard back from you."

"I didn't know I was suppose to respond."

He sighs. "That's not the point." More silence. "Anyway, did
you ever call Dad?"

"I thought you said you were going to stay out of that." *I don't
even know how to dial to Belize. And does Exit Strategy have a land-
line?*

"Don't get defensive, Taylor." Nathaniel's voice takes on a parental tone—a sort of Verdiesque melody punctured with staccato
inflections. He's been perfecting it since grade school. "I'm asking
you a question."

"No. No, I didn't call Dad." I hear the typing start again.

"Well, you might want to do that, Taylor, because even though
the man's moved to Belize, he still was gracious enough to provide you with half of your DNA."

"Excuse me?"

"Forget it. Did you get the check I sent you?" I put my head in my hands.

"Yes. Yesterday. Thanks."

"Good. Deposit it right away, and let me know if you need more help with rent."

My face feels rough, unpolished, against my palms. "Okay."

"What about Mom? Have you spoken to her recently?"

"She's left me a few messages over the past couple weeks. She said you told her to call."

Type type type click click click.

"Yes, yes, that's right. I did. I sent her an e-mail earlier this month and told her to call you. I mentioned that Saturday morning's probably the best time to reach you because you'd likely be in bed, completely useless, nursing a hangover. Have you called her back yet?"

"No, not yet."

"Well, fuck, Taylor, do us all a favor and call the woman back, okay? Lord knows she's going through enough right now, and the last thing she needs is the neglect of her youngest child."

I debate whether I should detail to Nathaniel the events of the year that I spent at home; of the crying and the notes and the movies and of Katie breaking down in front of that restaurant's— Cleo's—closed doors and dead lights and how he hadn't seen any of it.

"Hello? Taylor?"

"I'm here."

"Call her, okay?"

"Yeah, okay, Nathaniel. I'll call her."

"Good. Good. I mean, thank you. But good." Type type type click click click. "Okay, I've got to go. I've got some work I need to finish before the reservation tonight. But we'll see you in the city, soon?"

"Yeah, sure. Soon."

"Great. Have a good weekend, Taylor. *Call Mom.*" I say "You, too," but the phone's already gone dead.

And so with this heaving sigh I again scroll down in my address book until I reach Katie's name and, after two minutes of hesitation, I press "call." The phone—her cell phone—rings three times, and I start to thank God for allowing me to just leave a message when she picks up.

"Hello? Hello, Taylor?"

"Hi, Mom." I hear a crash in the background. "Jesus, what was that?"

"That was Kitana, or whatever the hell her name is. The Asian one. In purple."

I scratch my forehead and silently curse Nathaniel for guilting me into doing this. "Mom, what are you talking about?"

"Mortal Kombat: Armageddon, Taylor. That's what I'm talking about. Try to tap into your own generation, *dear."*

"Since when are you playing *Mortal Kombat?"*

"Shit," she says harshly. "That *bitch* just threw some fan at me. Do people do that, Taylor? Do people *throw* fans?"

"Can you please press pause or something?"

She sighs irritably and the crashing and the booming in the background silence. "Fine. Yes. Paused." Then, "I've been playing *Mortal Kombat* since Suzanne bought it for me last week. Dr. Thompkins said it'd be therapeutic."

"Good . . . good, I guess. How is everything else at home?"

"It's beautiful. Just really beautiful. There was a whale out in the cove today, just out in front of the house."

I grin. When I was younger, when we first moved into the Laguna Beach house, Katie and I would sit for hours on end scoping the sea for whales. We never saw any.

"And how's Suzanne?"

"Oh, God," she says with a laugh, "you know Suzanne. She keeps me up to no good. No good at all."

"Yes," I answer, "that's what I'm afraid of."

"Taylor"—her voice gets older, a little more sincere—"things are *fine*. They're fine."

"Did you ever meet with that financial adviser?"

"Once." Her voice goes offhand again. "He was a miserable man. *Horrible,* actually. Told me again that I should sell the house."

"And?"

"And I sold a Matisse instead, and I'm learning to shop at Safeway and Costco, and I haven't stepped foot into a Whole Foods in a month, and, like I said, *I'm fine.*"

I'm almost tempted to agree with her; I'm almost tempted to say that I haven't heard her sound like this in far too long.

And then, "I heard from your father two days ago. He called from Honduras."

My mouth runs dry and I remember that bench—that goddamn bench—in Rittenhouse Square.

"Taylor? Taylor, are you still there?"

"Yeah, I'm still here. What'd he have to say?"

"He said he missed me. He was calling from a pay phone outside of a bar."

"And what'd you tell him?"

"I told the son of a bitch he wasted a quarter and not to call this number again."

"Good," I tell her, "that's good." And she tells me that Dr. Thompkins said the same thing, that he was proud of her, and I explain that I'm tired and have a headache and need to get some rest. She tells me that's fine, she needs to rip Kitana apart anyway.

I set down the phone on a tiny coffee table and lay down, fully clothed, on my bed and stare at the ceiling, which is fractured with cracks. *He wasted a quarter.* I grin at Katie's bold audacity. But then, then suddenly those images of Juliana pushing me against a wall, and of that gin-filled tumbler shattering in slow motion against the floor of the porch, start invading my mind. And it's not until those visions start searing my eyes that slow tears start creeping down my own face, and I start considering whether guilt, in its many forms and iterations, is at its malicious worst when we consider the things for which we've wished, the things that we've accomplished, or the empowerment they've brought us.

X

o."

Kelly's voice pierces like sabers through the solid oak door of Grayson's office. "Absolutely not, Peter. Send someone else. I came to Washington to be a professional, not some *goddamn* babysitter."

My desk is cluttered with Post-its and letters and files that need to be put away, and my head is muddled, just some puzzled mess, from the lack of sleep of the night before.

"I'm not telling you, Kelly. And don't raise your voice at me. May I remind you who hired you?" This is Peter. I catch a sound that could be his clenched fist tapping on Grayson's desk. I rub my temples and I sign into my Gmail and I think of the hundred times, of the thousand times, that this exchange has likely occurred and will likely occur in the future.

"*Crepes-for-fucking-change*, Peter. Crepes. For change."

Two e-mails. First one from Chase. It's a sentence: "U alive, champ?" Alive, indeed.

"Juliana's a grown woman. She doesn't need a press staffer to make sure she pours on Nutella correctly."

Next one. From Nathaniel. Also, one sentence: "Thx for call-ing me + Mom, love you."

I can hear Peter sigh on the other side of the door, and the tapping on the desk ceases for an instant. "I know she's a grown woman. But with everything that's happening, with all of this UCI shit, with the Latham, Scripps, Howard deal"—*What Latham, Scripps, Howard deal?*—"I just need to make sure she doesn't . . ."

I delete Chase's e-mail and respond to Nathaniel's with one sentence: *No problem.*

"You need to make sure she doesn't what, Peter? Slice her fin-ger while cutting bananas?"

"I just need to make sure she doesn't fuck up, Kelly." The tap-ping starts again. "She can be such a goddamn liability sometimes." He starts talking to himself, now. "Why that woman can't just learn how to play the goddamn game is completely beyond me. *Completely fucking beyond me.*"

I hear the old rusted knob on the great oak door creak and rasp and I quickly close out of my Gmail. Kelly, outfitted in a blue blazer that hasn't seen tailored renovations since 1984, emerges from the office. "Then get someone else to be her coach, chief." She starts pounding on her BlackBerry and walks by my desk and through the office's front door without looking at me, but man-ages to slip in: "Taylor, the clips, please. Or we'll hire a chimp to do them for us."

"It's times like these when I wish that bitch wasn't so good at her job." I turn and see Peter, who is looking balder than before, leaning, arms crossed, on the door frame leading into Grayson's office.

"Sounds like things were getting pretty intense," I say, open-ing the *Los Angeles Times* Web page ("Fires Whip through Malibu Again").

Peter shakes his head and takes a few steps over to the fax

machine and begins fingering through the loose leaflets of paper resting in the machine's tray.

"It wasn't intense. It was just Kelly." And then, "And honestly, I can't really blame her." He continues to flip through the cover pages and letters and bill sponsor requests. I've always had a soft spot for them, fax machines: the discarded, redheaded stepchildren of technology's baby boom. Theirs was a day in the sun that was, in all actuality, more like an hour; a lunchtime that was quickly eclipsed by the advent of e-mail and PDF files and instant messaging. "I mean, I've been to a lot of ridiculous fund-raisers in this town, Taylor," Peter says with a chuckle, "but this one—this one takes the cake. *Crepes for change.* Jesus. Someone needs to find jobs for Bunny Howard and Kitty Scripps."

I skim the story about the fires in Malibu. A B-list celebrity is quoted using monosyllabic words and phrases to describe what a tragedy it is to see such beautiful mansions engulfed in flames. "This is a Bunny and Kitty thing?"

Peter continues to search through the stack of faxes. "I'm surprised you had to ask. You haven't seen a fax come in from LSH, have you?" I shake my head no. "Why those men can't simply send me an e-mail will forever confuse me."

I swallow hard and keep my eyes on the computer. "So why is Mrs. Grayson going to this thing?" I hear Peter sigh and curse the fax machine again.

"I don't know. Grayson's insisting on it. Says that it'd be good for Juliana. He keeps making the argument that it'll be good publicity to have her out there at these pointless charity events. She usually puts up a bit of a battle when it comes to going to these things. But this time, this time she almost staged World War Three. Said she wouldn't be caught dead there.

"Grayson won. She backed down." He looks up from the machine. "You know, a few years ago I read this article that was more of an exposé of one of these circuses, and it said that the gowns worn by two of the women in attendance cost more money than was actually raised. Granted, I read it in some liberal rag. But still."

"So is she going to go?"

"Huh?"

I swallow harder. "Juliana. Is she going to go to this thing?"

Peter rubs a hand over his bald spot and shrugs. "No clue. All of the legislative aides have hearings all day. Grayson's day is packed, according to Janice. And Kelly"—he laughs—"I think it's safe to say that Kelly won't be going with her. And I'm not going to send her alone. Not when Bunny and Kitty are there, along with every other bored Washingtonienne. God only knows what would come out of Juliana's mouth." Then, again, "You're sure you haven't seen a fax from Paul Scripps? I was expecting one this morning."

"Yes, I'm sure. There've just been the sponsor requests and the letters from Florence Rivers."

"Ah, Florence. Still complaining about Those Damned Mexicans?"

"Still complaining."

"It's hard not to love that woman."

Peter moves back to his desk and I trace the open windows on my computer screen with my mouse's cursor and tap my dying loafer nervously against the old, embattled floor. I haven't spoken to Juliana in two weeks, not since she told me with those sad eyes, those eyes that appeared as though they'd seen Troy burning all along, that I was a benefit with diminishing returns.

Guilt, I've found, which we too often experience with equal amounts of sadism and masochism, causes us to engage in the strangest of acts—none of which seem to be driven by conscience. For example: during moments of desperation, moments during which no other voice would soothe whatever anxiety I was feeling, I had tried calling her twice: once on her mobile phone, and once more—in a brash play—on her home line.

Concepción answered and I hung up in a panic without saying a word.

"You know, Peter"—I feel and see the words creeping from my mouth before my ears actually hear them—"if Grayson's so insistent on Juliana going to this thing, I don't mind accompanying her." Peter opens up the top drawer of his desk and pulls out a scratched pair of glasses.

"I may be a tough boss, Taylor, but I'd never subject you to Bunny and Kitty unless lives were at stake. Believe me."

"No." My voice, which is truthfully no longer my own, but is rather the audible output of a different brain—a separate set of neuroses unconnected to my better judgment—begins developing more confident undertones. "No, I don't mind. It'll get me out of the office. And I know Bunny and Kitty. Chase, remember? Chase is my best friend." I cringe through the word like it's salt on an open wound. "I really don't mind."

Peter lowers his glasses on his nose and gives me a look that, for an instant, causes me to fear that I've betrayed myself. "You're not dressed appropriately," he says, turning back to his computer. "You'd have to be in a suit. And wrinkled khakis don't count."

"I have one," I'm pleading now, at least in my own mind, or in this different one. "It's really nice. A Hugo Boss. I could take a cab back to my apartment and be changed and ready in thirty minutes." Then—and oh, and then, "I think it'd be a fantastic opportunity for me."

"Here it is," Peter says, his eyes fixed on his computer.

"Excuse me?"

"Looks like Paul Scripps learned how to use e-mail."

"So can I go?"

"Huh?"

"Can I staff Juliana at the fund-raiser?" He doesn't look up from the computer but rather waves a hand.

"Yes. Yes, go. But change into your suit. She's expecting Kelly to meet her at the P Street house in forty-five minutes. Just tell her I sent you instead." He continues reading the e-mail and his face slackens.

"Where is it?"

"The Ritz. M and New Hampshire."

I log out of my computer and my heart hurts and is overworked and my forehead is starting to sweat again.

"And Taylor"—Peter finally looks up—"be a gentleman."

He turns back to the glowing screen.

"Pay for her cab. I'll reimburse you."

"What are you doing here." It's a statement more than a question as Juliana—adorned in a sleeveless, metallic Elie Tahari dress—stands in her open doorway, staring at me. "Peter told me that Kelly was coming."

I brush my hair out of my face and smile—a gesture that falls flat on Juliana's pursed lips. "She got caught up in something. So he sent me instead."

"I'm not sure that was the best idea," she says, removing her arm from the doorjamb and allowing me to slip past her into the house. The door, that bright yellow portal, is more garish, more blinding, in the light of day.

"I disagree." I shut the door behind me and I lean in to kiss Juliana's flushed cheek as she, in an evasive move, ducks her head and walks into the kitchen.

"We'll have a drink before we leave," she says, pulling her midnight hair into a tight bun before pinning it into place. "We should be at the Ritz in twenty minutes. The silent auction starts at one thirty after lunch. Gin, right?"

I laugh nervously. "Yeah, Juliana. Gin. That's what I've drunk the past four times I've been here." I follow her into the kitchen and watch her for a moment as she reaches into the freezer, almost frantically, for three cubes of ice that she then places into a blue opaque glass. "You need help?" I place my hand onto the small of her back, and she jumps, dropping the glass to the floor.

"Shit," she says with a hiss. *"Shit."* She steps precariously around the broken glass and then crouches to pick up the jagged shards.

"Here," I say, crouching as well, "let me help."

She brushes away my hand and replaces a dark strand of hair that's become loose. "No, you'll cut yourself. Why don't you go wait in the foyer, Taylor. We'll have a drink once we get to the fund-raiser." She looks up at me and her eyes are dull and sad and she forces a smile that makes my stomach churn and jolt.

I stand up slowly and I tell her that yes, okay, I'll wait for her in the foyer. She says thank you, and that she'll only be a moment, and I flatten down the creases that have formed on my jacket and move into the empty, echoing room.

The light showering in from the windows creates warm, isolated islands on the otherwise cold floor. I stand on one of these islands, and I rock back and forth on my heels and stare at the Pollock hanging above the stair's curving banister—all these lines colliding and then retreating and then colliding again. I follow one of the streaks, a black band of varying width, through loops and twists and collisions and turns until finally it disappears off the left side of the canvas.

"It's a print." Juliana reenters the foyer, carrying a small bronze clutch. She's redone her hair. "It's not an original. If you were wondering." She stares at me and then at the ten feet of space between us. "Shall we hail a taxi?"

Crepes for Change lays bare no surprises. Bunny Howard and Kitty Scripps, undoubtedly with the help of their husbands' never-ending expense accounts, stand in matching Polo dresses and pearls in the center of the West End Bistro, the restaurant connected to the Ritz Carlton. They greet and kiss and smile and laugh and sip and smile some more as throngs of women and small clusters of men flow seamlessly among the tables. Though one may be led to believe otherwise, the benefit's goal is to raise money for undereducated children in Afghanistan. ("Everyone deserves to read," Kitty Scripps was quoted saying in the *Post* yesterday.) At various stations erected along the restaurant's walls, attendees feast on sweet and savory crepes being sold for fifteen dollars each (three for forty dollars).

Crepes, at least at my last reading, do not play an essential role in Afghan cuisine. But these are the sort of details I've learned that Washington is apt to overlook.

Above each station is a picture of a smiling though highly un-dernourished child wearing a Latham, Scripps, Howard T-shirt.

I stand awkwardly with Juliana in the restaurant's entrance, my arms folded tightly in front of me, her hands white-knuckling her clutch. She brushes off a caterer offering a sampling of cana-pés topped with gray foie gras and some undistinguishable puréed meat. Juliana does, however, stop a man carrying a tray topped with flutes of champagne.

"I suppose I should make some sort of donation, or at least bid on something useless," she says after taking a large swallow. "I'd like to see these children wearing something other than an LHS T-shirt, if nothing else." And then, more to herself than to anyone else, "John will never hear the end of this."

"What would you like me to do?" I say quietly before she fin-ishes the champagne in a second sip.

"Behave yourself."

I watch Juliana walk across the restaurant—past Bunny and Kitty—as small clusters of women magnetize toward one another and begin whispering. The hem of her gold dress sways defiantly and she places her bronze clutch under an arm as she deliberately

ignores the scorns and gawks of gossips and admirers and everyone in between.

It's not an original. If you were wondering.

I stop the man carrying the champagne tray and take a flute
for myself. And as I watch the crystal glasses disappear from the
pewter serving plate at an alarming rate—as the demand out-
paces the supply—my churning stomach and my racing heart
shoot these destructive signals to my brain, to that region of my
cortex that never made it past thirteen years old, that say the opposite economic phenomenon is occurring in my unraveling life.
That, really, whatever I have been supplying to Juliana is now
becoming overstocked, oversupplied.

The sweat from the flute starts to wet my fingers and I watch
as Juliana smiles and kisses a Spanish-looking man on the cheek,
and I keep my eyes locked on them until she shoots a look at me
that tells me I'm not adhering to her original order ("behave"), so
I move instead to one of the crepe stations where a man who is
neither Afghan nor French pours batter onto a steaming pan. I let
my eyes follow the steam and smoke waft upward from the pan
until someone taps me on the shoulder and says, "Hey, stranger."

Annalee is dressed like Bunny Howard and Kitty Scripps—
Polo dress and pearls—though she is undoubtedly more beautiful
and her smile is inarguably more genuine. I haven't seen her since
Hal's party at Smith Point, since that night, and her absence in my
life has been deliberate, as has the absence of everyone else.

"I haven't seen you in a while," she says, lightly kissing my
cheek and then looking at my suit. "Who knew Mark men cleaned
up so nicely?" I laugh and look down and then raise my eyes again
to see Juliana standing in a corner with Kitty Scripps.

"I certainly didn't."

She reaches up and straightens my lapel and she brushes
something off my chest and then she smiles sweetly again. "Well,
Nathaniel would be proud. What are you doing here, anyway?"

I fumble over my answer but finally explain that through a series of mishaps and cancelations and angry press secretaries, I was sent to staff Juliana Grayson. "But what about you?" I say. "Shouldn't you be at the magazine?"

"I'm covering the event for the next issue."

"I didn't know you got promoted to reporter."

"I didn't." She smiles. "Truth is, Patricia asked me to come with her. She said there were some women she'd like me to meet. So she put in a call to the magazine, and they ended up giving me the assignment."

"Patricia Latham?"

Annalee raises her flute of champagne and clinks it against mine. "The one and only." I had always thought of Patricia as innocuous, ever since that dinner at Striped Bass. She was the lifeless form, the accessory, hanging off Kip's cuff-linked arm.

But then, people—creatures—can take new forms when placed in different elements.

"Speaking of," Annalee says under her breath and then nods behind me to Patricia, who is waltzing toward us with Bunny Howard.

"*Taylor,*" Patricia says, grasping my forearm with a hand adorned with as many diamonds as Cartier could possibly muster to sell her, "what a pleasant surprise."

"So pleasant," Bunny echoes, smiling.

"I don't think any of us had any idea that you'd be here," Patricia continues. "But really, we couldn't be more pleased. Just last night at dinner Chase was telling us what a wonderful time he's having now that you're in D.C." I nod and swallow more champagne and Annalee looks away and Bunny smiles.

"Are you here for Congressman Grayson?" Mrs. Howard asks.

"Peter, our chief of staff—"

"I know Peter."

"Right. Well, anyway, our press secretary couldn't make it to staff Juliana, the congressman's wife—"

"I know Juliana as well." Bunny's grin widens and I loosen my tie.

"So Peter sent me instead." Bunny nods slowly and holds her grin. The caterer with the tray of canapés stops alongside our group, and as Annalee reaches for a cracker topped with a small mountain of foie gras, Patricia clears her throat and Annalee withdraws her hand. Patricia smiles.

"That's wonderful," Bunny says after the caterer has left. "Just wonderful. Usually she shows up to our little gatherings with Fernando." She studies my face for a reaction and taps a large ring against her crystal glass. "In fact, Patricia, wasn't it just last week? Right after Kitty, Juliana, and I got back from New York, that she arrived—*late*—at that dinner party in Bethesda with Fernando?"

Patricia nods and smoothes a wrinkle out of Annalee's dress.

"Of course," Bunny continues, "I'm not one to gossip. Never have been. But Fernando. I understand he's the son of an ambassador. But *really*, Juliana, what of her husband, you know?" She cocks her head to the right and moves a strand of blond hair behind her left ear.

"May I refill your drink, Mrs. Howard?"

"Thank you, Taylor. That'd be lovely."

I never return with Bunny Howard's drink because, honestly, neither of us expected me to. Instead, I leave the West End Bistro, trading it in for the Ritz's lobby bar, which, at three-fifteen in the afternoon, is nearly empty, save a small handful of insignificant lobbyists. Briefly, I consider calling Peter to tell him that I won't be returning to the office today, that the fund-raiser was taking longer than expected, that Juliana had taken a keen interest in the

plight of Afghan children and how paper-thin pancakes may serve
to alleviate their trauma.

But I don't.

Rather, I order a scotch and spend what remaining mental
energy I have trying to decide from which Latin American country Fernando hails, and then what sort of things he'd been whispering in Juliana's ear, and, if for once, guilt was becoming more
masochistic than sadistic. And why—God, why—was it all still
worth it?

"A little early for scotch, isn't it?" I don't have to turn to see
Juliana sitting on the stool next to me. "I thought Peter sent you
to staff me, not to get drunk on liquor you can't afford at the bar
next door."

I shrug and swirl the crackling ice in my glass. "Bunny Howard led me to believe you didn't exactly need my staffing." Juliana
looks down and sighs and shakes her head and orders bourbon,
straight, in a tall glass.

"I'm sure Bunny Howard could make a person believe a lot of
things," she finally says.

Behind us, two gentlemen finish their drinks and then shake
hands and exit into the oppressive summer air. The door swings
shut behind them and blocks out the sounds of the street.

"What do you want me to believe?" I say once the world's
gone silent again.

"It doesn't matter." She stares straight ahead and rests her elbows on the bar. "Because you're going to believe whatever you
want to believe. It doesn't matter what I tell you."

The door behind us opens again and I hear honking horns
and screeching brakes and voices—so many voices not saying
anything at all. I wrap my hand around Juliana's wrist, and she
pauses before bringing the glass in her other hand to her lips. "But
I believe you're different. I know that we're different."

"And that's where you're wrong." She lays a twenty-dollar bill on the bar and she closes her clutch bag and stands up. "But as I said, Taylor, that doesn't matter."

"Yes," I say, and my heart, I swear my heart is about to detonate and take half of the Ritz with it. "Yes, it does matter, Juliana. It does. And I know that we're different. And I know how you look at me, and I know we need each other."

She casually but deliberately reaches up to fix the pin in her hair. "No. You need the idea of me. That's what you need. That's all anyone ever needs." She readjusts a slight silver bracelet on her wrist. "But the truth is this: I'm not different. And neither are you. You can put deceit in diamonds, or you can put it in pearls. But it all looks the same when the lights are off." She stares at me for a moment longer before walking past the overstuffed leather chairs and the small mahogany tables, and then, before she reaches the door, she turns to me once again and says:

"You're on a sinking ship, Taylor. We both are."

XI

June 26, 2007; 8:30 A.M.

On Tuesday, I arrive at 1224 Longworth at 7:30 A.M. to write a one-minute speech on elementary-school playground fights that the congressman is planning to deliver during that morning hour of the day's House session that is typically reserved for these types of irrelevant remarks. I walk into the office and find that the lights are already on and the daily newspapers—the *Times* and the *Register* and the *Hill*—are disorganized on the chipped coffee table in the front office and that four Starbucks coffee cups are already littering Peter's desk. The door to Grayson's office is closed and I can hear three different muffled voices that converse in an invariable volume that's punctuated with a raised voice every minute or so. The words are just sounds and syllables—nothing I can make out—so I turn on my computer and start filtering through the research I pulled yesterday in reference to the congressman's one-minute.

"Mr. Speaker," I begin typing, though really the only thing I can focus on are those voices, garbled and hooded, behind that heavy oak door. *"In this time of war and bloodshed, I wish to direct the attention of this House to another battle being fought—one that's unfold-*

ing before us on the playgrounds and basketball courts of our nation's schools. Bullshit bullshit bullshit, garbage garbage, garbage." I drag the cursor over the prose until it's entirely highlighted and then I hit delete and I watch the text disappear before I turn back to look at the oak door.

At eight o'clock the door creaks open, and Peter emerges from the office, sweating, and behind him, the two Pauls—Scripps and Howard—file out in alphabetical order wearing identical suits and sporting faces that are as cold and as stoic as I remember them at the races. Peter nods a hello to me and asks me how the one-minute is coming and I tell him that I'm almost done and he says great and then wipes his brow and returns to his desk. The Pauls thank him for his time and tell him to let them know, and then one of them says:

"How are you liking the job, Taylor?"

"Fine," I tell him. "I really enjoy working for a man like Peter."

"Who wouldn't? I heard you attended my wife's fund-raiser. What a fantastic cause that is," he says, before the other one whispers something in his ear and they both nod and say their goodbyes.

I wait for the front door to click shut and for the Pauls' footsteps to echo down Longworth's halls before I turn to Peter and ask what the meeting was about.

"Nothing," he says. "Nothing. Just boring lobbying stuff." Then, "You think you can get me that speech to look over in ten minutes?"

A day after I write his one-minute speech, John Grayson asks me if I'd like to join him for lunch.

The night before the lunch date, which is set to take place on Thursday at 1:30 P.M. at this small Thai restaurant just next to the Capitol South Metro stop that Grayson describes as "casual" and "low-key" and "perfect for guys like us," my mind is a disaster—a wasteland of just so many worries and concerns. I'd left something there, I think, a credit card receipt, maybe, or we hadn't been careful, Juliana and I. We'd been careless, blasé, *flippant.* I open the small closet in the studio and tangle through the hangers until I find the blazer I had been wearing the last evening I was at Thirtieth and P, the night Jack brought that kid Chris to Local 16. It's intact; no missing buttons. Out of the inside pocket I see Juliana's letter, her gorgeous disaster one, which I tear up into tiny shreds and place in the garbage.

My palms are sweating when the waiter, who is small and grinning and just altogether disconcerting, brings us our menus. The congressman was right: the restaurant is "low-key" and "casual," though I'm not sure if I'm in a position to say whether it's for "guys like us" because—and I'm blinded here by his hair, which looks even more brilliant, more extraordinary, up close—I'm finding myself knowing less and less about the "guy that I am" and am starting to believe more and more that whoever he is is far from a "guy like him."

"The pad Thai's fantastic," Grayson says as he flips through the menu. I nod slowly, unsure of what to say to this man who (a) signs my paychecks and whom (b) I've just recently made a cuckold. *It looks delicious—I love bean sprouts: Have you found that your wife moans louder when she's on top?*

Grayson asks me if I've decided on what to order and I tell him that I have—the pad Thai—and he winks and tells me good choice and then flags down the grinning waiter, who takes our order with more glee, more unbridled energy, than anyone I've ever encountered in the service industry.

"He's got quite a smile, doesn't he?" Grayson says once the waiter is out of earshot.

"Yes, sir, he does." Grayson lifts his napkin off his lap and I notice the stump at the end of his right hand.

"Please, Taylor, call me John. Or, if that makes you uncomfortable, call me Mr. Grayson. But please not 'sir,' or 'Congressman.' Okay?" I shift uncomfortably on the red vinyl chair.

"Okay . . . John."

Grayson laughs and runs a hand through that perfect hair. "No one ever seems to be comfortable with that to begin with." A group of interns eating two tables away from us gather their heads together and whisper. "So how are you liking things in the office so far?" I tell him that they're fine and I shift again. "Peter says you're doing excellent work. I'm sorry this has taken so long."

"You're sorry what's taken so long, sir?"

"Hey," he says, feigning a stern voice, pointing the stump at me. "What'd I tell you about calling me 'sir'?"

"Sorry . . . John."

He laughs again. "I'm just joshing with you, son. Just kidding around. I mean that I'm sorry that this lunch has taken so long. I hate that most of our interactions have been over the phone. See, I try to take all my new staffers out to lunch as soon as they start. It's just something I like to do. Of course, with my little . . . well"—he pulls at his collar and laughs—"my little, let's just call it 'mistake' at UCI, I haven't been engaging with my staff as much as I'd like to." The grinning waiter arrives with our drinks—a water for me, an iced tea for Grayson. "In any event—you're enjoying things? Everyone's treating you nicely?" I nod. "And outside the office . . . are you enjoying Washington?" I nod again. "Good, good. My wife mentioned she met you at the Gold Cup. In the Latham, Scripps, Howard tent?" He laughs and sips his tea. "If you're running with that crowd, son . . . well, you're doing better than I am."

Our food arrives, and after a few bites Grayson asks me how my pad Thai is and I tell him that it's delicious, even though it's actually a bit cold and the chicken is a bit overcooked.

"So tell me, you're from the district, is that correct?"

I tell him that yes, I am from the district, from Laguna Beach.

"Really?" He wipes his mouth. "Where in Laguna Beach?"

"South Laguna," I say. "Do you know the restaurant the Coyote Grill? It's really very sma—"

"They've got the best fajitas in town," he says with a smile.
"And my friends and I used to go surfing—God, it seems like forever ago." He stops for a moment. "Anyway, we used to go surfing
at Tenth Street."

"I hate those steps."

He smiles and leans across the table a bit, laying nine fingers
on its edge. "So do I. There's nothing worse than hauling a surf-
board up those things." We both laugh and, for a moment, it slips
my mind that I've transgressed this man in one of the more em-
barrassing fashions available.

"Are your parents still there?"

"One of them." He nods slowly.

"Divorce?"

"Yes, sir. Sorry, yes, John. Last year."

"I'm sorry to hear that." He clinks his wedding ring against the
glass of iced tea and waits and thinks and doesn't let the words fall
from his mouth until he's ready. "Though, Taylor, I'm going to be
honest with you, sometimes that's for the better." I stop eating for
a moment and allow the dish to get colder than it already is and
I consider going into it all—Belize and everything else—before I
realize that he's talking about himself. "Anyway, enough of that.
Brothers? Sisters? Tell me more about life in Laguna."

I tell him that yes, I have one older brother. "He graduated
from Princeton. He's in New York now. Banking."

"Ah, one of those." Yes, yes, I say with a laugh, one of those:
summa cum laude, swimmer, taller than I. I tell him that geneti-
cally speaking, I got the shorter end of the Mark stick. He tells me
that's nonsense. "There's one of those in every family," he says.

"Mine's called Rupert Jr." He waves his right hand at me. "And he's got all ten fingers."

The waiter brings the check, which Grayson signs for, but not before he's completed telling me the story of how he lost that goddamn finger, and how Rupert Jr. took over a family empire—a city on a hill—that John had originally envisioned for himself, and how *between you and me, Taylor,* he had never really expected to end up here in the first place. So he knows what it's like, believe it or not, he tells me, to feel like you're always finishing in second place; even congressmen, he says, feel like that. Then, with a swoosh of ink against the carbon paper of the receipt, he excuses himself from the table, telling me that there's a vote on the floor in twenty minutes, but that I'm welcome to stay and finish my water and take my time getting back to the office. I stand as he stands, but he tells me to sit, and he shakes my hand and tells me that he's glad he was able to schedule in time to do this.

And once he's out the door, and once I've given up on a resolution to laugh or cry at the pitiless tricks of irony, I stumble back, past the grinning waiter, into the restaurant's narrow bathroom, lock the door, and vomit.

I wet my hands and place them to my face, and the cool water calms my forehead, which feels like it's breaking out in a fever. Someone—another customer, I imagine—has been knocking on the door for the past minute and I've just let him or her pound away as I try to straighten myself out.

"Is someone fucking in there?" the person knocking finally says.

I dry my face with a paper towel that's rough and granular and feels like sandpaper. "Yeah," I answer. "Sorry. I'm just finishing up."

"You've been 'finishing up' for the past five goddamn minutes, man."

I tell the person to give it a goddamn rest and that I'll only be a minute more. I swing the door open and am greeted with the glaring face of one of the interns who had been whispering about Grayson during lunch.

"It smells like fucking *puke* in here," he says, twisting his nose in knots.

"Must've been the guy before me." The kid heaves a sigh and brushes by me, and I leave the restaurant and grab a handful of mints on the way out.

Outside, out on the street, the sun is eclipsed by giant gray clouds that cast dark shadows over the dome of the Capitol. I sit down on the curb and light a cigarette, which has become something of a habit lately, and I'm halfway through it when I hear someone call my name from across the street. Looking up, I shield my eyes from what sun the cloud has failed to mask, and I see Vanessa, brown hair pulled back, staring down at me and smiling.

"Hey, I think I know you," she says, though, this is only partly true. In the past five weeks I have exchanged a number of e-mails with Vanessa Ramírez, though most have been cursory and casual; brief recognitions of mutual existence. For some reason it's the only type of interaction with her that I've been able to muster. We had lunch together once, in the cafeteria, but it was a brief affair because she had some obligation at a labor hearing. And although she'd pushed for more meetings, more lunches, I had declined. "Long time no see. I didn't know you smoked."

"I don't," I say, stubbing out the cigarette on the curb, "or, not really. Or, not frequently I guess is more accurate. Anyway,"—I squint and continue looking up at her—"what's up?"

She laughs and readjusts her purse. "Nothing's up. I just feel like I haven't seen you in forever."

"That's not true. We had lunch last week."

"It lasted fifteen minutes."

I don't have the heart to tell her that, really, fifteen minutes is all that this current version of myself could stand.

"Taylor, Taylor, Taylor," she says after she's watched me light another cigarette. "Why is it that lately, whenever I see you, it looks like you're in need of some serious drinking, or that you've just come from some serious drinking?"

"Couldn't tell you." She watches me a bit more and I turn away from her gaze and watch the smoke drift aimlessly.

"Well, look . . . I have a staff meeting I have to get to." She fidgets with the purse again. "But do you want to get a drink tonight? Maybe Sonoma again? I want to know what's going on with you. Your texts—which, may I add, have been limited to nada and chilling, haven't revealed all that much."

I initially turn down the invitation, but then at Vanessa's urging and repeated appeals I agree, and we decide on the early side, and besides, her smile is just so damn sweet that the whole thing would probably do me some good. She makes me promise that she'll see me at seven o'clock, and then she tells me to stop smoking, before heading back up C Street toward the Capitol. There's no wind, just those peculiar clouds, so the smoke from my cigarette doesn't move in any particular direction. It just rises and falls like some ethereal haze.

Grayson isn't in the office for the rest of the afternoon, and Peter, pleased with my ability to spin a subject as mundane as youthful harrying into a legitimate national security threat, tells me—*instructs me*—to leave the office at six o'clock.

"You've been working harder than Kelly," he says at five forty-five. And then he looks back toward her desk and whispers, "And trust me, you don't want to become Kelly."

"I heard that, you son of a bitch," she calls over the partition. "Anyway, get out of here."

I thank him, and head over to Sonoma an hour before I'm supposed to meet Vanessa. The bar's largely empty, so I walk upstairs
and settle into the same table that Vanessa and I shared the first
time we met here, over a month ago, when I was a different person and before there were bruised circles under my eyes.

The waiter asks me if I'm expecting anyone else, and I tell him
that I am, but that I'll have a glass of the pinot gris (sixteen dollars) in the meantime. He nods, and after I finish two glasses in
ten minutes, he asks me if I'd like to simply order the whole bottle,
and I tell him sure—why the hell not, right? And then I ask him
about the music, which is one of those never-ending acid-jazz
CDs that can be expected to be heard in a setting like this.

"You guys have anything else?"

"Like what?"

"I don't know. Like anything?"

He laughs uncomfortably and asks when my guest is expected
to arrive, and I tell him to just get me that bottle, that she'll be
here soon.

At seven-fifteen I've got two fingers of pinot gris left, and I've
heard electronica remixes of four portions of three of Beethoven's
symphonies when Vanessa, guided by the waiter, finds me upstairs. She tells me that the place looks familiar, and I tell her I
thought so, too.

"Sorry I'm late," she says, sitting down across from me. "Alvaro called and I couldn't get him to shut up. He's volunteering
in an ER on the Lower East Side, and he's got all these crazy
stories." She sets down her purse and looks at the waiter. "The
chardonnay, please."

"You want the bottle, too?"

She responds with a bemused look before noticing the nearly
empty pinot gris, half-illuminated by a candle on the table.

"No, thanks." She smiles. "A glass will be fine." He nods, relieved, and walks quickly back to the bar. "Getting an early start,

are we?" She raises one eyebrow and looks at me before turning off her BlackBerry.

"I got here at six. Peter let me out of work early."

"I see."

"Why'd you order the chardonnay again?" She gives me the same bemused look that she gave the waiter and removes a dark strand of hair from her face.

"Because I like it? And it's cheap?"

"I told you last time, it's not any better than the cheapest chardonnay on the menu." She leans back and crosses her arms. "Don't look at me like you're my mother."

"I doubt you'd talk to your mother like that," she jabs back.

"You're right," I say. "I wouldn't want her to have to take a Klonopin with an Ambien chaser." I rock back and forth in my chair and I avoid her eye contact. At the tables surrounding us, two other couples have been seated and are discussing the summer's unbearable heat.

"I'm sorry," I finally utter. "I don't know what's gotten into me lately."

The waiter sets down Vanessa's chardonnay and empties the rest of the pinot gris into my glass.

"It's okay," she says, though it's understandable that it's not. Outside, through one of the bar's windows, I see heat lighting flash between clouds. I don't have a solid grasp of the meteorological happening, but I've heard that the principle that heat lightning is silent is, incidentally, incorrect. I've heard that, contrary to what many people have been led to believe, thunder does accompany the flash, it's just that the atmosphere in which it occurs is so dense, so impenetrable, that the booms and the cracks that one would typically expect to hear are refracted into the ether. "So where have you been?"

"I've been around," I say quietly as I watch the electricity jump silently between the masses and I sip the last of the pinot gris.

"Yeah. I gathered you've been around. 'Chilling.' I'm asking *where* you've been around." I set the glass down and sigh and start rubbing my temples.

"I don't know, Vanessa. In Georgetown. I've been out with Jack a few times." She mutters something disapproving that I can't hear. "I'm sorry, I couldn't hear you. What'd you say?"

"I said I never liked that kid."

"You barely know him, Vanessa."

"I know him well enough to know that I don't like him." A hair falls into her face, but she lets it hang there, lifeless, as she looks into her glass of wine. "I just never really thought you were like them," she finally says, as if it's some hypothesis that she's been waiting to expound on from the moment she saw me sitting on the curb earlier in the day.

"Well, apparently you haven't known me for that long then."

"No. No, you're right." Her voice loses its edge. "I suppose I haven't." She looks at me for the first time in minutes and then says, "Your eyes look different. You should get more sleep."

"You're probably right." Those silent strikes continue to illuminate the world around us.

Vanessa finishes her glass of wine in silence and starts tracing circles with her finger around the stem's base. Internally, I wrestle over a way of telling her that all of this isn't really a matter of not feeling like myself, but rather, it's more of a matter of feeling *out of* myself, but before I can invent the proper means to convey a concept that I don't truly appreciate, the waiter arrives, and I tell him that I'll have a glass of whatever the most expensive scotch is that the restaurant carries—straight, no ice.

"Do you really think that's necessary?" she asks once he leaves.

"Yes."

She makes a move to stand up, and I ask her what she's doing.

"It's obvious you've got no interest in talking, Taylor." As the drink arrives she nods to the glass of scotch, amber and smoky. "And I refuse to sit here and watch you get shit-faced. I've got other things to do." She turns on her BlackBerry and slings her purse over her shoulder before I convince her, beg her, *plead* with her to stay—for just as long as it takes me to finish my drink; and, in the meantime, can we please, *for the love of God,* talk about something other than me? Because, frankly, nowadays that particular subject has one of two effects on me: boredom or nausea. She sighs and sits down.

"Fine."

My shoulders slump in relief and I take a sip of the scotch, which, after the bottle of pinot gris, goes down easily. "So . . . how's Alvaro?"

"He's fine. Busy."

I nod in an effort to show her that I'm listening, that I'm *trying.* "How are you guys doing?"

Vanessa crosses her legs and rests an elbow on the table. "We're fine." And then, "The long-distance thing gets hard after a while."

"Right," I say. "I've never done it before, but I can imagine."

She sets the other elbow on the table and begins espousing about bus ticket prices, and roommate dilemmas, and parental concerns, but how love—at least *this* kind of love—will eventually conquer all of that. She *knows* that. She's *sure* of that much, at least. But however moving it might be, her dissertation is lost on me because I'm staring at the way the space between the fourth and the fifth buttons of her pinstriped shirt reveals just enough of her bra to catch my interest.

"You know what I mean?" she says finally.

"Yes. Exactly."

On Pennsylvania Avenue, outside the restaurant, we walk without speaking for a few minutes under those heavy summer clouds that are still coughing up silent sparks. Finally, after three blocks, she stops and says, "Sorry about tonight. I didn't mean to come off like I was your . . . I don't know. Like I was your, like, *mom* or something."

"It's fine."

She takes a step closer to me. "It's just that I'm worried about you, Taylor. It's like you've always got these bags under your eyes. And I never hear from you. Or, hardly ever, at least. And when I *do* hear from you, your voice sounds different, and all you can tell me about is going out with Jack, or this absolutely *absurd* idea that life's just one, big cost-benefit analysis, or something god-awful like that, and I really don't know what else I'm supposed to do but—"

I don't know why I do this—or I suppose I do—but I grab her wrist probably a little too forcefully and I pull her face to mine and kiss her probably a little too vigorously. And for a moment, her body goes limp. But then, as soon as it does, she lays a strong hand against my shoulder and pushes me with enough strength so that I stumble backward, tripping over the roots of a tree, and thumping my head against the concrete sidewalk.

"What the *fuck* are you doing?" she yells, wiping her lips and staring down at me.

I rub the back of my head and wince when I feel a small patch of warm blood. "I don't know," I say, without attempting to stand up. "I just thought—"

"You just thought *what*?" My head throbs and I continue rubbing it.

"I don't know," I eventually articulate. "I don't know what I thought."

"Yes," she says with a nod, before walking away from me. "That's the one thing tonight that's been apparent."

On Friday, the day after the lunch with Grayson and the disaster with Vanessa, I call Peter at 7:30 A.M. and tell him that I'm not feeling well and that I won't be coming into the office. His voice is hushed and whispered—he's at a breakfast meeting at Latham, Scripps, Howard, he says, but that yes, that's fine, and not to worry about it. Grayson's in California, anyway, he informs me. For the beginning of the Independence Day recess. The office will be dead.

"Get some rest," he says before hanging up the receiver. "You've been working hard."

I thank him before hanging up and flipping the mobile shut. The pillows on my bed, which are soft and overstuffed with down, seem incapable of entertaining a comfortable position for my head, which now hosts a hard, painful bump the size of a golf ball. The thought of calling Vanessa has crossed my mind twice this morning, and each time I've phoned her only to reach her voice mail. From my outgoing text log, I see that I made a feeble attempt at reconciliation last night with a brief (and unsuccessful) message: "im soryy. Cnt explan myself latly."

There has been—much to my disappointment, but not to my surprise—no response.

And so I try one more time, and once again the call is directed to her voice mail. After she's given the requisite instructions ("please leave a message"), I muster enough strength and enough shame to pathetically beg her to call me so that I could at least attempt to explain myself. After tripping over the word "please," I hang up, and let the phone tumble from my hand to the floor, and I shift and I turn and I twist until I find a position that, while not relaxed, is at least painless, and I close my eyes and nod off for another three dreamless hours.

At ten thirty, the sun, terribly shoving its way through the curtains, paired with my cell phone vibrating against the parquet floor, awakens me. Startled at first, and then dazed, I reach down and pick up my phone, the screen of which is illuminated with a green backlight and, in gray text, reads *Chase Latham: work*.

Groaning, I hit a button on the side of the phone to silence it before throwing it to the ground and going back to sleep.

But that doesn't last long, partly because the sun's just too bright, too goddamn strong, and partly because the phone continues and continues and continues to shake and rattle noisily alongside the uneven floor. Each time it's Chase, and each call is succeeded by notification of both (a) a voice mail; and (b) a text message. Eventually, after the fifth call, I struggle with great effort to get out of bed and lurch into the small, detached kitchen for something to eat. My refrigerator contains three items: a slice of cold-cut turkey, an eighth carton of milk, and four bottles of Sam Adams's Summer Ale. After brief deliberations I settle on the slice of turkey and some of the summer ale, which I always forget doesn't have a twist-off cap, and then I move back into the living room and turn on the news, which features B-roll footage of clear, sunny beaches but warns of THE WORST HURRICANE SEASON ON RECORD. My phone starts vibrating again, and after the third ring I switch the television to mute and flip open the mobile.

"What's up?" I answer after a brief—but intentional—pause.

"He's alive!" Chase yells on the other end of the line, mocking old Hollywood's Frankenstein. "He's aliiiiiiiive."

"Yeah . . . Ha, yeah, I'm alive."

"Where've you been, bud? I've been worried that your Commie friend stole you away from us."

I can only assume that he's referring to Vanessa. "Been working hard, I guess."

Chase, ever the human polygraph, doesn't buy this explanation and he snorts. "Sure, bud, sure."

In the background, I hear him tell someone—his secretary? Does Chase have a secretary? Probably—that he needs thirty copies of *this*. "So how've you been?"

"I've been fine."

It goes on like this for about five minutes, with Chase weaving these elaborate stories about the parties I've missed and about the incredible, phenomenal, absolutely *ridiculous* dinners at which he wished I'd joined him, and it all sounds so wonderful, so impossibly *astonishing*, that for this brief second I forget the broom closet and the yellow door and the walloped lump on the back of my head. Although, then:

"You think you can meet me for lunch, champ? Say, one thirty at the Palm?"

"That might be hard to pull. I've got these two one-minutes to write for—"

"Nice try. It's Friday. And I spoke to Peter this morning when he was in our office. He said you were taking the day off—"

"Right, right, I just thought I'd get a start on them from—"

"And besides, I've got some big news. *Huge*, actually. And I want to share it with my best bud, first and foremost."

I can hear him; sense him, smiling in his office. "You said one thirty?"

"One thirty. I've got a reservation. I'll see you then." Then, before he hangs up, as if I've never heard of the Palm before, "Wear a decent shirt. It's a nice place."

The Palm is dark and stale and crowded with media types and lobbyists who have earned the freedom to turn their lunch hours into three-hour, booze-filled reprieves. After giving me a once-over with his eyes and tilting his nose up just so, the maître d' leads me to a table in the back of the restaurant, where Chase has already been seated and has taken the liberty of ordering me a Bombay and tonic.

"I was worried you got lost," Chase says as he stands up and gives me a hearty handshake and flashes that trademark smile.

"Sorry." I slip into the booth and the sweat pooling on the back of my knees becomes cement gluing together the seat's leather and my khaki pants. "There was a delay on the Red Line."

Chase waves away the maître d', who is now offering us both menus with grand hand gestures and a series of bows.

"We'll start with the steak tartare," he says, "and then we'll both have the filet, Pittsburgh-style, and a bottle of the Veuve. And did you say there was a delay on the Red Line?" He makes a tsk-tsk sound with his tongue. "That's what you get for taking public transportation."

"Right. Okay. What are we celebrating?" I ask once the maître d' has exited.

Chase sips his bourbon and sucks in streams of air between clenched teeth. "Patience, champ, patience. We'll get there. First: How have you been, buddy? You look sick. You've got those, you know"—he reaches under and points to his left eye—"those dark circles or whatever. And you look thin. You been eating enough?" Yeah, I tell him, I've been eating enough—it's just work and stress and the usual bullshit, all of which have been keeping me from the gym. "Well, you've gotta change that," he says, poking me in the stomach. "Those abs don't grow on trees!" Then he says with a solemn nod, "But I hear you, champ. It's a busy time of year. My schedule's been packed. Absolutely *packed*."

Five minutes later, another waiter, one I haven't seen yet, announces our steak tartare and sets it on the table with two sterling silver forks, which dully reflect the low light of the restaurant. He then asks if we'd like the Veuve now, or with our steaks. Chase instructs him that we will wait until we receive our entrées.

Inside my pocket, I feel my phone vibrating against my thigh. As Chase tells the waiter to hold off on the Veuve, I retrieve the mobile and read the new text message I've just received. From Vanessa: "Leave me alone." I close my eyes hard and I silently curse myself and I wish that Chase had told the waiter to bring the champagne immediately.

"Buddy." Chase causes me to open my eyes. He looks at my cell phone. "A little respect, please? I told you, we're in a nice place." I mutter something resembling an apology and put the phone back in my pocket. "Thanks. So," he says after taking the first bite of the tartare, "Jack mentioned he saw you out once or twice?" I look up from my gin and think about the last time I saw Jack, huddled in the back corner of Local 16, talking discreetly into Chris's ear before leading him out the back door of the bar.

"Yeah, I've seen him once or twice."

"That's what he said—just out in Georgetown or something?"

"Right"—I finish the gin—"just out in Georgetown. This is great tartare."

"Best in town," Chase says, shifting his attention to the impeccability of his culinary decisions. "That's one thing you learn while working at LSH: what to order, and where." I respond with a weak laugh and tell him that on the Hill, you learn to order turkey sandwiches and nachos with extra cheese. "Don't sweat it, pal," he says, wiping his mouth. "We'll get you out of there soon enough."

Our steaks take what Chase calls an "unacceptably" long time to prepare, with which I'm inclined to agree, especially considering that Pittsburgh-style refers to a cooking technique in which the meat is barely prepared at all; black on the outside, while still retaining an icy-blue center. "Fucking finally," he says under his breath, when the waiter arrives with the two plates, "and how about that Veuve, pal?" The waiter nods nervously and apologizes and disappears to retrieve the bottle.

"So you going to tell me what this is about?"

"Try your steak first. You'll love it. Guaranteed or your *goddamn money back*." I slice into the meat and pare off a piece of cool flesh.

"Yeah, it's great."

"I told you you'd love it." Chase chews through the sentence, his mouth still half-full. Our waiter scuttles back to the table sweating and apologizing and holding a bottle of Veuve and a bucket of ice. He prudently removes the cork and fills two flutes. "Ah," Chase says as the waiter dismisses himself, "perfect."

"So? Now?"

He grins and punches me in the shoulder. "Look at you—like some kid on Christmas. Fine, fine. Now. But first you've got to promise me—and I mean it, *promise* me—that you'll come out to the Eastern Shore for the Fourth. It's going to be a joint celebration: part Caitlin's going-away shebang, part Independence Day bullshit."

"Yeah, sure, whatever."

"C'mon, Taylor. *Promise.*"

"Fine. I promise. Now *fucking tell me.*"

Chase's mouth twitches and I see the beginnings of that Cheshire grin and I cut at my steak unnervingly and shovel pieces of it into my mouth. "I spoke to your Uncle Jack last week."

"My Uncle Jack?"

Chase rolls his eyes and laughs. "*Yes. Your* Uncle Jack. Annalee's father? I'm sure you've met him."

"Cut the bullshit, Chase. Of course I've met him." He laughs again and tells me to calm down.

The last time I spoke to my Uncle Jack was before my parents' divorce. It was a day prior to his departure for a spa in Patagonia.

"The man's entirely impossible to get ahold of. Do you know he's been sailing in Croatia for the past four months? Before that he was doing some bike tour of western Russia. He's a man after my own heart. I practically had to hire a damn PI to track the bastard down." Chase pauses. "I shouldn't call him a bastard."

"Why shouldn't you call him a bastard?" From all of my recounts, Jack is, indeed, a bastard. And that's being kind. He'd deserted his family in all but name and had kept their complaints at bay with that mansion outside Chicago, and a steady stream of vacation homes and six-figure checks.

At least my father, his younger brother, had the decency to file for divorce.

"That's where the champers come in, pal." Chase raises his glass and tells me to do the same. "Because the old man is going to be my father-in-law, champ. I've asked Annalee to marry me. And she said yes."

Chase clinks—bangs—his glass against my own, and the liquid's bubbles rock and explode against the side of the flute and I swear that somewhere that wretched beast Light of Our Lives is laughing through these amber tears.

XII

July 4, 2007; 7:30 P.M.

Much like the family who owns it, the Lathams' Eastern Shore estate is a bold and expansive piece of land that's at once inviting and unnerving in its gallant strides toward perfection. The centerpiece of the fourteen acres of Talbot County land is the house itself, which I suppose shouldn't be referred to as much as a "house" as it should be a "manor": thirty-five thousand square feet, ten bedrooms, a maids' quarters, entertainment facilities, two formal dining rooms, a state-of-the-art kitchen, and Kip's prized wine cellar—all outlined and framed with royal red brick and splendid white columns, as if the place were some goddamn antebellum plantation. Behind the home is a rectangular pool whose water is kept clean and unsoiled year-round, and two tennis courts that haven't been used in God only knows how long but are maintained as if they were holding international competitions on some daily basis.

From the brass knobs on the whitewashed front door of the home, an elongated green lawn punctuated with small outbursts of flowers whose species I vaguely recognize and whose names I can faintly recall stretches and yawns along meandering paths that eventually lead you to a great wooden dock.

And it's on this dock—to which is attached some white boat that proves if seduction could be accomplished by nautical means, this vessel would be Marilyn Monroe—that I'm standing, holding a clammy gin and tonic, and I'm looking back at the white tents and the blazing torches and the guests who have been intoxicated with so much more than booze, which have all materialized in the garden. I'm alone on this dock, which rasps and moans as I shift my weight from leg to leg. Late last week I had tried my best to convince Chase that my attendance wasn't necessary, that I hadn't seen Caitlin in months, and that I'd prefer to celebrate with him and Annalee alone, in a more intimate setting. Each excuse was dismissed with the waving of a hand or the rolling of eyes and so here I am, on this dock, alone with my gin and tonic, staring back at something I'm learning to simultaneously desire and despise.

Almost by second nature, I fish my mobile phone out of my pocket and reread Vanessa's text message for at least the three hundredth time: "Leave me alone."

But then someone from the party sees me, and of course the person is Chase, and he waves and nods and saunters through the crowd, past a patch of African violets, toward the dock.

"There you are." He slows his gait once he's five yards away from me, and then stops right before he reaches the dock. There're ten feet between us. "Admiring the fifty-five-foot Millennium?" He nods to the white boat. "Dad paid a hair over two million for that thing. Had it shipped over from Como last summer. It's beautiful, isn't it?"

"Yeah"—I look back at the vessel—"gorgeous." I note the boat's spotless leather seats and unblemished paint job. "You guys take it out much?"

Chase tosses back a swallow of bourbon and shakes his head. "Not since last summer. You know Dad. Lovely things are meant to be seen, not heard." He laughs and searches my face for some recognition of approval. "You know what I mean, man. A fifty-five-foot Millennium provides a certain . . . I don't know . . . a certain security blanket."

"For what?"

"I don't know. For *things*. For *events*." He sighs. "You get your fair share of gin already, champ? You seem a little off your game. C'mon." Chase steps onto the dock and it whines. "Come on back to the party. Dad's about to make a toast to Caitlin." He pokes a finger into my chest. "And I expect one from *you* later on this evening about a certain special engagement. Deal?"

I don't provide an answer but I let him drape his arm around my shoulders and he leads me back to the tents and the lights and the alcohol. The garden is far more crowded than I had expected—two hundred people, maybe more—many of them faces I had seen during those times I had attended Chase's functions and soirees in Georgetown. Under the canopy of a smaller, detached tent, a five-piece band alternates between angular renditions of big-band standards and more rounded jazz numbers, but the band's efforts are obscured by the guests' piercing laughter, which comes in these perfectly timed waves and echoes off the brick of the mansion. I watch as a waiter, clothed in the Latham-approved white dinner jacket, unsuccessfully struggles to offer a group of women baked pastries swollen with Brie and strawberry compote. One of the women in the group is Annalee, and I hear her tell the waiter thank you, but no thank you, because she'll be trying on wedding dresses in the coming weeks. Her friends congratulate her and smile widely to conceal their jealousy, and then she shows them her ring, which I have not yet seen. Across the crowd, Caitlin throws her head back and laughs loudly at something Hal has said. Next to them, Hal's cousin, the seventeen-year-old, shifts awkwardly in a Lily Pulitzer dress. Then, as if Moses himself had descended upon a sea of tiny diamonds, the crowd parts as Kip shakes hands and makes his way to a microphone that's been erected unnoticeably just outside the tent, between the crowd and the bay, which is rather brilliantly reflecting the sun's fiery decline.

"Champ, here." Chase taps the base of a champagne flute against my arm and then hands the flute off to me, sloshing a bit onto my khakis. "Looks like Dad's about to make the first toast of the evening." Then, "Where's that bow tie I gave you to wear?"

I reach up with my free hand and touch my bare neck. "It was choking me," I tell him, just as Kip's voice begins to purr over the microphone.

"Ladies and gents, can I have your attention please," he begins, and the mass hushes almost at once. "First off, I'd just like to thank you all for attending our little gathering. I can't imagine a better way to spend my favorite holiday." He pauses and smiles. "It's so rare to be able to gather so many good friends in one place." The crowd nods and agrees and whispers among itself before clapping lightly. "I hope you've all had a chance to get something to eat and a bit to drink . . . Patricia's spent hours working with the caterers." People begin clapping again, and Patricia, alone and quiet in a corner, smiles and mouths "Thank you."

"Now, I'm sure that you're all aware of the other, very important reason that we've invited all of you out here today. But first, before I laud *very-well-deserved* praises upon her, I'd like to call our gorgeous guest of honor up here. Caitlin MacMahon? Where are you, sweetheart?" This time the guests erupt in whistles and shouts and thunderous applause. Caitlin, who was right next to the microphone all along, feigns something that looks like shyness but that instead just makes my stomach uneasy and then says, "Kip, you couldn't be sweeter" into the microphone before readjusting her strapless Polo sundress. Kip lays a hand on the small of Caitlin's back.

"Ladies and gentlemen, I'd like to proudly introduce you to America's newest—and inarguably *most beautiful*—diplomat. In a week, Caitlin will be leaving for Baghdad, where she'll be serving as—hell, Caitlin, dear, why don't you tell them." She gracefully runs a hand across her chocolate hair, which has been pulled back into a tight bun, and then she touches a string of pearls—as if to check if they're still there—that tightly hug her neckline.

"I'll be serving as the deputy attaché to the Treasury Department, and I couldn't be *more thrilled*." More claps and more whispers of approval and more raised glasses and, after surveying it all for a moment, I can't help but laugh. And I laugh and laugh and laugh until Chase finally leans over and asks if something's wrong because I look like I'm fucking losing it and I just shrug before telling him that it must be the gin.

Dinner consists of Cajun barbequed chicken prepared by French men wearing tall white hats, and also of Maryland crabs, which I've never particularly enjoyed, as the whole process of eating them just seems like too much work—too much effort—for too little food. I finish, unsatisfied, and give my plate to one of the many caterers before wandering back through the garden and then through the white door with the brass knobs and into the grand halls of the house, all ordained with paintings of Chase and boats and hunting dogs. A few people my age are gathered in the kitchen and are talking mutedly around a granite island. They quiet as one of them sees me pass, and I ramble through the halls until I find a door leading to the back porch, where Jack is sitting alone, smoking. He looks up upon hearing the door open.

"Hey." He turns back to his cigarette, which is half-finished but hasn't been ashed. Ten yards ahead of him, the pool glows like a sapphire in a patch of expanding darkness. I don't say anything, but rather sit next to him and reach for my own pack of cigarettes. "Having fun?"

"A blast," I say once I've got the thing lit, and I can't decode whether he believes me or not. We both sit like this, just smoking and staring at the lights' reflections snake and wrestle in the blue water of the pool. Beyond it, a group of children write their names in the air—all glowing and alit—with sparklers.

"The fireworks should be starting soon," he finally mutters, though I can barely hear him. "You won't want to miss them. They're gorgeous over the water." Behind us, through the door to the house, the ambient noise from the party waxes and wanes. "I'm sorry what I said that night. About being out of your league. Because I really don't know anyone here who—"

"Forget it." Then, "Are you going to miss Caitlin?"

And I think that he begins to say that he hasn't decided yet when the door swings open and Hal Hastings Jr. explodes through it.

"Jack, you son of a bitch," Hal slurs. "There are you."

"Hi, Hal." Jack turns back toward the pool and closes his eyes. "What's up?"

"My dick, that's what's up," Hal says with a laugh and slaps Jack on his back.

"Hilarious, Hal. Hysterical, actually."

"Yeah," Hal says, self-satisfied, "I've always loved that one. Anyway, I've got that cousin I want you to meet. The one that's about to turn eighteen. You got an extra cigarette?" Jack hands him a Camel Light and Hal sticks it between his wet lips. "Thanks. Now let's go. She's waiting out front. She said she thinks you're hot." He pauses. "I told her whatever. Let's go."

Jack clenches his eyes shut a moment longer before he stands up and says, "Yeah, sure, let's go." I watch as he straightens his back and then, without looking back at me, he follows Hal back into the gaiety and jauntiness of the house.

I finish my cigarette and wait until the sparklers across the pool have extinguished and the children have retired to the arms of their parents before I stand and wander alongside the estate, back to the front garden. Halfway along the tall brick walls, I cross a utilities shed—also outfitted in antebellum plantation architecture—in front of which a group of caterers are clumped together, smoking weed.

"She was fucking *smoking*," I hear one of them say as I approach.

"The girl the guy was talking about on the mike?"

"Yeah, man."

"She looked like a frigid bitch." He looks up and takes notice of me, walking by with my hands in my pockets. "What's up, bro?"

I nod and continue walking.

"It'll do her well in Baghdad," the other one says with a cough.

"*That's* where they said she was going?"

"Yeah, bro." He laughs.

"Fuck, man." He pauses and lets smoke drift from his mouth. They both look at each other and then erupt into fits of hysterics. "Well," he says once he's finally contained himself, "hope those pearls are screwed on tight." Each one laughs again and takes deeper drags off their joints.

In the front garden, under the tents and the torches, a wooden dance floor now blankets the grass, and a separate band is crooning covers of popular eighties hits. The bar is still serving mixed cocktails—gin, vodka, and such—though most of the guests have fixed themselves to champagne, which appears to have been supplied with no forethought of ration. On a separate corner of the floor, Hal's cousin uncomfortably sips from a crystal flute as Jack runs a hand through his sandy hair and grapples with failed attempts at conversation. I watch the heartbreak unfold for as long as I can stand it and then begin to turn away when Kip, rosy-cheeked and tan, grasps my shoulder.

"Mr. Mark." His grip tightens and I see Patricia standing, all shy and reserved, next to him. "Enjoying yourself, I hope."

"Absolutely, Kip," I say, trying unsuccessfully to break free of his clutch. "As expected, your home is beautiful."

"It's just a little place to get away." He grins and appraises the crowd he's gathered. "We enjoy it." Finally he releases my shoulder. "Chase said he had a difficult time getting ahold of you. Working hard for Grayson, I presume?"

"Yes. Always."

"You've always been such a hard worker." Kip's grin expands to a smile and I nod and smile in turn, though really I just want to escape. "Well, I've heard nothing but good things about your work in the office. In fact, just the other day, I was speaking with your chief of staff, and he mentioned how you managed to give Grayson's speeches some—what was his word? *'Zing.'* That's what it was—after that little incident in California. My guess is you won't be an assistant legislative aide for much longer."

"Thank you."

"Don't thank me." Kip points to my forehead. "Thank that Ivy League brain of yours! If you keep this solid work up, we'll find you a place over at Latham, Scripps, Howard in no time, son. *No time flat.*"

"That's very flattering, Kip."

"It's the truth, son."

"Can you point me toward the restroom?"

The white door to the bathroom, which is just to the left of the kitchen, is closed and locked but I can hear giggling voices on the other side of it, so I knock a few times after waiting for three minutes or so.

"Just a second," a girl says with a laugh. "We're just finishing up."

I lean against the wall, next to a life-size portrait of Chase and a golden retriever posing on a white dock. Moments later, the door sways open and two girls, both in pearls and sundresses and both wiping their noses, file out of the bathroom and excuse themselves.

"Sorry," one of them says as she brushes by me. The other one whispers "He's cute" into her ear. Her friend giggles and whispers something about me being Chase's friend and Annalee's cousin, which elicits more laughter from the other one. Behind them, still in the bathroom, Caitlin is leaning against a gold-plated sink and gazing into a huge mirror set back into an engraved frame.

"Hi, gorgeous." She keeps leaning against the sink, but turns her head to look at me.

"Hi, Caitlin." I wait for a moment, expecting her to move from the sink and vacate the bathroom. "Are you almost finished?"

She rolls her eyes back to the mirror and brings her fingers to the pearls again. "I've got to fix my hair and freshen up a bit, but you're more than welcome to come in here while I do so." Caitlin pauses, fingers still on the pearls. "We're friends, after all."

"I can wait."

"Don't be a child, Taylor."

My judgment continues to disagree with her but my bladder doesn't and so I enter the bathroom and close the door. She reaches past me and locks it. Once the door's latched and secure, she unlatches a small clutch bag and fishes within it for a small, clear Baggie of coke. I turn my back to her and I face the toilet (also gold-plated) and unzip my pants.

"You want some of this?" she says after snorting a pile of white powder off a small silver spoon.

"No, thanks," I say, staring into the golden bowl, and I realize that there's no way—no possible manner—in which I'll be able to piss because there are so many things just so terribly wrong about all of this.

"Suit yourself." She shrugs before doing another bump and putting both the spoon and the bag back into the darkness of her bag. She nods at the bowl: "Everything coming out okay? Or do you need some help?" She smiles and I zip up my pants.

"I guess I didn't have to go as bad as I thought." I slide by her and reach for the door's handle but she brushes away my hand.

"Tell me how much you're going to miss me, Taylor," she says, her eyes all glistening, "and don't you *dare* lie."

"Tons, Cailtin. I'll miss you tons. Shouldn't we be getting back to the party? I'm sure there are hordes of people who'd like to say good-bye."

I reach for the handle again, but she brushes it away—harder this time.

"*Tons?* That's *all?*" She smiles coquettishly and my stomach becomes upset all over again.

"More than tons. Millions of tons."

One more attempt at the door handle, and this time she grabs my arm and twists me around and backs me against the door. I turn my face to the side as she leans into me.

"Caitlin, stop."

She pushes and urges and starts breathing against my neck and then brings her knee up against my groin and I keep saying stop until, finally, I grab both of her thin wrists and push her away from me.

"I told you to knock it off."

For this scarcely noticeable instant, she stares at me, hurt, and the glitter in her eyes has morphed into this unbridled rage and it's only after she's slapped me that I realize that she's going to do it.

"You fucking piece of trash."

My cheek, numbed by champagne and gin, slowly begins to sting and the pain steadily increases.

"Do you know how fucking lucky you'd be?" She adjusts her top and replaces a strand of hair that's become loose from her bun. "Get the fuck out of here," she says with a hiss. "You don't *belong.* You never *have.* Go back to that bitch. Go back to your fucking spic girlfriend."

"Caitlin."

"What?" Her voice never breaks; it never increases beyond that level at which ridicule can be foolishly mistaken for legitimate anger.

"Your nose is bleeding." I walk out the door and gently shut it behind me.

Outside, people and places and things are exactly as I had left them: Jack and Hal's cousin still stand in the same corner of the tent, both looking down at their shoes, both unmoving, both silent. The band has reverted back to Sinatra-era classics, and, in the center of a large circle of onlookers and admirers, Chase dances with his mother to a protracted rendition of "I Get a Kick Out of You." As the song ends, the crowd claps and Patricia smiles shyly and Chase gives an overstated bow. I leave the front porch, my observatory perch, and move to the bar, where I order a gin and tonic before following one of the side paths that run adjacent to the tent, and then past a long row of geraniums, whose petals are just these splashes of reds and pinks underneath the torches' fire.

The music from the tent fades as I wander deeper into the garden and closer to the docks. But the torches continue to provide light along the path, and eventually I can hear my steps and the rocking and sloshing of water against wood. As I get closer to the bay, closer to the tiny piers, I make out the outline of a figure sitting on one of them, in a reclined position, its legs dangling off the side and into the black water. Soon a head of blond hair materializes, and then the drooping back of a linen dress, and finally Annalee's tan, defined shoulders and bronzed arms. She doesn't hear my approach, and then only notices me once I kick off my shoes and sit down on the wooden planks next to her.

"What's up, cous?" I say once I've dipped my feet into the Chesapeake.

"Taylor." She looks up and smiles sweetly. "I didn't even hear you walk up."

On her left hand, one of the largest diamonds I've ever seen gleams against the moon's light. Small puddles gather around our ankles as they sway in the calm bay.

"Are you having a good time?" I finally ask, fearful of her response.

"I'm having a great time. I really like it out here. It's pretty." And then, "I think Chase is really going to miss Caitlin." She slowly cocks her head to one side. "They've known each other for so long. What about you? Having fun?"

My cheek has stopped stinging and I assume that it has returned from its red hue to a normal flesh tone. "It's been interesting. The house, though. The house is really impressive."

"It's Chase's favorite place in the whole world." She laughs quietly and the rock on her hand continues to reflect so many of the night's lights.

"I suppose I haven't formally congratulated you yet." I swallow after staring at the diamond for a few more seconds. "It's a beautiful ring."

"Thanks." She raises her hand off the dock and holds it out to a length at which we're both able to admire the stone. "It was Chase's great-grandmother's. It's a mine-cut three-and-a-half-carat diamond with cerulean sapphire baguettes laid into a filigree platinum rectangle setting."

I nod and then laugh. "I have no idea what any of that means," I confess.

She pauses for a moment and then laughs as well. "Me neither. That's just how he told me to describe it." She holds it out for a bit longer and it stares back at her.

"Are you excited?" I ask quietly.

"Very. The engagement party is next weekend. Kip has reserved the ballroom at the Four Seasons." She sets her hand down and looks back to me. "You'll come, right?"

"Yes. Of course."

Annalee kicks her feet, sending small splashes into the summer's weighted air. "Why don't we watch the fireworks from down here?" she suddenly says. "I feel like I haven't seen you practically since you've been *born*. We used to talk almost every day, and now . . . I don't know, it'll be so incredibly crowded up there." She's almost pleading with me now, and I shift uncomfortably. "And it's so peaceful and quiet down on the docks."

"Of course, Annalee." She turns back toward the bay and her blond hair tumbles down her back and I smile sadly and, in the moonlight, I can't help but think how she looks like some porcelain doll that's about to break. And then the air gets heavier and finally, "Annalee, about Chase."

"Yes? What about him?" She keeps facing the horizon, which at this late hour is nearly impossible to decipher.

I stumble and stammer over the words, which seem to be taking up too much space in my dry mouth. "I'm just not sure if he's been the most faithful. I don't know if he's the right guy for you."

The statement, the pronouncement, sucks the oxygen out of the night like fire in a closed room until Annalee, eyes still locked onto the distance, says, "I know."

"What do you mean, 'I know'?"

Her body's position doesn't change, but her voice lowers. "I know you think I've changed, Taylor. But I'm not blind."

"Then what are you doing?"

She keeps staring at the horizon. "Annalee"—she finally turns and looks at me and I'm surprised to see that her eyes are dry—"why are you doing this, then?"

She stands up, straightens her skirt, and searches for her sandals. "We should go back to the house and watch the fireworks.

Get something to drink, maybe?" She smiles down at me and offers a hand to help me up. I stand without her assistance.

"No." I shake my head. "No. I need to know why you're doing this. You can't do this. I can't let you." She's on the other side of the dock now, and she's found her sandals, and she slips them on and then turns to look at me. Overhead, the first firework, orange and gold and bright, bursts into a million tiny sparks.

"You can't *let* me? I need your permission to do this?" She shakes her head. "No. That's not how this works, Taylor. That's not how this happens. *You can't let me do this?*"

The next firework detonates as I take a step toward her and take her left hand. "You can't," I tell her. "You can't you can't you can't you can't. He'll kill you, he'll tear you apart, he's torn me apart." The third, the fourth, and the fifth rockets boom and illuminate our eyes with purples and greens and blues.

"What else am I supposed to do?" she screams, over the fireworks' calls. "Rely on my father in Croatia? Call Nathaniel? Call *you*? Because the last time I checked, you haven't proven to be very adept at picking up the pieces of your own pathetic life." She rips her hand away from mine and looks at the diamond and then at me and then back at the house and then tears flood her face. "I'm not leaving this, Taylor. I'm not. And stop telling me that you are. Stop telling me that, because I don't believe a *fucking* word of it," she says.

"Fine," I tell her. Then, *"Do it. Marry the son of a bitch."* The sky's become bright with the gaudy Technicolor of celebration. I yell in order to be heard, and my voice, I can tell, is like so many tiny daggers. "You know how this all plays out if you don't stop it. So don't ever come to me." She turns away from me and she starts walking back toward the house. *"Don't ever come to me,* Annalee, to talk about regret. Because you're going to end up like the rest of them. So, like I said, marry Chase. End up like Katie and Frank. End up like your parents."

"And what makes you think that you won't?"

"You have to stop this."

"I can't."

"Why?" My throat is aching from competing with the rockets' laughter.

"Because it's done," she says. "Because I'm scared of not having it. Because I can't."

Annalee watches me and I watch her until finally she breaks, until finally she's torn apart into so many fractured pieces. "I hate you!" she screams at the house and the tents and bright, happy torches. "I hate you I hate you I hate you I hate you." But no one can hear her, because above us the fireworks bang and roar to the oohs and aahs of the starry-eyed crowd.

July 8, 1987; 5:30 P.M.
July 6, 2007; 5:30 P.M.

*N*athaniel!" *My mother's voice carries over the Pacific waves, whose white foam mixed with the beach's sand crust our feet. "Don't take him too far! We're leaving soon! We need to be at your aunt's by seven o'clock!"*

Nathaniel grips my hand harder and turns back to Katie, who is standing a little more than a hundred yards down the beach. I look up at him as he squints and blocks the sun's rays with a hand and calls out to her.

"I've got him, Mom! We're just going to see the tide pools!" An immense wave crashes at our ankles, and Nathaniel swings me up off the sand so the rushing water doesn't sweep my feet out from under me. "Close call!" he says once he's set me down. "You almost became a fish."

"Just be careful!" I hear my mother fading behind us. "Those rocks are slippery, and I don't want him cracking his head!"

"Can that happen?"

"Can what happen?" He takes my hand again and we pad along the wet sand toward the tiny set of tide pools that spot the cove's walls.

"Could I really become a fish?"

"Sure," Nathaniel says, nodding his head authoritatively. "Happens

all the time, actually. Why don't you think Sarah Friedman's at school anymore?" Nathaniel's mind works in peculiar ways.

It's July and the days are idle and long, but the sun—although balanced tall in the sky—the sun's light is getting tired and soft. The waves, blue and recurrent and churning, keep pounding at our feet, and Nathaniel, forever diligent to the task laid bare before him, continues to lift me off the ground each time the whitewash causes me to stumble. Close call, he keeps saying. You almost became a goldfish. Or, that could have been bad, he tells me, because a school of guppies has been calling my name.

"Are you sure I'd be a goldfish?" I ask him as we near the tide pools.

"Positive," he responds with another authoritative nod.

I think about it for a moment and then look back at his tan, freckled face. "What would you be?"

"A shark," he says without thinking, but rather swooshing me into the air again as a wave crashes. "Whoosh!" He rocks my tiny body in the air for a moment before setting my feet back down upon the sand. "But I wouldn't eat you, so you don't have to worry."

"Why not?"

"Well, first of all," he takes a first step onto the smooth rock leading up to the small pools, which are turning gold and silver as the sun inches closer to the horizon. "First of all, I'd make sure you were a tough goldfish." He clambers a few more steps up the rock.

"Goldfish can be tough?" I say, my head cocked and my feet sinking into the sand. Nathaniel sighs and puts his hands on his bony hips.

"Of course they can. Look at Alvin." Alvin was a small, miserable creature Nathaniel had won for me at a school fair nearly two years ago. He'd insisted that Alvin was a fantastic specimen of marine life, all robust and sturdy and vigorous. When Nathaniel first presented him to me, I had spent two full days with my nose pressed hard against Alvin's small glass bowl, waiting patiently for some indication of the fantastic or the extraordinary. In the end, though, the small brute didn't do much,

aside from float and shit and eat and—occasionally—swim. Two weeks after his arrival, my mother flushed him down the toilet when I was at school. Fish, she told me as she cooked halibut for dinner, were meant for the sea. Just you wait, Nate told me, we'll be reading about Alvin in the papers soon enough. "Now will you come up here? There are some things I want to show you." *He reaches a hand down the slippery rock and pulls me up alongside him with a single heave.*

"Why else wouldn't you eat me?" *I secure my footing on the edge of one of the small pools, a minuscule puddle inhabited by a single sea anemone and a lazy hermit crab.*

"Because we're brothers," *he said matter-of-factly.* "The police will arrest you if you eat your brother. It's not allowed."

I nod understandingly. Makes sense to me, I think.

"Now look at this pool, Taylor." *He grasps my right hand again and uses his free one to point into the puddle.* "This is the most famous tide pool in North America. You can ask anyone."

My eyes widen as I stare at the crab sitting motionless in its shell. Below us, down the sand, far away from the most famous tide pool in North America, other families are packing up baskets and bags with towels and shovels. In the water, beyond the breaking of the waves, two surfers float on their boards without the slightest traces of ambition. Katie, farther and farther and farther away, sways her hands in the air and shouts words and orders that vanish somewhere in the air between us. I crouch down next to the pool, my knees at my chest, and dip a small, pink finger into the water.

"Don't do that." *Nathaniel kneels next to me and gently removes my hand.*

"Why not?" *I ask, startled.*

"Because that's theirs," *he replies patiently.* "That's their place." *He sighs and sits back on his heels.* "And you wouldn't like it anyway."

"How do you know?"

"I went into a tide pool once," *he says, looking off to the horizon.* "Before you were born, of course."

"What was it like?" I ask readily. Nathaniel shrugs and doesn't answer. "Nate, what was it like?"

"Where?" he asks.

"In the tide pool." *I stomp my foot impatiently.*

"Just really crowded, I guess."

And we sit there a little longer as the sun skulks cowardly to the water and as Katie continues her plea for us to return.

"Do you think we should go back?" I look up to ask him.

"No," Nathaniel says, resting his chin on his knees. "No, not yet."

Outside, over the narrow green breadth of the National Mall, the light is waning. Aside from the dust balls and the books and the aging computers, I'm the only one in the office; Congress is still on recess for Independence Day, and half of the staff has used the free time to escape to oases outside the Beltway. I've moved a pile of papers to one side of Peter's desk, and I'm sitting Indian-style on the other corner, just watching as cars and trucks and bikes and people make their way up Constitution and Independence, up the two sides of the Mall. And for this instant the clock's second hand is paralyzed somewhere between eleven and twelve, and my mind's just sort of paused, and I've forgotten about the invitation sitting on the desk next to me, the one that tells me I'm cordially invited to a celebration of the engagement between Annalee Mark and Chase Latham—which, when you stop to think about it, will probably just be really crowded, anyway.

July 11, 2007; 7:30 P.M.

Taylor *Mark*. Why, *look . . . at . . . you.*"

"Hello, Mrs. Howard.

"What'd I tell you?"

"My apologies, *Bunny*."

"Kitty, come over here this *instant* and look at how Chase's friend Taylor looks in this *gorgeous* tuxedo." Bunny brushes an invisible piece of lint off my tux's satin lapel before Kitty swirls into the conversation, just this big explosion of midnight blue silk and pearls and self-tanner wielding two glasses of champagne.

"You're right, Bunny: *gorgeous*." Kitty nods up and down and picks another piece of invisible lint off the opposite lapel. "*Stunning*, really. What is it . . . an Armani? A Gucci? Or *goodness*, what is it all the young people are wearing these days? Paul *Smith* or something-or-other?" She hands one of the glasses to Bunny, who sips and nods and sips and nods.

"Watch it, lady." Bunny sways, taking a swig. "We're still 'all the young people.'" This elicits much laughter and champagne toasts and smiles.

"It's a rental."

They both look at each other, awkward and confused and

drunk, and then Bunny turns to me and says, "*Well*, whatever fool said that clothes make the man was absolutely, *positively* lying. It looks like a million dollars on you, Taylor."

I tell them that no, no, it doesn't, and I excuse myself from the conversation.

Originally, Annalee told me, Chase had wanted the engagement party to take place at Café Milano; that, really, he had said, there wasn't a better place for them to make the formal announcement. Kip, though, told him that the choice was tasteless and immature and crass, and that any restaurant or locale that featured music and intricate Flash animations on its website would not be hosting an engagement party for which *he* was paying. And so, instead, the patriarch had charged Patricia with finding a suitable venue by which all vital invitees would be impressed and awed and she found this: a secluded terrace at the Four Seasons with views of Rock Creek Park and the illuminated streets of Georgetown that can comfortably fit seventy-five people but is currently playing host to eighty-two.

During the past few years, as more and more and more of my acquaintances have slipped rings on their trembling fingers and have walked down those petal-drenched aisles, I've learned that engagement parties can run the gamut from casual lunches to these black-tie affairs drunk with ostentation, and I'm not particularly surprised that Chase's revelry falls into the latter of the two categories. The guests, who hover around chest-high tables adorned with large candles encased in glass, have been handpicked by Kip and feature eight congressmen, two senators, a federal judge, and a string of lobbyists. And their wives.

I pull at my collar and stand at one of the tables—one that's set far off in one of the corners—with Jack, who is edgily holding the hand of Hal's cousin, who seems unsteady on her six-inch heels and who has just finished her second flute of champagne.

"I'm going to get another glass," she says, wobbling on the

spikes of her stilettos. "You want another one?" She gently lays a hand on Jack's arm.

"Yeah, sure." He shakes her hand off, agitated. "Whatever. Get Taylor one, too."

"Actually," I tell her, "I'm fine. But thanks."

The girl smiles and steadies herself on the table's edge before pitching toward the bar.

"What are you, boycotting or something?" Jack asks, though really it's more of a statement than anything else.

"I don't know." I run a hand through my hair, which I still haven't had cut and which is beginning to fall over my eyes. "Something like that." I change the subject: "She's nice—Hal's cousin."

"She has no idea what she's doing. She acts like a kid."

"That's nice though, don't you think? I mean, between her or Caitlin—"

"She's underage."

"Whatever. It's not like you're going to be sleeping with—"

Jack ends the sentence with a look, with these *daggers* that could kill lions and dictators and anything in between. Once he's made sure that the sentence has been buried incomplete, he reaches into the inner pocket of his tux's jacket (incidentally, Gucci) and produces a small pad of paper and begins scribbling.

"What are you doing?" I finally ask once he's jotted down a few sentences.

"See that man over there?" He nods to a gray-haired man, this corpulent pink fellow busting from the seams of his suit, who's standing in the middle of the terrace and who is whispering in the ear of a woman much younger—and much thinner—than he.

"What about him?"

"He's a congressman from Louisiana. And that's not his wife."

"And?"

Jack replaces the notepad into his jacket and nods at Hal's cousin, who is returning—*trying* to return—with the champagne.

"And I've got a column to write on Monday."

Contrary to my orders, the girl has brought back three flutes of Veuve and is trying to balance them all among her newly manicured nails, which, given the stilettos and the crowd and the low lighting, is no easy task, and causes her to come out more like a tightrope walker at an elegant circus than an underage guest at an engagement party. "You sure you don't want one?" And I feel badly for this girl for so many more reasons than simply this exercise in couture gymnastics, so I say sure—but just this one.

So we sit there, the three of us, as Hal's cousin complains about how painful her shoes are, and how boys just don't *get* the lengths to which a girl will go to impress them, and how someone—was it Caitlin? Yes, it was, it was Caitlin—had absolutely *insisted* that she wear these Christian Louboutin heels that are absolutely the *tallest* thing she's ever worn.

"They're cute, though, don't you think?" The three of us look down and stare at the white and tan leather.

"Adorable," Jack says before nodding to the other end of the terrace and excusing himself from the conversation by saying that he's spotted a features editor from *Capitol File* to whom he's been meaning to pitch a story.

"He *hates* me," the girl mutters, crestfallen. "It couldn't be more obvious." She brings the flute to her painted lips and I try to remember what I was doing on the eve of my eighteenth birthday. But they've been washed away, those recollections, and lately I've become concerned that the apparitions replacing them are pictures like these; pictures of a young girl careening into a world she doesn't understand, wearing shoes she cannot fill, being led by a man she can't understand, who doesn't understand himself.

"I don't think that's the case." I take a weak stab at comfort.

"Besides, don't you think he's a little too old for you to begin with?"

She sets the flute down on the table but keeps holding onto its stem. "That's what I told my cousin, but he said that Jack would be a good person to know. You know, to get, like, invited to all the *really* good parties and stuff." She starts twirling a strand of straightened blond hair around one of her slight fingers. Suddenly she looks up at me. "I mean, I wouldn't be *here* if it weren't for Jack. Hal wasn't even invited."

I want to tell her that I'm starting to have my own misgivings about what's so great about *here* in the first place, but instead I shrug, I nod, I sip, and I notice how Jack isn't talking to an editor from *Capitol File*, but standing alone at the bar.

The light's going, but a heavy cloud cover has only allowed for the most mediocre of sunsets, just a few dull strokes of tangerine and violet. I've watched for the past hour as Bunny Howard and Kitty Scripps have escaped to opposite corners of the veranda with each other's husband, whereupon they've managed to conduct conversations that expire in that gray area between flattery and flirtation. Hal's cousin sits at an empty table; her legs uncrossed but held tightly together, her face at once dejected and eager. Chase materializes and disappears in tempo with the evening, and each time he smiles and shakes hands and breathes in deeply so his chest fills his jacket and his father holds his broad shoulder proudly.

And it's during one of these stanzas that he passes me unfazed, and shakes my hand tightly and grins and tells me that he couldn't have done it without me, champ, that I'm the reason for this all, before he moves on to the next table and the next erupting flute.

And it's also during one of these stanzas that I see Annalee for the first time since confronting her on the docks on the Eastern Shore, when all those torches were glowing behind us. Her blond hair is pulled back up off her face, which once again looks fragile and dear and prized. Her left arm is linked to Chase's, and she politely accepts everyone's best wishes and congratulations and covetous stares with grace and smiles and thank-yous. Every few moments, she'll stop to readjust a strap on her white, sleeveless Chanel dress that hugs her chest closely and dips down in the back to reveal a slender back (the dress, I presume, she received from Patricia once the engagement was announced to the family), or she'll look into the three-karat stone and will remark to someone, in turn, how just extraordinarily lucky she is to be wearing it. But then once, she catches my eye from across the terrace, through the sea of black and white, and the blue of her iris glazes over, and I wonder if, for an unparalleled instant, she's caught herself alone on that white dock and has seen her future unfold.

But then the moment passes and she's hugged by the next guest and, smiling, she readjusts her ring, and I forget my boycott and I push my way toward the bar for another glass of champagne. Halfway there, I'm once again accosted by Bunny and Kitty, who tell me in a series of hand gestures and smiles that they simply can't *believe* how gorgeous Annalee looks, especially after they had to fit that Chanel dress—how many times was it, Bunny, five?—but that's besides the point; she looks *phenomenal.* And aren't I proud? After all, aren't I her only family in town? They'd heard whispers, they tell me, about a father clubbing baby seals in Siberia, and a mother who ran about with different men in different states, and of *course* they wouldn't even consider *prying* to ask if that's all true (but is it?), it's just that whispers and comments made behind manicured hands always cause such a *fuss.* In any event, she—Annalee—she's got me. And I'm such an upstanding young man. Right?

"Absolutely," I say to both of them. "Absolutely. And stories are often misconstrued about my Uncle Jack. He's been clubbing baby *Russians*. Not baby seals."

Bunny and Kitty laugh apprehensively and say things to each other in quieted undertones as I move past them to the bar, where Jack's standing, accompanied by a tall glass of clear liquid that— by this point—I know better than to say is water.

"Jesus," he grumbles into the tumbler once I've worked my way over to him. "What'd you say to those two?"

I look back at Bunny and Kitty, who are speaking frenziedly to each other and to anyone else who will listen.

"I told them that Annalee's father spends his spare time clubbing baby Russians."

Jack smiles and nips at his vodka. "Nice job." His smirk becomes an understated but sincere laugh. "Really nice job."

I reach for another flute of champagne; there are so many of them standing in perfect straight rows on the bar like tiny kamikazes who don't know any better than to perish for some goalless cause.

"I noticed you paying your respects to our future bride and groom."

"I was caught in the line of fire," I say, leaning against the bar. "Believe me, if it weren't for the fact that Annalee is my cousin, and that I'm the one who introduced the two of them in the first place, I'd just as soon skip this whole thing."

"It really bothers you that much?"

"What?"

"I guess I mean that all of this gets to you that much? It hits you that hard? Come on, Taylor. You want me to believe you haven't made some ethically questionable judgment?"

Her dark hair flares out like spiderwebs on the white sheets and I place the flute on the bar with probably a little more force than is necessary and the base cracks, leaving this line that zigzags toward the stem.

"That's not the point."

"But isn't it part of it?"

"Forget it." But then, no. My voice lessens in volume but amplifies in intensity. He doesn't blink, doesn't move. "You don't see anything wrong with any of this? You don't find anything wrong with the fact that they're getting married?"

He shrugs and preserves his sturdy, straightforward stare.

I start: "You don't see anything wrong with the fact that you're using that poor girl—Hal's cousin?"

Overhead, one of the clouds shifts to expose the moon, which isn't full, which is only half there.

"Look around you." Jack suddenly grabs the lapel of my jacket and seethes. "You think anything's going to change with these people? You think this all ends well? Look me in the eye and tell me something will change here—something will cause any of this to move in a different direction."

I want to but I can't.

"Look me in the eye, goddamn it." He lets go of my lapel and then says, "Your morals don't buy things here, Taylor."

"Then what is this?" I finally ask, once he's calmed down.

"This?" He grins slowly. "This is just discretionary spending." Then, "And whether you like it or not, pal, it looks like your man is about to ask you to make a down payment." He motions to the middle of the terrace, between two tables, where Chase is standing, holding Annalee's hand, and asking for the guests to please quiet down and to make sure that they've got enough champagne, because he'd like to have a special friend of his say a few words on this *absolutely wonderful* occasion.

"And I told him earlier this evening," Chase is saying to the delight of the crowd, "that he's the reason for all of this. See—what was it, two and a half years ago?—Taylor introduced me to Annalee at this bar up in Philadelphia." He leans over and kisses Annalee, who is looking down, on the cheek. "Plough in the Stars. That was the name of the bar. And I'll be honest, I feel like I ploughed my own star that night." Women swoon at the statement, which, if you really stop to think about it, isn't so much romantic as it is grotesque and pornographic. "Confession time, though: I was too drunk to ask for her number." The crowd laughs and says things such as "Oh, college" and "Who hasn't been there?" "So the next day, Taylor gave me her number and encouraged me to call her." Chase smiles across the crowd. "And now I'd like him to say a few words."

There was this time when I was ten years old, I must've been in the fourth grade, when, during a geography lesson, my teacher asked two of her students—one of whom was me—to participate in a series of debates regarding the shape of the planet. The premise of the deliberation was this: Is the world round, or is it flat? My opponent, a straight-A teacher's pet with fiery red hair named Bethany Frick, was to defend the mind-blowing proposition that there was more beyond the horizon, that the earth was round, while I was told to defend the opposing position. The whole charade was ridiculous; I complained to my family that night over dinner, it was *impossible*. I was to be mocked, I told them; I was having a shit time at school, and this was going to make things inarguably worse.

"You've got to sell it," my father said as he cracked open a beer and shut the refrigerator door with an elbow. "Your old man could sell a king his crown if he had to." He took a swallow of his beer and pointed at me and sat down at the table. "And believe me, buster, you take after your old man."

Katie shook her head and set a bowl of steaming green beans on the glass table. "This is exactly why I've been pushing for private school for so long."

"Katie—"

"Don't 'Katie' me, Frank." She took her place next to my father and flattened a cloth napkin against her lap. "Taylor, have you ever noticed any strange smells coming from your teacher's office during recess? Or have her eyes ever been, you know"—she flutters her fingers in front of her face—"bloodshot? Red?"

"You're being ridiculous, Katie."

I watched as she filled her glass with burgundy wine.

"Having a child debate a flat earth, Frank? You're trying to tell me a woman would tell a ten-year-old to do that without the help of some illicit substances?"

"Mom—"

"Wonderful, the prodigal son has something to say." Nathaniel starts separating the beans from the carrots from the whitefish on his plate.

"I was just going to say that I'm sure there's a purpose behind the assignment." He turns to me and speaks slowly. "Taylor, I'm sure Mrs. Powell would just like you to see how things were like in 1492. I can help you prepare some things after dinner, if you'd like."

Regardless of if I were prepared or not, the exercise was horrible and torturous and frankly worse than I had expected. While Bethany Frick went on and on and on about ships appearing as dots on the horizon, I stood behind my podium, distraught, and stared back at a sea of incredulous faces.

"It was a nice try," Mrs. Powell later told me. "The point wasn't for anyone to believe you."

So that's sort of how I'm feeling as I'm poring over these faces that are just older and more polished and preserved. They're smiling back at me and I'm holding a slippery crystal flute and I'm supposed to tell them that the world is flat, that ships don't round out over the horizon, but nose-dive off its edge.

"Well, come on," Jack whispers into my ear. "Let's hear it, *champ.*"

And so I start, and these words, these affected, phony, bastard words, just stumble and hesitate, and I know if I even sigh the word "congratulations" I'll become sick, because no one in this room deserves an olive wreath, and that includes me, so instead I say,

"I do remember that night, Chase, I do. It was the second semester of our junior year, and I had just returned from a semester abroad in Paris." *I adore Paris,* someone says. *But who doesn't?* another answers. "Annalee had finished Duke and she was working here in D.C. I was feeling a bit homesick, see. I don't have any family in D.C., aside from Annalee." Across the terrace, Annalee ducks behind Chase, who yells something that sounds like "You're family to me, champ," and of course the crowd laughs. "So, she was kind enough to come to Philadelphia for the weekend. She's always been a kind person, Annalee. Even when we were children. Growing up, we spoke quite a bit, even after her family moved from California to Chicago. And even then" and I stop for a moment as Annalee and her white Chanel gown and her three-carat diamond leave the terrace as unobtrusively as they had entered, but only a few of the guests notice and they begin to whisper and hush in small clumps—"even then she was a saint. And it's interesting, when you stop and think about it, I suppose"—I laugh nervously and shift my weight—"how all of these things have come to pass. I remember when I first got here—when I first got to Washington. I went to the Gold Cup, probably with many of you." The crowd nods, *yes, yes.* "And there was this horse—Light of Our Lives—"

"I lost money on that bastard!" Chase cries out.

"That didn't finish one of the races, because he died when he was running it." A woman near me gasps and Jack mutters "nice." "So I've been thinking a lot about that damn horse lately, and why he couldn't finish that race, or why he didn't *want* to finish that race.

"And I guess I've never been a huge believer in fate; this idea that someone's weaving our lives—or that horse's life—together without much of our say. You know, this concept that things happen, and that we're pulled into different places by . . . by some magnetic force. That'd imply we don't set things in motion, that we don't get things rolling. Which we do. Which we definitely do. Which I did. But once we start those things in motion, they don't want to change, and the faster they go the harder and harder it is to change them. So maybe inertia's a better word." The crowd shifts and I can tell that they're moving toward the bar and that they're beginning to lose interest. "Yes, I think that it is. I think inertia is better. And so"—I raise my glass but by this point the crowd has dissipated and is striking up unrelated conversations, and so I end up saying under my breath and into my own flute—"and so here's to our own inertia, Chase." But he's not listening. He's too busy speaking with a woman I've never seen and who is wise to Annalee's absence as an unexploited opportunity.

"A dead horse and some physics. Beautiful," Jack says, clanging his glass against mine. "Really. *Beautiful.*"

I shove Jack out of my way and he says "easy" while I finish my champagne. Once I'm done, once it's gone, I just throw the crystal to the ground and it breaks into so many jagged shards. My bow tie's become loose anyway, so I rip it open so its two ends dangle wilted and defeated on my chest.

Before I'm able to push, to *force* my way through the crowd, I feel Chase's strong grip on my shoulder. "Champ," he says with a hiss into my ear and he spins me around, "you all right?" He looks down at the fragments of the champagne flute and smiles. "A little too much bubbly?"

"Fine," I say as I grab one of the ends of the bow tie and rip it from my neck.

"Easy, pal," he says. "I know that thing's a rental, but they'll charge you an arm and a leg if you ruin it."

"I appreciate the advice, as always." I try to spin back away.

His grip gets harder and his eyes narrow. "What's wrong with you, man?" he whispers. "What the *fuck* is your problem?"

I grab his fingers and pry them from my shoulder. "Nothing's wrong," I say, and out of the corner of my eye I see Kip and Patricia approaching our confrontation. "Though, frankly, Chase, I can't say the same for your happy bride-to-be." They're standing behind him now—the happiest parents of the happiest son bred by the happiest society in America. I increase the volume of my voice. "Because the last time I checked, Annalee has never been keen on the idea of getting on her knees for someone in a broom closet. But thankfully you've got others to take care of that for you, right?" I point to the girl he's just been flirting with—*some blond whore*—and Chase stares back, and I lose track of what I'm saying, and it just starts flowing, just so many words from so many years. "And you know," I continue, my voice a raspy snarl that's being heard not only by Kip and Patricia, but by at least half of the guests in attendance, "I've always got your interest at heart. You know that, don't you, *champ*? So I asked Annalee for you, I asked her what she thought of marrying someone so phenomenally *beneath* her."

Chase's face is red and the clinking of glasses has stopped. "Don't talk to me about being low-rent, Laguna."

"And it appears that she's willing to make some sacrifices that I'm no longer willing to make."

Really beautiful.

The veranda's thick with people—just so crowded, anyway—and I lace through them until I've heard my name whispered at least twenty times, and until I've made it off the terrace and through the glass double doors that divide it and the inside world.

Leaning against the glass doors for a moment, I feel my shirt gum with the sweat on my back and stick to patches of my skin. I stay here for a minute, breathing like this, regretting like that, until the lobby's soft piano music fanning into and out of the guests' calm conversations becomes agonizing, echoing in my eardrums, and I ask a bellboy if he could direct me to the closest restroom, which he says is down the hall and to the left.

The hall is long and flanked with floor-to-ceiling windows that look out onto the terrace, which from this vantage looks blissful and happy and safe. Between each window is a large maroon vase—practically the size of me—that holds an assortment of freshly cut flowers, and the most dominant variety among the bunch is the lily. And standing next to one of these vases looking out onto the terrace is Annalee, who, in her white Chanel dress and honey blond hair, almost resembles a lily herself. She's wiping something from her nose, and I see that there's a drop of blood on her shoulder, and I delicately take her hand and tell her that I'm sorry for him and that I'm sorry for her and that I'm sorry for me.

"It's fine," she says blankly. And then, after a few moments have passed, "It looks so much prettier from the outside looking in, doesn't it?"

"Yes, I suppose it does."

It's empty, the bathroom, all quiet and serene, and I take a hand towel and, after wetting it with cool water, I place it against my burning forehead. I stay like this—leaning against the marble sink with a white cloth fixed to my face, staring into the mirror but not particularly seeing anything—until one of the guests from the party (a senator?) breaks the silence. I excuse myself and, under his glares of disapproval, place the hand towel in a wicker basket and leave the restroom. She's gone, Annalee, once I emerge again into the hall. So I look through one of the towering windows onto the courtyard and I see her, this white lily, attached to Chase's arm.

⤜⤏

And now, to conclude the present chapter of this gorgeous disaster:

From the hallway overlooking Annalee's blossoming and waning and kissing and dying I move to the hotel's bar, where I order a glass of Glenfiddich, no ice. I chase that beverage with two more of the same. And although I should be, I'm not surprised nor floored nor generally fazed when Juliana Grayson sits on the stool next to me. Her mascara is streaked and her hair undone. But of course she doesn't tell me why she has become the catastrophe that she had once predicted, and instead we drink in silence—me, scotch; she, bourbon.

Then, thirty minutes later, after more drinking and less speaking, I find myself spending the last cents of my moral capital pressing Juliana's shoulders against the oak walls of a stall in that same bathroom, her hair exploding in a ragged mess against the wood's dark grain and her breathing hot and low and toxic on my neck.

We finish and redress without speaking, awkwardly moving around one another without brushing elbows in the bathroom's cramped stall. She's crying, I notice, she's crying again. But I don't say anything, I stay silent as I tuck in my shirt and smooth back my hair. The stall door opens with a creak, and we walk across the bathroom—she, crying; me, silent—toward the outside world. And it's not until now, it's not until I open that door, that portal to what's encroaching, that I realize that the gravitas of what's surrounded me is suddenly upon my shoulders. Because on the other side of that door is Chase. And he begins to smile when he sees my unkempt hair and the stains on my pants, and Juliana, with her head bowed and her dark hair pulled back, brushes past the two of us, wordless, because she knows and I know that all of the returns on the benefits of this particular arrangement have vanished completely. And Chase smiles wider, and I see something behind his eyes that's born from that black place that's between excitement and envy. Envy. That most fucked of emotions that, when left in the hands of those who have never experienced it, has the ability to expose some of the uglier traits of humanity.

XV

July, 15, 2007; 7:00 A.M.

Capital Catfights

Jack A. Buchanan

From the sounds of it, the claws are out and the fangs are ready on Capitol Hill. *Politik*'s learned that Democratic Queen Bee Nancy Pelosi (D-CA) has formed a group of members—primarily men—in their thirtysomethings to get her dirty work done on the floor. And apparently some of the other mean girls on the left side of the aisle aren't happy about it.

"The whole thing's like high school again," Congresswoman Maria Reyes (D-NY) told *Politik*. "Just with better suits and nicer jewelry." We wonder: on Wednesdays, do they wear pink?

Guess Who . . .

. . . GUESS which Golden State congresswoman was spotted at Cobalt, D.C.'s favorite gay bar, judging a certain tighty-whitey competition?

. . . GUESS which Big (and) Easy congressman was seen canoodling with a honey half his age, half his weight, and (we're guessing) *not* his wife at an engagement party on Friday night?

. . . and finally, GUESS which well-coifed Orange County congressman might need to have a conversation with his newest staffer on Monday morning? Last time *Politik* checked, shagging the boss's wife in a stall at the Four Seasons wasn't part of an office assistant's job description.

XVI

July 15, 2007; 9:15 A.M.

And this is how it ends:

The picture of John and Juliana Grayson that sits on Grayson's grand desk in 1224 Longworth had to be taken four times. He had just won reelection, and she was just told that half of her time, if not more, was going to be spent in Washington. Both of them were having trouble producing believable smiles.

"It was three days after our marriage," John says calmly. "On our honeymoon in Maui." Behind us, the doors are closed and locked but I know that at least half of the staff members have their eager ears pressed against the door, listening for faint traces of what will define me because every three minutes I hear Peter tell them to give the congressman some respect. Grayson reaches under his desk for two glasses engraved with his initials. "They were wedding gifts," he tells me, laughing. He asks me if I want some scotch and I look at the clock—nine-fifteen in the morning—and I predict that after this conversation, I'll have very little to do for the rest of the day, so I tell him that yes, please, that'd be perfect. He uncorks a labelless glass bottle and fills each tumbler with the tawny booze that matches the color of his hair.

"I don't do this often," he says, excusing himself, which makes me uncomfortable. The fact that he's excusing himself.

"Don't do what, sir?"

"Drink at nine-fifteen in the morning. Especially when I'm voting."

"I see."

He leans back in his overstuffed leather chair and smells the scotch, which is smoky and pungent. "Supposedly this is some good stuff," he says. "My father-in-law gave it to me on the night of my wedding. Macallan Fine and Rare Collection. The bottle went for $10,125. He gave it to me with the glasses." And we both sit there for a moment, sipping and sniffing. "But who knows?" he says. "These things are so often overpriced."

Slowly he rocks forward in the chair and, upon standing up, he moves over to the office's bookshelf, which for the first time I'm noticing isn't filled with volumes of political histories, but rather with fiction set in far-off places, like *Treasure Island* and *Robinson Crusoe*. "God," he says, laughing, "that was an awful wedding. It was at the Balboa Bay Club. Have you ever been there?" I nod and tell him that I have. "It was pouring rain. And it was freezing. I don't think anybody wanted to be there. And neither Juliana nor I wanted to come back here." He takes another drink of the scotch and walks over to the window, the one overlooking the Mall. "It's different here, Taylor, you know? It's just different. But you probably know that." I tell him that, yes, I've learned that, but I stop before I begin explaining this new belief, this philosophy I've found myself mulling over, something that says that it's less where we are and more who we've become.

Grayson walks over to the picture on his desk and lifts it up in his free hand and there's this part of me that can't help but wonder if he's silently damning that thirty-second birthday of his, and that little redheaded girl he saved. "Things don't happen for a reason, Taylor. You know that, right? Otherwise she wouldn't have married me. She'd been against the idea for three years. *Three years.* And you wouldn't have come here, and they wouldn't have done what they did, and we all wouldn't be—well, we all wouldn't be *in this mess.*"

He pauses and I can hear both of us breathing and it seems as though he's preparing to deliver a speech—a monologue—that he knew, eventually, at some point or another, he'd be forced to give.

"You know, eight months before the wedding, when I proposed formally, it seemed like things might work out between us. She'd calmed down. I wasn't finding these . . . these clues . . . these things that I had seen when we first started dating." He brushes some dust off the picture with his thumb. "'Let's do it, John,' she said. 'Let's do this.'" He sets the picture down. "I asked her why, and she told me that she was 'ready to be safe.'" He laughs, and it's sad and haunting, and I look down. "I guess the three years it took her to build up the enthusiasm to marry me should have thrown up some red flags. It's just that, after everything that had happened with her brother, and after having known her for so long . . ." His voice trails off into a whisper, and then he looks up at me: "Have you ever been in love, Taylor?"

Before I can answer he laughs and shakes his head. "Jesus. Listen to me. 'Have you ever been in love?' I sound like some goddamn after-school special."

I tell him that it's a legitimate question, and that yes, that maybe I had been in love, but just once, and that it had ended badly.

"You convince yourself of these things, you know?" I nod and tell him that yes, I was beginning to understand that. "I know the reputation I've got around here. I know people think I'm not the brightest bulb. But that doesn't mean that I don't know what Juliana does—or what she's always been doing—while I'm not there. But during those eight months before the wedding, Taylor,

I swear to you, she was different. She looked at me differently.

"You're probably wondering when I could sense that things were going sour again, when they were going back to the way they were." I tell him that I don't think I'm in the position to be wondering, and his voice gets stern and then goes soft again. "No, you're not. But truth is, I don't know if I can entirely blame you for this, as it is.

"Anyway, I don't remember. Because, really, you don't remember things like that. They say that you do; they say you can pinpoint these exact moments when things start going wrong—as if they're milestones, like your kid's birth, or graduation." He shakes his head. "That's all a lie, though. When shit happens, it's more like an avalanche. You don't remember one flake of snow, you just remember it all rushing at you at once. Anyway, I'm guessing that it happened during one of the toasts at the reception, because that evening, the night before our honeymoon, there was this bitterness in the way we kissed. Like she had realized what she'd done. Like if she'd realized that harmless wasn't exactly safe."

He stops and looks into his glass, which has become empty, so he refills it with more scotch. A siren whines down Independence Avenue.

"We didn't see that much of each other during the honeymoon, if you can believe it. She'd wake up early and go to yoga, or spinning, or somewhere else where I wouldn't be caught dead, and I'd sleep late and then go to the beach. We'd meet for dinner every night, and talk about our days, and she'd leave out details that'd account for entire hours." He drinks half the glass and shakes his head. *"On our fucking honeymoon."*

A light on the clock above Grayson's desk illuminates, signaling that a vote is about to take place on the House floor. He looks up at it and finishes the rest of the scotch.

"Funding bill," he mutters. "More damn people asking for more damn money for bridges to nowhere and six-lane highways in counties that have five damn cars." He doesn't give any indication of leaving his office. Instead, he refills my glass.

"About halfway through the honeymoon, maybe four days into it, when I knew that nothing had changed, I sat her down and I told her"—and I could be wrong here but this shine on the edge of his left eye makes it look like he's tearing up, which just makes me so *goddamn* uncomfortable that all I want to do is run or disappear or be completely consumed by my own guilt, or maybe all of the above—"and I told her, 'You know, Juliana, we don't have to do this.' It broke my heart to say it. I said we could call the whole thing off; that if she wasn't happy, that if this wasn't what she *wanted*, then we could—"

"End it." He looks up at me.

"Yes, end it." The light on the clock extinguishes. "She told me I was being ridiculous. She said she wouldn't have walked down that aisle if she hadn't wanted to marry me." He laughs again—this time sadder than before. "I don't know who the hell she was trying to convince, but it sure wasn't me. I just figured—hell, I don't know what I figured, but whatever it was, it was dead wrong."

And here's where I realize that for all his bumbling faults and hot microphones and moments of misguided dictation, that John Grayson isn't so different than I, or Katie Mark, or Nathaniel, or Annalee, or Light of Our Lives, or any other unfortunate beast that's tried to push back against the stubbornness of destiny, or who has essayed to will a different course from the fates. Because, really, it all comes crashing down in the end.

"She stayed with me because of the money," he says.

"Sir?"

"Her father, Charles—he's a longtime friend and business partner of my father—but," and he refills his glass, "I'm sure the two of you have discussed that. In any event, Charles told Juliana that she wouldn't see a penny of her trust if she got a divorce."

"I'm sure that's not the only reason that she—"

"It is, Taylor," he says matter-of-factly. "She told me one night after she'd been out. I asked her where she'd been, and that she smelled like vodka. She told me that it wasn't any of my business. And then—Christ, you know how this all goes down—she starts yelling and fighting, and ends up saying something that she won't remember in the morning but that I'll never forget."

"Why'd didn't you leave her?" I ask, looking down, after it seems as though so many minutes have crept by.

"I couldn't," he begins, "I couldn't throw her to that pack of wolves, to Bunny and Pony or whatever it is those horrible women are called. Especially after everything that's happened. After all they've done." He traces a finger—one without a wedding band on it—around a coaster sitting on his desk.

"She may not love me, Taylor. And she may be lost. And she may never find whatever path it is that she's supposed to be following. But I had a hand in building this cage for her, and I'll be damned if I'm going to throw open the door so she can be destroyed by the rabid monsters on the other side."

And then, once it's clear that he's finished, and once it's clear that I've just been one more knife that's been stabbed in this man's bloody back, I ask him an obvious question that has an even more obvious answer: "So what's going to happen to me?"

"You?" He looks up from his desk. "You, son, are fired. And you can thank your friend Chase for that. Beyond that? What's next?" He sips his whiskey and shrugs. "I couldn't tell you."

As I stumble under those Ionic columns that support Longworth's entrance, everything seems a little less grand, a little less powerful, a little less impressive. And then I'm sitting here, an unlit cigarette in my hand, and my cell phone vibrates, and I know that it's Chase, and I know that he's going to ask me to meet him at the bar at the Palm, and I will tell him that I will go, because I have to, because there are certain things that need to be done, because, really, I need to empty my hands. But I'll hang up the phone before he's able to call me champ.

He's alone when I get there, hunched on a stool, nursing a Bloody Mary. He's discarded his jacket onto the empty stool next to him, and his tie's loose and weekly knotted in a half Windsor. I'm getting the sense that he's been sitting here most of the morning. I don't say anything, but rather just take a stool close to him and order a club soda from the bartender.

"Thanks for waiting to call until after I was fired," I say eventually without looking at him.

"Anytime, champ," he says without looking at me. "Thanks for causing a scene at my fucking engagement party. My mother hasn't spoken to me since that night. And Bunny and Kitty—*those miserable fucking women*—won't stop calling the house."

"And that's why you did this? Because I caused a scene?" I thank the bartender for my drink and take a large swallow but I'm still facing forward, staring at a row of half-empty bottles.

"Politics, I suppose," he answers.

I don't answer him so instead Chase orders another Bloody Mary and we sit in silence like this, alone, for fifteen minutes. Every so often I'll look over at Chase, whose eyes are dull and empty and whose lips are dried and cracked.

"How's Annalee?" I finally ask.

"I haven't heard from her since Saturday. She's away."

"Where?"

"New York or Chicago or something. Wherever her mother is. She talked about going to Croatia, to meet her father, but I talked her out of it." Then, "She ruined that Chanel dress with that goddamn bloody nose."

"I'm sure your marriage will experience more expensive casualties," I say, and he tells me to stop being cute, which, really, is fair. Because I am being cute. Because I've been wanting to say something like that to Chase Latham for as long as I can remember.

"You know he almost called off the wedding?" Chase says after removing a celery stalk from his tall glass. "Kip almost called off the goddamn wedding. He told me I was an embarrassment, that he was too busy to explain his son's behavior to the people who mattered; that Annalee should be a *privilege,* not a *right.* I asked him if that's how he looks at Mom, and he hit me, Taylor. He *hit* me. Across *the fucking face.* 'Keep your skeletons where they belong,' he told me, 'in their fucking closets.' He almost called off the wedding *because I fucking got caught.*"

"I'm sorry," I say, once he's done, once he's through. "But I couldn't let—"

"No," he says, taking a bite off the celery stalk. "No, you're not sorry. And you shouldn't be. And neither am I." He sets down the stalk and turns to face me and, for the first time since I've known him, Chase Latham, America's golden boy, looks old. "And you know why I'm not sorry?" he says through clenched teeth and with heavy eyes. "Because I *won.*"

"Chase," I say, standing up, "this isn't a game."

"Yeah, pal, it is."

"Then it's a sad one." I shake my head. "It's sad and it's pathetic and it's mundane."

"And you, sir, are the worst for having played it."

He asks me to sit down, to listen, because this is it, his last *lesson,* his final *appeal* to a side of my personality he's managed to create and mold and hone over the past six years.

I order a vodka soda and he begins telling me about Saturday night, about how, after Annalee had left to be with her mother, his father had taken him to a suite at the Four Seasons that had originally been reserved for the betrothed and had backhanded him—twice—as Patricia had stood by and had watched silently. "I told him I'd fix things," he says. "At first he told me that would be impossible. He told me I'd fucked up for the last time—and what was worse, I'd embarrassed them." He winces but continues, "But then," and here Chase lays a hand on my shoulder and his eyes light up a bit, but not to that same brightness I've always known, "I told them about your little romp in the bathroom with Mrs. Grayson, and they seemed to settle down a bit."

"I don't see how that has anything to do with this."

He sucks down the last drops of his Bloody Mary and orders another. "I'll give it to you: getting blow jobs in the broom closet of Smith Point is pretty despicable—but having your wife fucking your office assistant? That takes the cake." He laughs to himself. "And isn't this what this is all about? Finding someone who's done something just *that* much more despicable than you? Shame trumps shame. So I guess in that sense, you won.

"Besides," he continues, "Bunny and Kitty—hell, even my mother—have been after Juliana Grayson for years." I ask him why and he shrugs. "I don't know. Boredom, I guess? Jealousy? There's something about Juliana, something that she has that those other women don't . . ." He trails off here. "But I suppose you already know that. Anyway, Bunny and Kitty. Those women have nothing better to do with their time . . . and fuck, man, just *look at her.* She doesn't belong in a place like this. She shakes things up. She doesn't know her *place.* Talk about skeletons in your closet . . . that woman has a walk-in wardrobe full of them, man. The problem, though, how I understand it, is that Bunny and Kitty have never actually *caught* Juliana doing anything wrong. Sure, everyone knows she sleeps around. But they didn't have any *proof.*" He laughs quietly, sadly. "Jesus, I remember one time, they tried to slip a tape recorder into her purse at this charity event. It was so Junior League. I mean, a *tape recorder?* Are you *kidding me?* On some level I feel bad for her, Juliana—and you, I guess. Hell hath no fury, right? And trust me: those women have fury. But it's like Dad said the other night: if you have skeletons, keep them in your closet."

"So that's it?" I stand to leave.

"Easy, *champ*. No, that's not it. Give me a little credit." He loosens his tie further and his face gets red. "LSH has been having problems with your boss—or, I guess, your *former* boss" (he drives this point home a number of times) "for a while now."

"Over what?" I ask, incredulously. "I find it pretty hard to believe that John Grayson would be at the center of anything earth-shattering, Chase."

He laughs and smiles that Cheshire smile—though this time it's smaller, and he looks at me. "I know, right? Jesus, Lindsay Lohan is involved in more scandals than that man. Anyway, apparently one of our clients is this big land developer. Deidrich and Howe, ever heard of them?" I tell him no. "Yeah, neither had I until we started doing work with them. In any event, they've had their sights set on building this golf course in Grayson's district, on this marshland—the Back Bay?—that's apparently pretty heavily protected. A wildlife reserve or something."

I think back to the jokes and the letters and the calls made on behalf of the Back Bay in Grayson's office. The cause du jour of the bottled-blond housewives of Newport Beach. It's so upsetting and so disappointing and so perfect. Just so perfect. "You're kidding, right?"

"I wish I could say I was. Believe me, if you're going to be involved in a scandal, you might as well add a little umph to it, right? Coke smuggling or something." He swirls ice around in his empty glass. "Unfortunately, in this case we're just dealing with herons and coyotes and shit." His voice gets more earnest. "But it's a big account for LSH. And Dad says that Deidrich and Howe had been threatening to take their business elsewhere unless Grayson got on board with the course—which, I'll add, Mickelson is designing. Pretty cool, right?" I stare back. "You know who he is?

Phil? Anyway. So, on Sunday, Kip came to me and said that my knowledge of—*ahem*—your little hanky-panky could be of some service."

"And so?"

"And so." He stops here. But just for a moment. "Christ, man, you know the rest." I tell him that yes, yes, I probably do know the rest; that this is a small, angry history that's been written so many times before. But despite all that, I wanted to hear it anyway. He shrugs and nods and continues. "I called Grayson at home—the fucker is listed, can you believe that?—I called him at home and I told him what was on the table."

"Herons and coyotes and shit."

"Well, yeah." Chase stumbles here. "And the fact that the entire town was about to know that a certain office assistant had been dipping into his wife."

"Okay."

"And you know what the fucker did?"

"No."

"He *laughed* at me. Can you believe that?"

"Honestly?"

"Honestly."

"Yes."

He nods a few times and stares at me and then continues, "So I hung up on the asshole and called Jack—who, by the way, I think is queer, anyway. That's what Caitlin's saying. I guess she saw him walking around with some *obviously* gay dude in Dupont. He's just been acting *off,* don't you think?" I tell him that it's none of our business, and I ask him what Jack said.

"He was weird about it at first," Chase admits as he reaches for a bowl of nuts that's been sitting, untouched, in front of us. "But he eventually just convinced himself. Said it'd be better for you in the long run." He pauses and shakes his head. "I don't know who that kid thinks he is. He acts like he's some arbiter of what's good and evil in this town, and what's worthy and what's not, and yet all he does is write a fucking *gossip* column."

We sit awhile longer, and the waiter asks me if we'd like another round. Chase asks for another Bloody Mary and some more nuts. I tell the waiter I'm fine and that I'll be leaving soon.

"And the wedding?" I finally ask, at once knowing and dreading the response.

"It's still on," he says flatly.

"Does Annalee know how this all went down?"

"No." He turns to me again. And I'm not sure about this, and looking back, I'm probably wrong, but the lower lids of his eyes are reflecting light as if they're wet, and his voice gets softer— pleading in a way that I'd never heard before. "And she won't. She *won't.*"

I tell him that I'm done—done with him, done with her, done with *this*; and that, really, I had tried to tell Annalee, that I'd tried to warn her, but that the fireworks had been too loud, and there had been too much to drink—that, to be honest, there had always been too much to drink.

I stand, eventually, finally, and I slide my blazer over my shoulders. "Think about me as you're playing the back nine, Chase."

"Will do, champ." He turns and faces the bar, with its low light and its grand wood and its half-empty bottles.

So this is how I leave; out of the darkness of the restaurant and into the bright, hot sun. I leave him seated at the bar, accompanied by his pride and his envy and his desperation.

As I do so, as I walk away, I realize it will be those three things that will forever prevent Chase Latham from understanding the entrapping loneliness that I've felt for the past six years. And how it's that same hungry void that is creeping ever so slowly, but now just a bit faster, into his happy life.

Epilogue

From: Jack.Buchanan@politik.com
To: Taylor.Mark@gmail.com
Subject: Fwd: Bisous from Baghdad!!

T,
Hope New York is well and not too frigid. Read below—
from Caitlin. Hate me now as I'm sure you must, and thank
me later for rescuing you from being a recipient of corre-
spondences such as these.
—JAB

From: Caitlin.MacMahon@gmail.com
To: [Recipients undisclosed]
Subject: Bisous from Baghdad!

Dear All,
First things first: Chazy, am absolutely devastated I won't
be able to make the wedding. Pleaded and begged with my
supervisor, but apparently there's some peace talk going on
that weekend, etc., etc., etc. Needless to say, the priorities
in this place need to be realigned! All my best, though, to
you and Annalee (no doubt the luckiest bride in D.C.'s history!). Also, Chazy, if you remember (and I know you won't,

you big lug), tell her that I say to nix the lilac bridesmaid dresses but to keep e-mailing me suggestions. God knows I've got nothing to do here! In any event, moving on . . .

My loves, my loves, my loves! How I miss you all sooooo *dearly.* Firstly, allow me to say that the saying's true: the zone is always greener on the other side of the (heavily guarded) fence. I'm finding out rather quickly that "deputy attaché to the Treasury Department" sounds a lot better at Smith Point than it does here in B-Town, but such is life, I suppose. Lots of paper pushing and the such, surely Princeton prepared me for more than this.

In terms of accommodations, my apartment wasn't completed upon my arrival. (We're on Iraq time, as we say.) So I've been staying in—how shall I say this while paying deference to the government that brought me here?—an "ill-equipped" trailer. (By "ill-equipped" I mean "no bathroom." Which basically means that I've got to trek to the housing complex in order to shower, etc. And believe me, walking two hundred yards in 100+ degree heat is not what I expected to be doing in my Manolos.)

Aside from the aforementioned mishap, things are . . . well, things. I've learned that (a) Bose noise-canceling headphones do *not* reduce the deafening explosions of IEDs (much to yours truly's disappointment—sectarian violence makes it absolutely *impossible* to sleep). Also, (b) finding a proper manicurist in the Green Zone is a task that should be reserved only for those deserving of the worst imaginable punishment. I've managed to find this lad who is a translator for the military (I'm pretty sure he's gay—but didn't ask, and he didn't tell—don't want to lose the only man in this hellhole who knows how to properly paint a nail!) who does a decent job. And finally, (c) contrary to what you may believe, "Green Zone" does not imply "organic." Was positively *shocked* when I arrived and discovered canned beans and unrecognizable veggies served from aluminum trays. But don't fear, my loves, your girl will survive. She always does! Until we speak again—adieu, you *gorgeous beasts.*

Bisous and xoxo and all that jazz,
Caitlin

Acknowledgments

My infinite thanks goes to the many people—some of whom are listed here, others whom I've overlooked on account of my own carelessness—who have helped make this book happen.

First, to Richard Pine and Colin Fox: Richard, whose faith, patience, and guidance are the pillars of this novel; and Colin, an incredible editor, and (undoubtedly more important) an incredible friend.

To Al Hunt, David Eisenhower, Yaroslav Pelikan, and Laura Nichols, who all have the diligence to teach me how things are—and how things should be.

To my friends and colleagues: Jill, Klair, Jon, Nathaniel, Clare, Yona, Ross, Sarah, Emily, Amanda, Paige, Teresita, Jennifer, Daniella, Anna, Debbie, Ben, Cory, Meghan, Jennifer, Krissy, Lauren, Liz, Dave, and the countless others who were harassed to read these pages time and time again. There's no way to adequately thank you, so at least let me buy you a drink.

Andrew Tejerina and Jessica Kirshner have both been blessed with that breed of patience that saints envy.

Again, to my family—Mom, Dad, Reid, and Katie—for suspending enough disbelief to trust me when I said that all this wasn't about *them*.

Finally, to Libby O'Neill: for everything.

About the Author

Grant Ginder was raised in southern California and graduated from the University of Pennsylvania in 2005, where he was an editor at *34th Street*, the school's humor and culture magazine. He currently works as a speechwriter at the Center for American Progress and resides in New York City.